Readers love the Blood series by SHIRA ANTHONY

Blood and Rain

"…a supremely entertaining and engrossing read. It's a vampire swashbuckler, full of romance and evil deeds, that includes thwarted, star crossed lovers and the stuff heroes are made of."
—Scattered Thoughts and Rogue Words

"I am completely invested in her fascinating characters and in the world she has created for them, both past and present, and can't wait to discover the past that is slowly unfolding through this intriguing set of stories."
—Prism Book Alliance

Blood and Ghosts

"The way Shira tells a story is perfect, your emotions are right in tune with the book, and at times I was wondering if I could take it!"
—Bike Book Reviews

"…devilishly good. This is a completely new approach to tales of vampire lore."
—Hearts on Fire Reviews

"Everything is in here. Good versus evil. Regret and pain. Love and loss."
—Boys in our Books

By SHIRA ANTHONY

The Dream of a Thousand Nights
Once Upon a Time in the Weird West
With Aisling Mancy: A Solitary Man
Take Two
With Venona Keyes: The Trust

BLOOD
Blood and Rain
Blood and Ghosts
Blood and Eternity

BLUE NOTES
The Melody Thief
Aria
With Venona Keyes: Prelude
Encore
Symphony in Blue
Blue Notes
Dissonance

DREAMSPUN BEYOND
#4 – Finder's Keeper

DREAMSPUN DESIRES
#2 – First Comes Marriage
#32 – Forgotten Paradise
#51 – Swann's Revenge

MERMAN OF EA
Stealing the Wind
Into the Wind
Running with the Wind

With EM Lynley
A DELECTABLE NOVEL
Lighting the Way Home

Published by DREAMSPINNER PRESS
www.dreamspinnerpress.com

BLOOD
AND
ETERNITY
SHIRA ANTHONY

REAMSPINNER
PRESS

Published by

DREAMSPINNER PRESS

5032 Capital Circle SW, Suite 2, PMB# 279, Tallahassee, FL 32305-7886 USA
www.dreamspinnerpress.com

Blood and Eternity
© 2018 Shira Anthony.

Cover Art
© 2018 Reese Dante.
http://www.reesedante.com
Cover content is for illustrative purposes only and any person depicted on the cover is a model.

Trade Paperback ISBN: 978-1-64080-743-3
Digital ISBN: 978-1-64080-742-6
Library of Congress Control Number: 2018934248
Trade Paperback published July 2018
v. 1.0

Printed in the United States of America
∞
This paper meets the requirements of
ANSI/NISO Z39.48-1992 (Permanence of Paper).

DRAMATIS PERSONAE

HUNTERS

Adrien Gilbert. An immortal hunter and the youngest son of the fabled Gilbert Clan of vampire hunters, Adrien Gilbert saw his mother murdered by a vampire when he was just a boy. Adrien never wanted to become a hunter and always believed his older brother, François, was the more powerful son. Adrien was given immortality by the ancient vampire Nicolas Lambert. Adrien loves Nicolas.

François Gilbert. Adrien's older brother, François is a hunter who willingly became a vampire after falling in love with the powerful and solitary vampire Charles Duvalier.

Jacques Gilbert. Jacques is the father of Adrien, François, and their sister, Isabelle. Much of Jacques's past is shrouded in mystery. Once a powerful hunter in his own right, Jacques has not been himself since the murder of his wife by a vampire.

Isabelle Gilbert. Adrien and François's little sister, Isa was also trained as a hunter, although she chose to pursue a life with humans.

Verel Pelletier. An immortal hunter, Verel Pelletier has installed himself as the new regent of the Council of Hunters. He is ruthless and cunning and does not believe in the vampire-hunter treaty that created the Council. Pelletier advocates the use of vampire blood to enhance his followers' powers.

Roland Günter. An immortal hunter and former teacher of Adrien and François Gilbert, Roland has long been a vocal opponent of Verel Pelletier and his cronies. Roland and his longtime companion, Thomas Fournier, keep a low profile, working behind the scenes against Pelletier's forces.

Thomas Fournier. Roland Günter's longtime companion, Thomas is a powerful hunter in his own right.

Victor Sauvage. Another of Roland Günter's students, Victor saves Adrien in a barroom brawl in Paris and becomes one of Adrien's strongest allies.

Antonio Giovanetti. A hunter and Verel Pelletier's right-hand man and proxy, Giovanetti is more powerful than most hunters, although he is not an immortal. He serves as acting regent of the Council of Hunters after Pelletier disappears.

Claus Bremen. A hunter and researcher for Pelletier's faction, Bremen perfected the means to enhance hunters' powers by using vampire blood. Bremen is heartless and cruel and doesn't hesitate to torture for pleasure alone.

Robert Aguillon. Former regent of the Council of Hunters, Robert Aguillon was once quite powerful but in recent years has become feeble and struggles to maintain control over the Council.

VAMPIRES

Nicolas Lambert (Rousseau). An ancient vampire (born a vampire, not created from a human), Nicolas is the youngest son of the Lambert Clan. He is several hundred years old but is relatively naïve in the ways of the world since he has been sheltered by his older brother, Jean. Nicolas offered himself in marriage to Rosina Rousseau to cement a fragile peace between their warring clans, but learned that he is actually a Rousseau himself and was born on the day Verel Pelletier murdered his parents and older brother. Nicolas loves Adrien Gilbert and gave Adrien immortality.

Jean Lambert. An ancient vampire, leader of the Lambert Clan, and Nicolas's older brother, Jean Lambert appears cool on the surface, but he genuinely loves Nicolas and wants what is best for him. In spite of his reservations, he permits Nicolas to offer himself in marriage to end the war between the Lambert and Rousseau Clans. Jean and Blaise Rousseau share a history that reignited the war between the clans, and while Jean finally tells Blaise the truth of what happened the day they were to be married, he keeps his distance from Blaise.

Rémy Desgrieux. A distant relative of Nicolas and Jean, Rémy is a loyal Lambert Clan member and a good friend of Nicolas. Despite their rocky start, Rémy and Adrien Gilbert become close friends.

Paul Rousseau. Nicolas's brother, whom Pelletier killed to obtain immortality.

Stéphane Rousseau. Nicolas's father, who was killed in a fight with Verel Pelletier's men on the day Nicolas was born.

Anaïs Rousseau. Nicolas's mother, who was killed in a fight with Verel Pelletier's men on the day Nicolas was born.

Charles Duvalier. Transformed from human to vampire against his will, Charles is old and very powerful. Charles shuns vampires and hunters alike, and he blames himself for transforming François Gilbert into a vampire. In spite of this, Charles loves François deeply.

Caroline Vestry. Charles Duvalier's creation, Caroline would do anything for Charles and would defend him to the death. Caroline also cares deeply for François Gilbert and believes François will make Charles happy.

Blaise Rousseau. An ancient vampire and the eldest surviving son of the powerful Rousseau Clan, Blaise hides a painful past and a broken heart. His wedding to Jean Lambert was interrupted by Verel Pelletier, who murdered Blaise's brother and parents and blamed their deaths on Jean. Blaise loves Jean Lambert, but after nearly two centuries of being spurned by Jean, he has accepted the fact that he and Jean will never be together.

Rosina Rousseau. Blaise's younger sister, Rosina is a strong-willed ancient vampire who is quick to anger but loyal to a fault. She begrudgingly agreed to marry Nicolas Lambert to ensure the treaty between their clans, only to discover that Nicolas is her brother. Reynaud Rousseau. Uncle of Blaise and Rosina, Reynaud became Rousseau Clan leader after his brother's murder. Reynaud believes in the need to keep his clan strong, even when his choices lead to dire consequences.

SERIES RECAP

Vampire hunter Adrien Gilbert lost his mother to a vampire attack when he was a young child. When his brother, François, is killed by a vampire, the Council of Hunters sends Adrien to execute the vampire who murdered him, Charles Duvalier. Duvalier, however, proves difficult to locate, so when Jean Lambert, head of an ancient vampire clan, offers to give Adrien Charles's location in exchange for his help, Adrien agrees. Adrien is tasked with escorting Jean's younger brother Nicolas to Paris to marry Rosina Rousseau as the price of peace between the warring clans. The last thing Adrien expects is to fall in love with Nicolas.

Adrien locates Charles but is startled to discover that François is alive and well... and is now a vampire. Overwhelmed with hatred for Charles, Adrien tries to kill him but is quickly defeated. While Adrien regroups to lick his wounds, his brother ventures outside of Charles's protection and is captured by the Council of Hunters, who, under Verel Pelletier's direction, imprison and torture him to experiment with his half-hunter, half-vampire blood.

Charles, Nicolas, and Adrien join forces to save François. During the fighting that ensues, Adrien is mortally wounded. Unsure of what to do but unwilling to allow Adrien to die, Nicolas gives Adrien his blood, and with it, the "gift" of immortality. Adrien is angry with Nicolas, but he also can't deny his feelings for him. Adrien finally delivers Nicolas to the Rousseau Clan in Paris and the wedding is scheduled.

Just before Nicolas is to take his vows of marriage to Rosina, Jean Lambert reveals the truth about Nicolas's birthright: Nicolas is the son of Stéphane and Anaïs Rousseau, whom Pelletier and his men murdered the day Nicolas was born. Jean raised Nicolas as his own brother in order to keep him safe from Verel Pelletier and the hunters who threaten to destroy the vampire race. The wedding is stopped, but a fierce battle between vampires and hunters ensues.

During the fighting, Nicolas saves Adrien from Pelletier's attack, but is killed. While Adrien is out of his mind with grief, his immortal gift reveals itself and he turns back time to a few minutes before Nicolas's death. Adrien and Pelletier fight again, but Pelletier is too powerful. Before Adrien can kill Pelletier, Pelletier kidnaps Nicolas.

For more than a century, Adrien and Jean search for Nicolas, but to no avail. Adrien sinks into a world of grief and self-hatred. He dreams he hears Nicolas calling his name, but when he wakes, he's alone and miserable. A voice in his head drives him to the verge of insanity, and he wants nothing more than to die. A desperate Jean drags Adrien to Paris, where the Council of Hunters is about to choose a replacement for the missing Pelletier.

SECOND TIMESTREAM—PRESENT Day

During the Council meeting, something strange happens. Time shifts, and Nicolas appears alongside his uncle Reynaud Rousseau. In this new timestream, Pelletier is said to have died a hero trying to save Nicolas's parents and brother, while Roland Günter is vilified as the man who murdered them. An enraged Adrien, believing Reynaud to be keeping Nicolas prisoner, attacks Reynaud and nearly kills him while a horrified Nicolas looks on.

SECOND TIMESTREAM—PAST

Time shifts once again, and a confused and desperate Adrien awakens in his childhood bedroom. He's seventeen again, and he and his brother attend the Council's ball in Lyon. Adrien realizes he's traveled back in time. At the ball, he meets Nicolas. Nicolas is inexplicably drawn to Adrien, and the two of them become lovers. Adrien shares his blood with Nicolas and Nicolas sees the truth about Adrien and their time together in another timestream. But Adrien is suddenly wrenched from the past, abandoning Nicolas and leaving behind a young, clueless Adrien who despises vampires.

SECOND TIMESTREAM—PRESENT DAY

Adrien wakes up in Jean's Paris apartment to discover that he has returned to the present just a few hours after the incident at the Council of Hunters. Roland explains to a confused and heartbroken Adrien that when hunters become immortal, they develop powers from their vampire blood. Immortal hunters call these powers their "demon," because the powers take on a life and personality of their own. Only by learning to control the demon can the immortal hunter survive and become stronger.

Adrien isn't particularly interested in learning to control his demon. He wants to find the Nicolas he was forced to abandon in the past. When he does, however, Adrien learns that when he returned to the future, the Adrien he left behind knew nothing about Nicolas and despised vampires. Nicolas, in a desperate attempt to keep this clueless Adrien safe, married Antonio Giovanetti, Pelletier's right-hand man.

After Nicolas and Adrien finally meet, Giovanetti becomes suspicious. In order to protect Nicolas, Adrien pretends to try to kill Giovanetti and Nicolas pretends to reject Adrien. Adrien, Roland, and Jean discuss Pelletier, whom they all believe is still alive.

Third Timestream—Present Day

Before Adrien can decide what to do about Nicolas, Giovanetti, and the absent Pelletier, he is once again thrown into a new timestream. In this version of his future, Adrien finds a Nicolas who calls himself Nico. In this version of the present, Pelletier and his followers massacred most of the ancient vampires more than a hundred years ago. Now only a few ancients remain, including Jean and Nico.

Nico and Adrien make love, and for the first time in a hundred years, Adrien is happy and the demon is silent. But in spite of his happiness, Adrien's heart breaks for this new world. His brother, François, is dead, as are Charles Duvalier and the other vampires Adrien counted as friends. Adrien is torn between going back to fix the two previous timestreams, and staying here with Nico in a world where nearly everyone he cared about has been murdered by Pelletier and his men.

Before Adrien can make his choice about whether to fix the past, Pelletier resurfaces with a single text message sent to Adrien's phone: *If you choose to stay here, I won't get in your way. Keep your sweet vampire. Live your perfect life.*

CHAPTER ONE
ALTERNATIVES

Miami, Florida—June 2014 (Third Timestream)

ADRIEN LUXURIATED in the soft sheets and wiggled his toes as raindrops gently tapped against the windows. The distant sounds of Miami traffic reached the high-rise apartment as more of a pleasant hum than an echo of the chaos in the streets below.

Adrien yawned and glanced at the man who slept naked beside him: Nicolas. *No, his name is Nico.* One of the last few surviving ancient vampires. A man whose friends and family—with the exception of his adopted brother, Jean Lambert—had been murdered in a brutal massacre at the Council of Hunters.

There would be no more ancient vampires born in this timestream. But in spite of the bleak world he'd grown up in, Nico was much like the Nicolases Adrien had known—kind, gentle, and loving.

If you choose to stay here, I won't get in your way. Keep your sweet vampire. Live your perfect life.

Adrien hadn't deleted the text, but he hadn't looked at it again either. He didn't need to; he'd memorized Pelletier's warning.

Fuck the bastard. He had decided even before he received Pelletier's text that he'd stay here with Nico. He hadn't spent the past century searching for Nicolas only to abandon him for the empty timestream he'd come from. It didn't matter that Pelletier had probably brought him to this place—the choice to stay was his own. He'd keep Nico safe. All that mattered was Nico.

He kissed the bare skin of Nico's back. The soft sigh he received in response made him shiver.

"Morning." Nico rolled over and smiled at him.

"Mmmm." For once, the low thrum of Adrien's bloodlust felt warm and comforting, like Nico's expression.

"Worried I might not be here when you woke?"

"The thought crossed my mind." Adrien wrapped his arms around Nico's waist.

"You worry too much." Nico pressed his lips to Adrien's neck—more a tantalizing promise than an invitation since they'd shared their blood again the night before. The press of Nico's cock on Adrien's thigh, however, demanded an answer.

"I love the rain," Adrien said as he squeezed Nico's ass and pulled him closer. "It's a great excuse to—"

Nico's cell played "Thunderstruck." Nico sighed and reached over the side of the bed, casting about with a hand for his jeans. "Shit." He snagged the phone after it stopped ringing and frowned at the screen. "Sorry about that."

"Let it go," Adrien said and began to lave Nico's left nipple.

The phone rang again. "Can't," Nico half moaned, half croaked. "It's Jean. I promised I'd call last night. He's probably worried sick about me."

Hearing Jean's name stung, once again bringing back the memories Adrien had seen in Nico's blood. Roland's death. The massacre at the Council of Hunters. Once revealed, memories left an indelible mark.

Nico answered and sat on the edge of the bed. Adrien had hoped he and Nico might share a few more moments of peace before reality replaced fantasy. He'd been naïve.

Adrien threw on a pair of sweatpants and walked over to the window. Rain fell over the city, creating long streaks of dark against the brightening sky like the legs of a giant spider. Adrien shivered and tried to think of something more pleasant.

"I'm so sorry. I should have called. Something came up unexpectedly and I...," Nico was saying as Adrien grabbed his own phone and headed down the hallway to give Nico privacy.

He tapped the screen. Still no service. And yet the message from Pelletier remained: *If you choose to stay here, I won't get in your way. Keep your sweet vampire. Live your perfect life.*

Something was off. He'd only been here a few days, but he was sure he was missing something about this place. Something about this timestream didn't make sense. *As if any of this makes sense!*

"Adrien?"

Adrien jumped at the sound of Nico's voice. He'd zoned out again. He couldn't blame it on the time travel; he'd been here long enough to adapt.

The unease he'd felt when he'd arrived had only deepened. It was starting to affect him, pull his focus.

Nico rubbed Adrien's shoulders. "I didn't mean to startle you."

Adrien sighed. "I'm a little tired." *A little jumpy. A little... something. I'm just not sure what.*

Adrien expected Nico's concerned frown. "Adrien, I—"

"Please don't apologize." Adrien forced a smile. "Whatever... *however* things are now isn't your fault." What the fuck was he doing, making Nico feel like shit about something he had no control over? *This is my problem. My choice.*

Nico pulled Adrien over to the couch and they sat, side by side, thighs pressed together. The contact felt good. Reassuring. The only thing normal in a fucked-up world.

Adrien hated the pain he saw in Nico's gaze. Had he put it there?

"What's wrong?" Nico asked. "Really."

"I'm not sure," Adrien answered. "Honestly," he added as Nico frowned again. He held up the phone and studied it. "There's something about place—this *time*—that feels strange."

"This time?"

Adrien nodded. "I haven't had cell service since I got here."

Nico laughed. "Isn't that just proof you need to change your cell phone carrier?"

Adrien chuckled in spite of himself. "Maybe. But the building...."

"What building?" Nico's put his hand on Adrien's arm. God, Nico felt so fucking good, solid and real.

"Before we met, I was headed to my office. But the security guard had never heard of me or my company." Adrien rubbed the bridge of his nose. "May I use your cell?"

"Of course." Nico handed him his phone.

Adrien opened the browser and typed *Adrien Gilbert*, then scrolled down the results. Nothing. He typed *Gilbert Industries*. Still nothing. He tried googling *François Gilbert*.

He hadn't expected much. François had, over the years, changed his name to avoid questions. Adrien tried several of the other names François used. Not a single mention. A quick check of Charles's names gave him nothing.

"Fuck."

He felt more than heard Nico's breath catch. "I'm sorry. I wish I knew what happened to them. In the aftermath of the massacre in Paris, many vampires went into hiding. Hunters too." Nico kissed the top of Adrien's head.

"None of this is your fault. I'm thankful you and Jean survived. Please don't doubt that."

"I don't." Nico kissed him again. "But you think…?" he prompted.

"I've got a bad feeling about this." How could he explain to Nico that this timestream felt completely different? That Pelletier had contacted him even though his phone still hadn't connected with a network? He wasn't sure he wanted Nico to know about that. Not yet, at least.

Adrien swallowed hard and typed *Saint-Gervais Wines*. Halfway down the list he read *Gilbert, Benoît*, one of the names his father had used over the years. He clicked on the link and sighed with relief to see his father's face.

"Your family's vineyard?" Nico asked hopefully.

Adrien nodded. "It's been in my family for hundreds of years." He clicked on the link beneath the photograph, but the page only displayed the address of the vineyard. No link to a webpage. Not surprising, since his father detested the internet. *Doesn't mean he's alive. Or dead.*

"Coffee?" Nico offered.

"I'd love some." Adrien barely glanced up from the screen.

An hour and two cups of strong coffee later, the only thing of interest he'd found on the web was a casual mention of a Benoît Gilbert at a regional wine-tasting conference held in Lyon in 1998.

Nico glanced over his shoulder from the kitchen, where he'd begun to make their breakfast. "Your father?"

"Yes. But nothing of anyone else." Adrien tilted the phone so Nico could better see it. "Nothing about me. Nothing at all. And you don't remember meeting me…."

"I don't recall having met you," Nico agreed. "But that doesn't mean anything. There are plenty of hunters I've never met. Hunters who fought on our side and survived the massacre."

"You said you and Jean buried Roland."

Nico eyed him cautiously. "We…. Yes. We buried him at a small church near the Rousseau castle. But why—?"

"Did my father come?"

"Jacques? Yes." Nico's lips parted as though he'd finally understood. "But that doesn't—"

"I would have come as well." Much as he'd struggled with his feelings for Roland, Adrien loved him like a father.

"I'm sure there's some good explanation for why you didn't come." Nico sounded far less sure than before.

Adrien shook his head. "There's only one explanation for my not being at my father's side. The reason my phone doesn't work. Why my company doesn't exist." He drew a long breath. *Say it. Just say it and get it over with.* "I don't exist in this timeline. Not anymore. I died, Nico."

CHAPTER TWO
GHOSTS

WHEN ADRIEN and Nico arrived at midday by car, Saint-Gervais looked the same as he remembered, with its mid–twentieth century apartment complexes and shopping centers built in a ring around the ancient dwellings he recalled from his childhood. At its center, like a beating heart, stood the tiny stone church where he and his parents attended Mass before his mother's death. After she was killed, Jacques refused to take Adrien and his siblings, although Isabelle still walked the mile or so every Sunday morning until she moved away.

As he and Nico drove onward, the buildings thinned and the hills beckoned, familiar and immutable. Adrien's spirits soared as his family's vineyard appeared on the horizon. With its deep green vines and rocky soil, it looked much as he remembered it from his last visit. How long had that been? The timelines blurred, the answer elusive.

"You need to go to France. Figure things out for yourself," Nico had told him two nights before. Adrien hadn't argued. Nico obtained a fake passport and driver's license for Adrien through a vampire who made a living helping other vampires avoid detection. They'd booked the first flight to Lyon and rented a car there for the short drive to his family's vineyard.

A small placard at the side of the road announced the entrance. The new building adjacent to the highway sported a sign that listed days and times of tours and wine tastings. Adrien's father had once talked of opening the place to tourists, but as with many of Jacques's dreams, his enthusiasm never seemed to be enough to sustain the project.

There were no cars parked in the paved lot, despite the fact that it was a beautiful early summer day. Adrien and Nico headed up the dirt driveway toward the main house on foot. Neither had spoken much on the flight. Nico seemed to have taken on Adrien's anxiety as his own, something Adrien deeply regretted. Still, knowing Nico was at his side made the uncertainty of what they might discover in France far easier to bear.

Throughout the past week, the demon lingered at the periphery of Adrien's thoughts. It seemed content to sit back and let Adrien explore the truths of this new timestream. Adrien was happy for the silence. For a change, he didn't want to fight.

Nico took Adrien's hand as they walked. Stones crunched beneath their feet, a familiar and reassuring sound that reminded Adrien of growing up here. "I always loved this place," he said as his family's stone house with its peeling green shutters came into view. "I often thought I'd live out my days here." He didn't add that he'd envisioned Nico at his side in that particular fantasy.

Adrien paused at the front door, unsure whether to knock, when he heard whistling coming from the storage barn farther uphill. Adrien recognized the tune as one he'd learned when he'd been quite young. His mother had taught him the song.

Il était un petit navire,
Il était un petit navire,
Qui n'avait ja-ja-jamais navigué,
Qui n'avait ja-ja-jamais navigué.
Ohé! Ohé!
There was a little sailor...
Who had never sailed....

He rubbed a hand over his mouth and glanced at Nico. "He's here. My father." *He's still alive.* He ran up the hill as he'd done a thousand times as a child. He caught the smile on Nico's face as he turned into the barn.

His father, who'd been sharpening one of his tools, stopped the machine and looked up. "What—?" The blade clattered on the metal plate beneath, ringing as it vibrated.

Adrien embraced his father without hesitation, reveling in his steady presence. "God, it's good to see you." He clenched his jaw against a sudden swell of emotion.

"See?" Jacques paled and exhaled a stuttered breath. "But I don't...." Tears brimmed in his eyes and he shook his head. "How are you here? How did you...?"

"It's a long story." Adrien chuckled. "One best told with a good bottle of wine when you're sitting down."

Jacques appeared to rally, then nodded and turned to Nico. "Nico, it's been a very long time. So good to see you. Not quite the surprise of seeing Adrien"—he offered Nico his hand—"but a pleasant one. How's Jean?"

"He's well." Nico shook Jacques's hand and smiled.

"It seems I owe you a debt of gratitude," Jacques said. "If I didn't trust my senses, I might be inclined to believe this is some sort of joke."

Adrien inhaled slowly. "I was right, then. The Adrien you knew…."

"Died more than a century ago," Jacques finished. "At least, I thought he did." He eyed Adrien again as if trying to comprehend.

"But you know it's me," Adrien said.

"Yes."

"I'm afraid I can't take the credit for Adrien's good health." Nico took Adrien's hand and gently squeezed it. "Much as I'd like to, that is."

Jacques raised an eyebrow. "Then how…?"

Adrien took a deep breath. "Nicolas gave me immortality." He glanced at Nico and added, "Not Nico. It's a bit… complicated."

A broad smile lit Jacques's face as he wrapped his arm around Adrien's shoulders. "A tale I want to hear," he said. "But for the moment, let me catch my breath, steady my shaking hands, and get us something to drink. I sure as hell need it."

As they sat around the kitchen table a few minutes later, Adrien recounted the basic facts of his recent history.

"Quite a tale," Jacques said as he refilled their wineglasses with a shaky hand. "And if I didn't know my son, a tale I wouldn't have believed."

"Not knowing your son," Nico said with a shake of his head, "I nearly killed him before he could explain."

Adrien put a reassuring hand on Nico's thigh and Nico smiled in reply.

"Good?" Jacques said as Nico finished the last of his wine.

"Excellent, thank you. Is this your own?"

"1996 cuvée." Jacques's expression became wistful. "My late wife once told me the only reason I wanted a vineyard was to enjoy the wine." He grinned and added, "She was right."

Adrien glanced around the kitchen. Framed embroidery, yellowed with time, decorated two of the walls. Delicate pottery sat neglected and covered with dust on a wooden shelf high above the back door. Charlotte's death clearly haunted his father as much as it haunted him.

"I haven't seen Jean since we buried Roland." Jacques sighed and rubbed his mouth.

"I'm sure he wouldn't blame you for that," Nico offered. "You're safer if you keep your distance."

They drank for some time without speaking, the room silent but for the ticking of the ancient grandfather clock in the nearby sitting room.

Adrien refilled their glasses, then drank deeply to steel himself. He told himself he'd come here to learn the truth, but now he hesitated. "What of Charles?" he finally asked.

"Charles?" Jacques frowned. "Charles Duvalier?"

Adrien nodded.

"I haven't seen him since the hunters drove him out of town more than a century ago. He was killed in the massacre at the Council of Hunters. Or so I'm told. Many of the vampires and hunters who died that day were burned beyond recognition when the Council Chamber was destroyed." Jacques studied his wineglass with keen interest, and Adrien imagined he was remembering the attack.

"Hunters?" Adrien asked.

"Dispatched from Paris," Jacques explained. "Not a carte, but an ultimatum. They said he was under suspicion of working to undermine the Council."

"François and Charles didn't leave Saint-Gervais together?"

"I don't know what you mean." Jacques appeared genuinely confused.

"After François was transformed, he—"

"Transformed?" Jacques stared at Adrien.

"François is dead, isn't he?" Adrien whispered.

Jacques nodded.

Adrien thought he'd grown inured to loss. He was wrong. It didn't matter that this wasn't his timestream; his grief was real enough. "How?"

"He was attacked. A few months before the massacre." Jacques sighed. "The Council said he was killed by a vampire."

"But you believe otherwise?" Adrien squeezed the bridge of his nose.

"He was working with Roland and Victor Sauvage," Jacques explained. "There were others too. They hoped to convince the regent that Pelletier was planning a coup. I can only guess that Pelletier learned of their plans and had them killed."

HEADSTONES CROWDED the small plot in the shade of the large sycamore tree. Whereas in his own timeline there had been only two, his mother's and sister's, there were now two more graves.

"My son—your counterpart—was killed by a vampire while on a mission to provide the Council with evidence that Verel Pelletier was using vampire blood to augment his followers' abilities," Jacques told him when he'd asked. "The Council covered up your death as it had many others."

He ignored the marker with his own name inscribed on it and pressed his palm to his brother's.

François, I'm so sorry. Nico's steady presence behind him gave him a measure of comfort, but guilt weighed heavily on his heart. If he had stopped Pelletier, none of this would have happened.

"You forget I can read your thoughts at times," Nico said softly. Adrien stood and Nico wrapped an arm around his shoulders. "You aren't to blame for this, Adrien."

"I can't let it go."

"Then don't." Nico's voice resonated with challenge. "Do something about it."

CHAPTER THREE
SHAKY GROUND

"TALK TO me." Nico wrapped his arms around Adrien as Adrien closed the drapes in their hotel room a few hours later. Jacques had offered to let them stay at the vineyard, but Adrien couldn't imagine sleeping there, not after what they'd learned. The house was too full of ghosts who knew his name.

"What should I say?" Adrien knew he sounded dejected. He *was*. Just as Pelletier had known he would be.

"There's something I'm missing here," Nico said. "Something you're not telling me."

Something Adrien hoped never to have to tell Nico. But Pelletier had taken care of that too. Nico had seen Adrien's past, and he was far too intelligent to believe what they'd learned today was a coincidence. "Pelletier knows about this," he said at last.

"Your finding me here?"

"Yes." Adrien turned and took Nico's hands in his, then met Nico's gaze. "And more."

"What more?"

"Everything. All of this. The Pelletier who took you from me. The immortal. He knows about this timestream. Best I can tell, he sent me here."

"Timestream?"

"Sorry," Adrien said. "I should have explained to begin with. Every time something changes, what follows changes with it."

Nico frowned. "I'm not sure I understand."

Adrien smiled. "It's taken me a while to understand it myself. Think of time as a path. You walk down it and you come to a fork in the road. Each fork is a different timestream. Mostly the same people, but each is slightly changed from the last."

"You mean that each choice someone makes creates a fork in the road?"

"Right. So maybe you decide you want to get married. That's the path on your left. Take that path, and in a few years you have children. But maybe instead you decide you want to remain single. That's the path on your right. Take that path…."

"And your children are never born."

"Exactly."

"Or in my case," Nico said, "I didn't meet you."

"And I never became immortal. I died."

"Why didn't we meet in this… timestream?" Nico asked.

Adrien shrugged. "Who knows?" If François died before Charles turned him into a vampire, Adrien would never have been looking for Charles and Nicolas would never have come looking for him. Or maybe François hadn't insisted Adrien come with him to the ball. "There are so many different reasons we might have never met this time around."

"So you believe Pelletier sent you to this timestream?"

"I… I'm not sure. Maybe. I didn't think he could do that. Maybe the thing inside of me… my demon… sent me. Either way, Pelletier *knows* I'm here."

"How can you be sure?"

"The morning after I found you again," Adrien replied, "there was a message on my phone. From Pelletier. I don't know how he sent it." He shrugged. "It doesn't matter."

"A message?" Nico frowned and tilted his head to the side.

"I'm sorry. I should have told you. To be honest, I wanted to forget about it. I was ready to move on…." *I was ready to stay with you here. Forever.*

Nico brought one of Adrien's hands to his lips and kissed it. No doubt he'd heard this last thought. "What did the message say?"

"That he wouldn't bother me if I wanted to stay in this timestream. He'd leave me alone. With you."

A flicker of fury lit Nico's eyes. "How generous of the bastard. So he wants you to stay here because you're a threat to him in your own timestream?"

"Maybe." Adrien wasn't sure he *had* his own timestream anymore. If you could affect many timestreams by traveling through time, weren't they *all* his own?

"If he knows you're here…. If he can travel through time at will, why not just go back in time and stop you from being born?"

"I'm not sure. I've wondered that myself." Adrien focused on the warm feel of Nico's skin and tried to shake off his dark thoughts. "Maybe he doesn't want to. He's always enjoyed games. Or maybe he can't. It doesn't matter."

"Of course it matters!"

"It only matters if I leave this timestream." He'd already made up his mind that he wanted to stay. Nothing else mattered.

Nico's hands slipped from Adrien's and he turned away, his face now hidden in shadow. The muscles in his shoulders tensed. "No," he said, his voice as soft as a sigh.

"Nico, I love you. I've been looking for you for so long. I can't—"

"No!" Nico spun around and grabbed Adrien by the upper arms. "I won't have you do this."

Adrien cupped Nico's cheek. "I want this. I want to be with you. I love you. I can't—I *won't* let you go this time."

"No." Nico's hard veneer crumbled, and Adrien saw his own pain mirrored in Nico's beautiful face. "I've seen enough of your soul to know what this will do to you. What it's *already* doing to you. Don't you see? It's brilliant. And it's fucking twisted. Pelletier takes away everything you care about—" Nico stopped Adrien's protest with a finger to Adrien's lips. "Everything but me and your father. All of the others are gone. Your brother. Roland. Charles. The Council. Then he tells you to enjoy what you have. Knowing it will eat at you. Knowing you'll suffer with regret and guilt."

"But I *do* have you and my father." The words echoed hollow.

"This is wrong." Nico rubbed the back of his neck and closed his eyes.

"Of course it's wrong," Adrien agreed. "To manipulate all of us for—"

"It's more than that. When I saw you on the street," Nico explained. "I *felt* something. I thought I knew you. Roland once told you there weren't any living vampires with this power, right?"

Adrien nodded.

"And now there are *two* hunters who can manipulate time? That can't be a coincidence." Nico clenched his fists, then said, "It's *not* a coincidence. This about my blood. Pelletier took the Nicolas you knew at the wedding. He *used* that blood. The Rousseau blood he coveted and killed my family for. He's probably still using it. And he's figured out a way to do what you've been able to do."

"Your blood." Of course. Pelletier had kidnapped Nicolas from the wedding over a century ago and kept him alive for his blood. If Nico was right—if it was *Nico's* blood that held the power over time—Nicolas was still Pelletier's prisoner. Somewhere. *Some time.* "Oh God." Adrien sat heavily on the bed, face in his hands. "I tried…. For so long, I tried to find him…."

Nico sat next to him and wrapped a gentle arm over his shoulders. "Adrien?"

Adrien leaned into the touch and sighed.

"Staying here will kill your soul." Nico's voice was rough with emotion.

"I need time to think." Adrien laughed as he realized what he'd said. Time. He had time in abundance, didn't he? "Time with you. After so long, I—"

"Shhh." Nico pressed a fingertip to Adrien's lips. "I'm here for you as long as you want me."

Chapter Four
Heeding the Call

THE NEXT morning Nico and Adrien said their farewells to Jacques and drove to Lyon. "I don't come here often," Nico told him as they walked the grounds of the Lamberts' mansion on the outskirts of the city. Where before the gardens outside had been carefully manicured, most had now reverted to a natural state. But it was the building that took Adrien by surprise, or what was left of it: a tumble of stones and charred wooden beams in and around which grasses and bushes grew.

"From the expression on your face, this isn't the way it looks in your time." Nico gestured Adrien past the ruined mansion toward the coach house a few hundred yards away, and they began to walk. "This is all that's left."

Adrien drew a long breath. "It's been some time since I've been here, but as far as I know, it's still standing."

"Jean chose not to restore it after Pelletier's men burned it down. Perhaps he believes it's best to leave sleeping dogs to lie, as the Americans say, or perhaps he just didn't have the heart for it." Nico shrugged. "I never asked him."

"Why did they destroy it?"

"To send a message to those who survived the massacre." Nico wore a grim expression.

Or a message to me, perhaps. A challenge Pelletier knew I'd have no choice but to answer.

"He sent creatures… abominations. Many of our kind perished as a result."

Before Adrien could ask what creatures Pelletier had sent, a human servant peered out from the coach house, then ran toward them and kneeled in front of Nico. "Lord Rousseau? Is that you? I didn't expect—"

"Pierre, my deepest apologies for not having called in advance," Nico said and gently pulled the man to his feet. "I hadn't planned on the visit."

"You know we are always happy to serve you and Lord Lambert," Pierre said and looked with suspicion at Adrien.

"This is Adrien Gilbert," Nico said. "An old and dear friend of mine. He is no threat to me or any other of our kind."

15

Pierre nodded but looked unconvinced. In spite of this, he took their bags, then left them alone after reassuring them that he would prepare them lunch.

"Pierre survived the attack on Jean's home," Nico explained. "He's wary of any newcomers, regardless of race."

"I understand." The Lamberts' Lyon mansion had once served as a home and safe haven to many vampires, many of whom willingly served or helped maintain the sprawling grounds. But instead of the nearly hundred men and women who had lived here in his own time, Adrien now sensed only a few.

"We probably should have sold the property long ago," Nico said, as if he'd read Adrien's thoughts. "But now's not the time to dwell on the past. We've been given a gift, you and I." Nico pressed his hands to Adrien's face and kissed him sweetly. "Come with me?"

Adrien nodded and let Nico lead him upstairs to a room furnished simply in the bright colors of Provence that reminded Adrien of the cool blue of the ocean as the waves broke under an orange sun. The windows looked out on the formal gardens, which, unlike those in front of the main building, were clearly lovingly tended.

"These tiny gardens are my own piece of heaven," Nico said brightly as he gathered Adrien into his arms. "Even after my true heritage was revealed, Jean made me feel at home in this place. There's little left of it now, but what there is I'm happy to share with you."

Adrien kissed Nico's neck and smiled when Nico shuddered in response. Nico was right: their time together was a gift, one Adrien had dreamed of for more than a century. He would savor it for as long as possible.

"RIDE WITH me?" Nico said after they'd eaten a hearty lunch of coq au vin, bread, and cheese. Outside, the sun had just started its afternoon descent, and a gentle breeze ruffled the drapes by the open window.

"I'd love to."

An hour later, wind blowing through his hair, Adrien felt far better as they rode through the woods to the familiar hot spring at the edge of the Lambert property. They dismounted and removed their boots and socks, then settled onto the soft grass at the edge of the pool and dipped their feet in. Past and present combined as he remembered himself here with Nicolas—a different Nicolas—more than a century before.

Adrien drew a long breath and glanced at Nico, who wore a strange, faraway expression. "What are you thinking about?" Adrien asked as he wiggled his toes and watched the ripples dance over the smooth surface of the water.

Nico offered Adrien a shy smile, then said, "I feel as though I've been here before. With you."

"We came here together," Adrien confirmed. "Although it wasn't in my own timestream. There is another timestream, one where I changed the future. Maybe you saw that in my blood."

Nico nodded. "Could be." He gazed at the water with a slight furrow of his forehead.

"You're not convinced."

Nico shook his head. "I can't explain it. I don't recall having seen it in your memories." Nico laughed softly, then added, "Of course I could experience your soul a hundred times and I'd never see everything hidden within your blood. I'm sure you're right."

Each time he'd taken Nico's blood, more of Nico's past became clear. Souls held so many memories, thoughts, and feelings. The explanation made sense, but was he missing something? If Nico's blood held the key to his power….

"It doesn't matter," Nico said after a moment's pause. "There are far more important things to do than contemplate memories."

"Such as?" Adrien lay on the grass and stretched his arms over his head. Later, there'd be time to think about what it all meant.

"Such as enjoying the present as fully as possible." Nico ghosted a finger over Adrien's lips, then laughed and joined him on the grass.

As the sun dipped below the horizon, Adrien chased Nico from the stables and through the back entry into the coach house. "I was only trying to help pick the leaves out of your hair," he said, laughing.

"I'm sure I can handle that myself—" Nico stared at the man standing in the hallway. "Jean," he exclaimed, running to his brother and embracing him. "I didn't expect you. I thought you were in Paris."

"When you mentioned you were stopping in Saint-Gervais," Jean said with a cautious glance in Adrien's direction, "my curiosity got the better of me. I'm sorry to have interrupted.

"Please don't apologize," Adrien said, offering his hand. "I'm Adrien Gilbert."

Jean shook Adrien's hand, but his eyes flickered with suspicion and his fingers twitched as he released his grip. "Nico," Jean said. "Explain."

"He's Jacques's son," Nico said. "And before you draw your sword, yes, I know he was killed more than a century ago."

Jean raised an eyebrow but remained silent.

"I couldn't risk explaining by phone." Nico glanced at Adrien and smiled.

"It's a long story," Adrien added. For just a moment, he'd enjoyed Nico's company without thinking about the future. *Or the past.* Jean's arrival was a jolt that sent him crashing back to reality. "One best explained by blood."

ADRIEN STUDIED Jean as he sipped his brandy and gazed at the fire. Since he'd given Jean his blood a few hours before, Jean had said nothing. Adrien guessed he needed time to digest what he'd seen and come to terms with its implications.

At last Jean set his cup on the side table and took a long breath. "When I received Nico's summons, I feared the worst. But what you've shown me is both more disturbing than anything I imagined and more than I'd dreamed possible."

"You understand what I have to do," Adrien said with a quick glance in Nico's direction.

"I'd given up hope." Jean's face remained unreadable, but his hand shook ever so slightly as he poured himself another drink.

"Even if I'm successful," Adrien said, "there's no guarantee your world will change."

Jean glanced at Nico, and a ghost of a smile spread over his face. "I don't expect to see the past repaired. But if the future you create allows Nico to live without fear?" He sighed. "We've spent far too long in the shadows wondering when Pelletier's men would finish the job and eradicate the ancients for good. It's not a life I wish for myself, let alone for my brother."

"One way or another, this *will* end. I swear it." Adrien spoke the words like the vow they were.

"I will help you, of course," Jean told Adrien.

"Thank you." Adrien poured himself a drink and sat facing them. "But there's only one thing I need from you."

"Name it."

"Keep Nico safe," Adrien said. "When Pelletier learns I'm not interested in his pathetic bargain, he may seek to harm you. *Both* of you. And if I'm not here to watch over him…."

"Of course."

CHAPTER FIVE
FACE TO FACE

"ADRIEN." THE demon's voice echoed in Adrien's mind, waking him from an uneasy sleep.

What do you want? Adrien slipped silently out of bed and padded into the sitting room, careful not to wake Nico.

"Right question, wrong person. What do you *want?"*

Adrien breathed in slowly, trying to calm his racing heart. *You know damn well what I want. You said it yourself—you're me, right?*

"I can think of a few things you might want."

Fucker.

"Did you think I wouldn't know all of your thoughts?" The demon's laughter rang in Adrien's ears. *"Time to make nice. You* need *me."*

Adrien clenched his jaw and gazed out the window at the clear night sky. The moon hung low and bright on the horizon, illuminating the fields below. The urge to run under that moon, to feel the grass under his bare feet, suddenly became more than he could resist. He pulled on the jeans he'd tossed on the settee and opened the window. The wind carried the delicate fragrance from the gardens. Adrien inhaled and pushed the demon away.

Fuck off.

"Not that easy." The demon pressed back, snaking tendrils of fear and doubt into Adrien's thoughts.

Adrien glanced back at Nico, sound asleep in the bedroom. A cold terror wound through his body, starting at his belly and working its way into his chest and arms. The bed shimmered and dissolved. For a panicked moment, Adrien thought the demon had once again sent him through time. He grabbed the sill to steady himself, as if he might will himself to remain here. But the room did not change as expected, and the usual nausea never came. Instead, the bed became a hard stone floor, and on it, Nicolas lay shivering, his clothing in tatters, his body thin and pale.

This isn't real.

"Isn't it?"

19

Cold clawed at Adrien's throat, causing him to gasp for air. *No. I don't want to see this.*

"*These are your thoughts,*" the demon said in a whisper. "*The thoughts you hide from yourself. Do you think hiding them helps him, Adrien? Do you think he doesn't suffer?*"

"Nico," Adrien said, reaching out to the ghostly figure.

"*Not Nico. Nicolas. The one you lost to Pelletier more than a hundred years ago. Or don't you remember? What do you think Pelletier does to him? Do you think Pelletier cares about anything but the precious Rousseau blood that courses through Nicolas's veins?*"

Adrien could smell the demon's cloying breath on his neck. And his words…. God, his words cut like a knife! This was everything he'd feared for Nicolas when Pelletier took him at the wedding. Pain. Hopelessness. Loneliness.

"*Wallow in your guilt,*" the demon hissed. "*It's better than facing the truth, don't you think?*"

He hadn't faced the truth. He'd pushed it away. The vision before him—was it a vision or was it reality?—was a nightmare.

He reached for Nicolas, but his fingers touched only the air. *A vision.* That's all it was—his own imagination, brought to life by the demon.

"*This is your truth, Adrien. The truth you deny. The truth of how Pelletier uses the man you say you love.*"

No. And yet he'd imagined this. He'd dreamed of this—horrible dreams he'd managed to forget that ate slowly away at his soul, devouring it piece by piece until nothing remained but a hollow, worthless shell.

"*You believe the truth is otherwise?*" The demon sniggered. "*Perhaps I should show you this Nicolas. If I did, what would you do?*"

Yes! Take me to him! He'd help Nicolas, care for him.

"*And if he's too far gone? If his mind has broken? Will you pick up the scraps and hope to repair the damage?*"

Adrien shuddered and covered his face with his hands. *Please. It can't be so. I would die if he suffered so deeply on my account.*

"*See? Guilt is easier, isn't it?*"

Give me your power. Let me fix the harm that's been done. Let me go back!

"*What price are you willing to pay for my power?*"

Of course the demon would demand a price, and a high one. *What is it you want?* Adrien already knew the answer. It had been there all along, but he'd refused to see it.

20

"*I want you, Adrien,*" the demon said, his voice now a sensual murmur. "*I want my freedom.*"

Like hell am I giving myself over to you. The last time the demon had taken control, Adrien had had to fight his way back to himself. He'd tried to kill Roland.

"*Give me tonight,*" the demon said. "*One night in your body.*"

And what do I get in return?

"*I will take you back, if you wish it.*"

Back where? To my own time, to chase Nicolas again? To the Nicolas who could never be his?

"*To the place you must go before you can change the future,*" the demon answered.

An answer, and yet not an answer. *Where will you take me?* Adrien demanded. *How do I know you'll keep your word?*

"*You'll trust me. You have no other choice.*"

He took a deep breath and uncovered his eyes. The hellish vision had vanished, replaced by the reality of Nico, peacefully asleep beneath the soft covers. Without the demon, Adrien would remain in this world where nearly everyone he cared about had been killed. Sooner or later, the guilt would destroy him, and with him, Nico. He owed Nico more than that. Not only Nico, but the Nicolas who was Pelletier's prisoner, and the Nicolas who had given up his future to marry Giovanetti. He owed François and Charles a future. He owed them all everything, even his life, if it would set things right again.

Tonight only, Adrien told the demon. *Tomorrow, you will do what I ask of you.*

NICO AWOKE with a start to realize Adrien was gone. A quick glance at the bedside clock told him it was about three in the morning. He pushed aside the niggle of fear that buzzed in his veins and reached out for Adrien's soul. *He's nearby.* His sense of relief that Adrien hadn't vanished as quickly as he'd appeared mingled with something else, a strange sensation he couldn't place. Something about Adrien. Something different.

He climbed out of bed and dressed quickly, then sprinted down the stairs and out into the gardens.

CHAPTER SIX
TAKING THE REINS

THE DEMON sensed the vampire long before he saw him. The vampire's blood called to him and made his cock fill with need. Delicious blood. *His* blood for the taking.

"Adrien?" The vampire stared at him from across the gardens.

Perfect. The demon licked his lips and strode over to Nico. "I'm sorry if I woke you," he said, choosing his words carefully and speaking in the hunter's voice.

"You will not hurt him."

The demon pushed the hunter's mind away and laughed. He wouldn't hurt the hunter's plaything. There was too much to be gained here from the plaything's blood and from his body. Still, it served the demon's purposes that the hunter feared what he might do.

Cooperate and I will not harm him.

The hunter pushed back against the demon's mind, but the demon held tight. *You promised me this*, he reminded the hunter.

"I woke and didn't see you. I was afraid," Nico said.

"Afraid I might have left?" the demon asked. He smiled as the hunter might have, then took Nico in his arms.

This close, the scent of blood made him dizzy. He tilted Nico's head to better display his lovely throat. The powerful muscles there elongated and the slight pulse of his artery grew more visible. He didn't wait for Nico's approval but licked a line over where the skin fluttered with each beat of Nico's heart.

"Adrien." Nico gasped, his pulse racing beneath the demon's tongue. The flutter of his heart seemed so weak. So fragile. All the more delicious.

How delicate that flesh there felt. How fragile these creatures were. It would be too easy to tear that flesh apart, to sever that beautiful head from its body. The demon smiled and grazed Nico's neck with his teeth. It would be a waste to destroy so alluring a creature as this. He must possess Nico. Use his body to derive pleasure. In this, at least, the hunter was not mistaken. This vampire was beautiful.

"Please," Nico whispered.

Nico's arousal pressed against the demon's thigh. The demon would taste that delicious cock before the night was through, but for now it would drink its fill. It growled again and ripped into the perfect flesh of Nico's neck, knowing it caused Nico pain, but knowing that pain created pleasure as well. The hunter's blunt teeth were ungainly things, far less effective than the pointed eyeteeth of a vampire. And yet perhaps they allowed for more enjoyment.

Nico's blood flooded the demon's mouth with heat. Almost immediately, the demon's thoughts became entangled with Nico's. Nico's fear upon meeting the hunter for the first time. The disbelief that turned to stunned surprise as the hunter had shown Nico the secrets of his blood. Already Nico loved the hunter, though he hadn't yet spoken the words.

Pathetic human emotions.

"Emotions give us strength," the hunter said. *"Without them we are animals, incapable of true pleasure."*

Perhaps. But emotions could break a man and destroy his sanity. The demon had hoped the vampires were stronger, but if Nico was any example, they were as fragile as their hunter kin. To survive, it must control the hunter. To allow itself to *be* controlled? That would be foolish or worse. The hunter cared nothing for his own life. He cared only for the lives of others.

The demon continued to drink. It tasted loneliness and pain. It avoided peering too deeply into the hidden rooms of the vampire's soul. There were things there it did not wish to see—a bitter taste that lingered at the periphery and tainted the sweetness of the blood. It forced itself upward, back toward the surface with its shimmering brightness and lust-filled edges.

"Adrien." The vampire shuddered and clung to the demon as it released its purchase and the broken skin began to knit.

It would forgive the vampire's use of the hunter's name. It had no name. It had been born from the vampire's power—Nicolas's power. It needed no name.

It pushed Nico roughly onto the grass and claimed his mouth without hesitation. Nico welcomed its tongue, pressing it against the sharp edge of his teeth so that it bled. Nico met its gaze, and the demon saw understanding there even before it heard the vampire's voice in his mind. *"I know what you are."* Nico, speaking through the connection forged in blood.

That only excited it more. Perhaps even if the hunter won the battle for control over this body, there might be a reason to continue to exist.

But I will not allow that to happen.

It smiled as it ripped the thin fabric from Nico's body to expose the smooth expanse of his chest. The earthy smell of the grass mingled with the scent of Nico's skin and the citrus soap he'd showered with hours before.

Nico gasped as the demon grabbed his ass and kneaded it roughly. Nico arched toward the demon, moaning, his cock grinding against the demon's member hard enough to hurt. The demon smiled and settled more of its weight against Nico, then moved until Nico laughed and nipped at the demon's neck. The sting of the bite felt good. Vampires liked to skirt the edges of pain in sex. Perhaps its own hunger for the same came as a result of its birth and the vampire's blood.

Nico licked the blood that dripped down its neck, then pushed the demon onto its back and claimed one nipple, then the other. He licked around the tightening bud, then ran his sharp eyeteeth over the same path. The sting felt so fucking good the demon cried out, causing several nearby birds to take to the air and rustle the tree branches as they fled.

"Fuck me." Nico met the demon's eyes. "Use me as you wish."

As if the demon needed permission! Still, the words sent a frisson a pleasure down its spine. The hunter wouldn't have stood for taking the vampire without consent, and somehow knowing the vampire wanted this made it that much sweeter.

The demon fumbled with the opening of the vampire's trousers and growled in frustration. This was the hunter's fault. If he would only allow the demon to use his body at will, moving the hunter's hands and fingers wouldn't be so awkward.

Nico's knowing chuckle should have incensed the demon, but instead it found the response endearing. A strange sensation of warmth flooded the demon's belly and made its way to its arms and legs. Pleasant enough, but the demon pushed away the temptation to let the feeling continue— something about it made the demon uncomfortable.

"Love is a powerful emotion," the hunter said, amusement sounding in his words like music spurs a dancer to twirl around a partner.

Love is weakness. The demon returned its focus to Nico, who by now had unfastened his pants. The demon slipped its hands beneath the fabric as Nico leaned forward and shimmied free. The demon squeezed the perfect globes of Nico's ass beneath its fingers and dug its fingernails into the smooth flesh.

"Mine." The demon reveled in Nico's naked body atop its own. The contrast of bare skin against the hunter's heavy jeans and sweater awakened its possessive nature.

"Yours, Adrien," Nico said. "Always."

"I'm not—"

"You're the same." Nico's eyes lit with determination, as though he might convince the demon through the intensity of his thoughts.

"Believe what you wish"—the demon cut into Nico's flesh with its fingernails—"but I *will* control him."

Nico pulled the demon's face to his own and claimed the demon's lips, his tenderness in contrast to the violence with which the demon still held him prisoner. The demon clenched its teeth in reply, but Nico slid his tongue between its lips and traced a gentle path over its teeth as he ghosted lithe fingers over the demon's cheeks, nose, and temples. The demon closed its eyes and allowed itself to experience the pleasure of the moment. It opened its mouth fully to allow Nico entry.

Nico's sweet mouth left the demon dizzy and weak. The kiss ended far sooner than the demon wished. A moment later Nico's sharp eyeteeth pierced the tender skin below the hunter's ear. That Nico dared to take his blood without asking took the demon by surprise, but the ecstasy of the bite eroded the edges of its anger. Acquiescence was far more pleasurable than the demon imagined.

Nico sucked and pulled at the hunter's flesh, taking his fill. The demon knew it shouldn't trust Nico, but it basked in the warmth of its submission.

I allow this because it is my choice. The hunter chuckled in reply, and the demon pushed the hunter away. *This night is mine alone!*

But it was not the demon who broke the delicious contact. Instead Nico withdrew, leaving the demon momentarily bereft. It reached for Nico, eager to fuck his beautiful ass. Nico slipped from the demon's grasp, got to his feet, and ran toward the forest. In the moonlight, his pale skin seemed luminescent. He turned around and smiled at the demon, then ran so fast the demon struggled to follow his movements.

A game, then. The demon liked games. Nico was its prey.

Nico ran naked in the dim moonlight that pierced the cover of the trees. The demon's cock strained against its clothing. It growled and pulled free of the fabric, tearing it in the process. Once naked, it resumed the chase.

Ahead, Nico waited on the low branch of a tree, his feet dangling over the path. "You're slow," he told the demon as it lumbered toward him. Nico was right. This was the hunter's fault, of course. If he would allow more regular use of his body, the demon would have had time to master running.

The demon hissed its displeasure and heard the hunter chuckle. *"I can help,"* the hunter told the demon. *"If you'll permit me."*

The demon considered the offer and was ready to tell the hunter to leave it be when Nico began to run again, disappearing a moment later deeper into the forest.

Catch him, the demon said. It didn't like the hunter joining in the chase, but it had yet to master the hunter's body and it saw no other option.

"My pleasure." The hunter slipped alongside the demon's consciousness and began to run, following Nico's scent past a dense stand of trees and emerging onto a glade bathed in silvery light.

Nico continued to run. With the hunter's help, the demon drew closer and closer, until Nico was within its grasp. It lunged and grabbed Nico by the shoulder, roughly tackling him to the ground and straddling him triumphantly. There, Nico lay on a bed of moss, the whisper of a smile on his lips. The demon bent down and stole a kiss before grasping Nico's cock and its own. It squeezed and ran its thumb over Nico's tip to wet it. It pumped them both and groaned with pleasure.

"He's beautiful, isn't he?" the hunter asked. Until that moment, the demon hadn't realized the hunter was still with him.

Leave, the demon commanded. The hunter acquiesced, leaving the demon once more in control.

Nico's smile broadened. "You and he would be far better served if you always worked together," he said.

The demon responded by biting Nico's lower lip and licking the blood that blossomed there. "The hunter is too gentle with you," it said and bit Nico's earlobe. Nico panted and gasped in reply. "But I know your kind like pain with your pleasure."

"My *kind* can't be so easily categorized," Nico replied. "My tastes are not so limited." He grabbed the demon and rolled it onto its back with surprising force.

So he was holding back. Interesting. Perhaps vampires were worthy of more respect.

Nico licked his lips and took the prize of the demon's cock in his mouth. Wet and warm, the contact sent shivers of pleasure throughout the demon's body. It arched its back and thrust deeply into Nico's mouth, fucking it as though it were the delicious ass it intended to invade before the night was through.

The glorious sting of pain as Nico's eyeteeth brushed the tender skin at the base nearly sent the demon over the edge. "Not yet," it said. "Not until I'm buried inside you."

But Nico didn't relent. He sucked harder and used his tongue to press the demon's member against the roof of his mouth. Would it be so terrible to acquiesce this once? The demon fought its mounting need for release until it felt nothing but Nico and wanted only to fill that sinful mouth with its seed. The demon came, its cries echoing back to him off the trees. It watched as Nico licked clean the shaft.

"Turn around," Nico ordered before the demon had a chance to catch its breath.

"I won't yield to—"

"Turn around." Nico didn't wait for a reply this time but forced the demon onto its hands and knees with unexpected strength.

The demon pushed back against Nico, but Nico easily held it there. "You forget where your power comes from," Nico said.

The demon laughed. "You've hidden this from him."

"I've hidden nothing. I'm physically stronger," Nico replied. "But your power? That remains to be seen."

"I am not *him*." The hunter was weak. Pathetic. Didn't Nico understand? They were different. *Separate.*

"You're the same. You'll understand this someday. There is no *you*. There is only *him*.

"I may allow you to take me," the demon said, ignoring this.

"You *want* this," Nico parried. "You wish to be dominated. You want to feel power other than your own." Nico nipped its shoulder, the sting causing the demon's softening cock to fill again.

The demon remained silent but bucked beneath Nico. Again Nico bit its shoulder, deeper this time. Nico sucked and licked the bite, each flick of his tongue sending fingers of pleasure throughout the demon's body. Gooseflesh rose on its neck, and it shivered.

Please.

"You are the same," Nico said in its mind. *"You are both the man I love."* He licked his way down the demon's back, pausing at its ass long enough to part the globes and knead them to the point of pain.

Please.

Nico's tongue brushed its hole, and the demon pressed against the cool wetness. Nico dug his fingers into the demon's buttocks until the demon shouted, but Nico did not yield. As the demon quieted, Nico pushed the tip of his tongue inward, opening the passage just a bit before withdrawing.

Please. Don't stop!

"I love you, Adrien," Nico replied silently, then pressed in again, farther, remaining there until the muscles began to relax.

I'm not—

Nico's answer was a wet finger tugging at the demon's entrance. Pain and pleasure, much like Nico's bite. So delicious.

Please. Yes! Please!

A second finger breached the demon.

Please. Please fuck me!

A third finger, scissoring, opening, making it want Nico's cock. Making it want to succumb to Nico's power. Want to feel Nico's power.

Nico!

"Adrien. Forever, Adrien."

The hunter's consciousness mingled with the demon's, but for once the demon didn't force it away. Memories floated free, touching the demon's soul. It struggled briefly, then allowed them to remain.

Nico pressed his cock against the demon's hole.

Please. Oh, please, Nico!

"Adrien."

I'm here. Yes. Adrien and the demon spoke in one voice.

Nico thrust inside and filled them, waiting a moment for them to catch their breath before beginning to move. Nico's hands caressed their bare back, traced the line of their spine, and followed his fingers with tender kisses.

Yes. Oh, yes!

"I love you, Adrien."

The demon thought to push the hunter away, but his presence seemed to intensify the joy of the union. Together, they moaned their pleasure as Nico increased the speed of his thrusts. The noises of the forest faded, the only sound in their ears the sound of blood, of hearts beating, and Nico's grunts.

I love you, Nico. No longer two voices, but one. *You alone, Nico!*

Adrien's climax exploded white and hot, engulfing him much like the flames of his beloved sword. He shouted, but the sound did not pierce the cloak of reality. Colors invaded his vision as the forest disappeared. He reached for future and past, felt them collide and separate again.

The realization of what he had just touched peaked, ebbed, then vanished as the world came flying back into perspective.

CHAPTER SEVEN
STUMBLING IN THE DARK

ADRIEN AWOKE to a headache that stabbed at his eyes, making his head spin and his stomach do backflips. He grabbed for something to steady himself and was rewarded with handfuls of soft sheets.

"Are you okay?" Nico frowned with concern.

"I… yes," Adrien croaked. His memories of the night before came flooding back. "Nico, shit, I'm so sorry, I can't believe I—"

Nico silenced him with his lips. "I make my own decisions," he said after the kiss broke. "You didn't do anything I didn't want. Although—" He kissed a tender spot beneath Adrien's ear. "—I'm hungry enough for three breakfasts this morning."

Adrien shivered, then closed his eyes and sighed. "I should have known better than to trust it."

"Trust it? The demon?" Nico kissed him again.

"It said it would take me back in time if I gave it my body." Adrien half expected the demon to laugh, but instead it remained silent.

"I don't understand the difference."

"Difference?" Adrien asked.

"Between you and the demon." He ran a finger over Adrien's lips and sighed. "Seems like you remember pretty much everything."

"I do. At the end, I… we…." His throbbing head won out and he sighed. "You're right. I'm probably overthinking this." A memory flickered at the edge of Adrien's consciousness. Something he needed to remember. *Something I have to understand.*

"Something wrong?" Nico asked.

"Nothing. Something happened and I thought…." Adrien rubbed the bridge of his nose. "It's nothing."

Nico rolled out of bed and pulled on a silk robe. "I'll tell the cook to prepare breakfast." Nico's eyes were tinged with the red of bloodlust. "Although if I weren't so hungry for food, I might…."

Adrien's face heated with arousal. *Fucking demon.* Had they really run naked through the woods? He swallowed hard and said, "I'll meet you downstairs in a few." He needed a cold shower first, although he guessed it wouldn't help much.

Nico grinned knowingly, then left the room. The sound of a whistled *Il était une bergère* echoed from the landing outside. Adrien made his way to the bathroom, splashed some cold water on his face, then rooted around in the medicine cabinet for something to help his headache and swallowed a double dose. As Adrien undressed and slipped into the shower, the demon sang the familiar words to the old children's song:

"Il était une bergère.... La bergère en colère, et ron, ron, ron, petit patapon. La bergère encolère, tua son p'tit chaton, ron, ron, tua son p'tit chaton."

There was a shepherdess who made cheese from the milk of her lambs.... The cat watched her with a mischievous look.... If you put your paw in it, you'll get a beating.... He didn't put his paw in it, he put his face in it.... The angry shepherdess killed her little cat....

"BREAKFAST IS ready," Nico said as he walked back into the room while Adrien dressed.

"Mmmm." Adrien stopped buttoning his shirt and gathered Nico into his arms. "Sure you don't want to wait a bit?" he asked as he tugged on the sash of Nico's robe. "I could make it worth your while."

Nico laughed and wreathed his arms around Adrien's neck. "You're going to be the death of me!"

Adrien released Nico and backed toward the bed, arms outstretched. "I promise breakfast won't be too cold."

Nico shook his head in mock resignation.

"Come on. Just a few minutes? Florette will forgive us if she has to reheat the croissants," Adrien said.

"All right." Nico pushed off his robe and stepped naked toward the bed.

ADRIEN PULLED a sweater over his head and slipped on his shoes. For the first time, he noticed Nicolas's gold pocket watch on the bedside table. The same watch Nico's counterpart had left for Adrien with a note inside: *I remember you.* Adrien picked it up and smiled.

"Where did you find that?" Nico asked.

"Isn't it yours?"

Nico took the watch from him and frowned. "I… no… I mean, yes, it *was* mine." He turned it over in his hand.

"What do you mean, *was* yours?" Adrien asked.

"Jean gave it to me on my twentieth birthday. But I haven't seen it in more than a hundred years." Nico shifted on the bed and met Adrien's gaze. "It was stolen when I went to study in London. At least I thought it was."

Adrien struggled to understand the implications. "May I?" he asked, reaching for the watch.

Nico nodded and gave the watch back to Adrien. Adrien was sure he hadn't seen it on the table before. Perhaps one of the servants had placed it there. But Nico appeared as surprised as he.

"Open it." The demon's voice thrummed with anticipation.

Adrien's hand shook as he clicked the watch open. Inside was a small scrap of paper. Gently, he unfolded it, willing his heart to stop pounding. The handwriting was Nicolas's.

"Nico," he said, his voice trembling in spite of his best efforts, "it's from you."

"Me? But that's impossible. I never…."

"*I need your help,*" Adrien read. In the upper right corner of the paper was a date: March 12, 2016.

"How…?" Nico was instantly on his feet.

"You didn't write this note?" Adrien gave the paper to Nico, who shook his head.

"The writing's mine, but I don't remember writing this. Besides, why would I write something and date it in the future?" Nico handed the note back to Adrien.

Had the demon left the note? Had he retrieved it from the other timestream? *That isn't possible.*

"You haven't even scratched the surface, Adrien. Let me show you what more I can do."

Time began to shift. Adrien heard Nico shout, "You can't take him!"

"No!" Adrien grabbed Nico's hands as the room began to fade and the familiar blue light blurred his vision. "I won't let you take me from him again. Not—"

CHAPTER EIGHT
AN INSTANT IN TIME

Paris, France—March 8, 2016 (Second Timestream)

"...NOW!" ADRIEN came back to himself. He looked around the room. *Not Nico's bedroom... but I remember this place.* His head ached. He wondered if he'd ever get used to time travel. *Probably not.* The dizziness and nausea began to fade, and Adrien realized he was holding Nico's hands. *Still* holding his hands.

The demon laughed.

What have you done?

"I've kept my promise. I've brought you to the place you must go before you can change the future," the demon replied. *"The rest...."*

"What the hell? Where are we?" Nicolas stared back at him. His hair was long again, tied back the way Adrien remembered it before he'd found himself in a future where he didn't exist.

"Nicolas?" Adrien's hand slipped from Nicolas's. In his other hand, he still held the watch and the crumpled note. He stared at it, uncomprehending.

"Nico," the man in front of him corrected. "Who else would I—?" Nico frowned and ran a hand through his hair, stopping as he reached the tie at his nape. "What the hell?"

"You're Nico?"

"I.... Of course, but...." Nico fingered his shirt. Not the T-shirt he'd worn before, but a silk button-down, open at the neck. "I don't understand. We were together.... You opened the watch...."

The throbbing in Adrien's head grew worse. "When I travel from one timestream to another," he said, struggling to focus, "I occupy my body in that time. Younger, older."

"Then the Nicolas of this time looks like this?" Nico asked.

"A different timestream." *Probably the one where you're married to that bastard Giovanetti.*

33

Nico paled. Adrien hadn't meant Nico to hear that particular thought. "I've seen that in your memories." He shuddered and Adrien pulled him close.

"Whatever this is," Adrien said, "I won't let him near you."

Nico relaxed against Adrien and nodded. "This body… it feels strange. A bit like wearing borrowed clothing."

Adrien chuckled in spite of himself. "You'll get used to it quickly enough."

After a long moment, Nico took a deep breath and slipped out of Adrien's arms. "I don't recognize this place."

"I do. This is—"

"My apartment in Paris," Roland said as he walked into the room. "But I don't recall inviting either of you." A crooked grin lit his face.

"Roland?" Nico stared, lips parted.

Roland raised a quizzical eyebrow and eyed them with interest.

"But…. The massacre…. The hunters…." Nico frowned. "You're supposed to be…."

"Dead?" Roland appeared amused.

"How…. How did you…?" Nico faltered.

Roland glanced at Adrien and said, "I'm aware of Adrien's talents. You might say we share a fair bit of history. Since you're staring at me like you've seen a ghost, it's quite simple to put the pieces together. Still, I'm at a loss to understand how Adrien managed to bring you with him. You aren't from this timestream, are you?"

"I… no."

"What is the date today?" Adrien asked.

"March 8, 2016."

Adrien met Nico's gaze. *Just a few days before the Nicolas of this timestream wrote that note.*

"I can't explain it." Adrien was relieved that Roland seemed to grasp the situation so quickly.

"Perhaps the explanation lies with someone other than you." Roland pressed his lips together and tilted his head to one side.

"Someone other than Adrien?" Nico frowned before adding silently, *"Does he believe that I'm the one who brought us here?"*

Maybe. My gift is from your Rousseau blood. Besides, I've never been able to bring someone with me before.

Nico rubbed the bridge of his nose but said nothing.

"There'll be time to discuss it later." Roland motioned them into the kitchen. "For now, why don't you both sit and let me make up for my inexcusable lack of manners."

Adrien offered a very confused-looking Nico a shrug and a smile. Roland would get to the point. Eventually.

"COFFEE WILL help your headaches." Roland set two demitasses of espresso in front of Adrien and Nico a few minutes later.

Nico inhaled the strong scent and sighed. "Thank you." He took a sip and set the cup back down.

Adrien grunted his thanks.

"The Roland I knew died fighting Pelletier over a hundred years ago." Nico swallowed hard, then added, "It's really good to see you again."

Everything felt surreal; Adrien's familiar presence was the only constant. Nico took Adrien's hand and squeezed it. *He's worried about me. Or what Giovanetti will do to me if he realizes I'm not his mate.*

"What did you mean that someone else may be responsible for bringing me here? And how did you guess I'm not the Nicolas you know?" he asked Roland, intentionally changing the subject to focus Adrien's attention on something other than concern. Not that he felt all that steady himself, but Adrien's worrying wasn't going to help them.

"Logic," Roland said with a wry smile. "While touching Adrien wouldn't kill the Nicolas I know, he couldn't hold Adrien's hand as long as you have or as often as I've witnessed it today," Roland said. "Not without a lot of pain."

Nico gently released his grip on Adrien. He stared at his hand. "Giovanetti. Of course. I married the bastard because I was afraid of what he'd do to Adrien. Jean was right in the end," he added as the memory continued to unfold. "It didn't help."

"You remember that?" Roland asked.

Adrien frowned. "You saw it in my blood."

"No. Not in your blood." Nico struggled to explain. "These aren't your memories. They're mine. But I'm not sure how or why." These were memories of another Nicolas.

"Fascinating." Roland rubbed his chin. He looked like a child who had just discovered a new toy. "You've never been able to bring someone with you when you've traveled through time, have you, Adrien?"

"No."

"Then the someone who brought me here…," Nico began.

"Was you yourself." Roland wore a self-satisfied grin.

"Me?" Was that even possible?

"Adrien's power comes from the Rousseau blood, after all." Roland picked up his coffee and sipped it.

Nico frowned. "But I did nothing."

"Are you sure?" Roland asked.

"Nico?" Adrien set his cup down and frowned.

"I…." Nico hesitated and tried to remember. "Back in my room, when you picked up the watch… I felt the demon. I… I knew what it was going to do. I couldn't let it take you. Not without me. I remember thinking that I would go with you rather than let it take you."

"Indeed." Roland grinned. "Adrien's gift is yours, after all."

Adrien rubbed the back of his neck. "You think Nico did this? But the demon—"

"Who's to say? Perhaps the demon is only part of the equation," Roland put in.

"Does it matter?" Nico was tired of trying to understand. He didn't care why or how. "The only thing that matters is that we stop Pelletier. Repair the damage he's done."

"It's too dangerous. Giovanetti will suspect something," Adrien told Nico. "He'll kill you if he realizes you aren't the Nicolas he married."

"He isn't in Paris," Roland said. "I'm afraid I don't know where he is."

"Probably planning something with Pelletier." Adrien looked genuinely worried. *"That would explain Nicolas's note. He must have gotten wind of something."*

"I can handle Giovanetti." Nico's stomach roiled at the thought of having to pretend to be married to someone like Antonio. "My counterpart might have submitted himself to the bastard for your sake, Adrien, but neither of us is weak."

"No." A muscle in Adrien's cheek tensed. "You aren't weak."

The words reassured Nico. Convincing Adrien that they should join forces in the fight against Pelletier and his men would be a challenge. Nico didn't doubt Adrien, but overcoming Adrien's protective nature would be a stumbling block. Adrien was stronger now, but Pelletier clearly had the upper hand. Together, they might defeat him. Alone, Adrien might not survive.

Roland poured more coffee and took a long sip from his own. "Charles and François went to Italy to investigate reports that Pelletier was seen there. Last I heard, they were headed back to Lyon to speak with Jean."

"Pelletier wants us know he's up to something," Adrien said. *And he probably knew the Nicolas from this timestream would try to contact me.*

Nico understood only too well what this meant. "He knows Adrien's accepted his challenge."

"Challenge?" Roland asked.

Adrien shook his head. "Pelletier found me in Nico's timestream. Maybe he even sent me there."

"He gave Adrien an ultimatum," Nico said between clenched teeth. "Stay with me and do nothing and he'd leave us be, or come out and play."

"He knew what choice you'd make." Roland seemed quite happy about this.

Nico brushed the back of Adrien's hand with his own. *Together. We're meant to do this together, regardless of what you're thinking.*

Adrien's nearly undetectable nod reassured Nico. Adrien wouldn't take off on his own and leave him unprotected in this timestream. At least not for now. Adrien would never do anything to endanger him. But if he thought being apart was safer….

"We're going to Italy." Adrien stood.

"We need to think this through," Nico countered evenly. "We don't want to tip our hand yet."

"I agree. You need to develop a plan first," Roland said. "You can stay a few days. Pelletier won't—"

"I can't stay." Adrien glared at Roland. Sweat beaded on his brow. He looked almost feverish.

"You aren't ready to meet him in a battle, Adrien." Roland spoke softly, but there was no ignoring the warning in his voice.

"I can't just stay here and… and…." Adrien teetered, and Nico caught him as he collapsed.

"What did you do?" Nico demanded as he settled the unconscious Adrien onto the couch. He pressed a hand to Adrien's chest. Adrien's heart beat slowly, steadily. A moment later he began to snore.

"He's fine. Just sleeping."

"You drugged him?"

"I bought us a little time." Roland was sanguine.

"Time for what?"

"Are you familiar with the story of the bull?" Roland wore the same coy smile Nico remembered. If Nico hadn't been so angry with him, he might have appreciated seeing it once again.

"Tell me." Whereas Adrien might have argued, Nico spoke the words he knew Roland wanted to hear.

"The bull is powerful," Roland said. "You can take it by the horns and argue with it. Perhaps it will lend you its power. Perhaps you will try to lead it through the valley and over the mountains. But eventually you will tire and it will gore you."

"Not a pleasant outcome." Nico had sensed Adrien's struggle, but he'd felt powerless to do anything to help.

"No." Roland refilled his coffee and sipped it.

In spite of Roland's outward calm, Nico sensed the power beneath churning and growing. Was that Roland's demon? Yet Adrien lacked Roland's absolute control.

"You cannot lead the bull, much as you believe you can." Roland swirled the coffee about in the cup. "You will always fail."

"Then how do you climb the mountains and pass through the valleys?"

"You don't." Roland set down his cup and leaned back against the cushions. "Because there are no mountains or valleys."

"None?"

Roland shook his head. "And there is no bull."

At least *some* things stayed the same, regardless of the timestream. Roland was as irritating as Nico recalled. "What are you going to do with him?"

"Even without a bull, the comparison is apt. Adrien is at least as powerful as a bull, and more stubborn."

Nico wouldn't argue with that.

"I'm giving him the opportunity to fight his demon in a place where neither of them will cause damage." Roland motioned to the sleeping Adrien. "Would you mind carrying him?"

"Of course, but—"

"You want to know if such a place exists." Roland tilted his head to one side and pressed his lips together.

Nico nodded.

Roland shrugged. "I suppose we'll find out, won't we?"

CHAPTER NINE
ON THE BRINK

"*ADRIEN.*"

Adrien rubbed his eyes. He'd been sleeping. No. Something else. He'd been talking with Nico and Roland and—

Something in the coffee. Bastard put something in the coffee.

How long had he been asleep?

"*They did this to you, Adrien.*"

Shut the fuck *up!* Piece-of-shit demon. He was tired of being manipulated. First by Pelletier, then Roland, then—

"*He* did this to you.*"

He? Nico? No. Nico wouldn't have done this. He trusted Nico.

"*How do you know you can really trust him? The ancients can hide their thoughts, even in their blood.*"

Fuck off. Adrien looked around. The darkness was nearly complete, but the place smelled familiar. Musty. Damp.

"*We're leaving.*" The demon stood.

What the hell? Adrien had no control over his body. *What are you doing?* Had the drugs weakened him enough that the demon could take control even without his permission?

"*Don't you understand? They betrayed you. You've risked your life over and over for them, and they* betrayed *you.*" The demon walked blindly in the blackness, hands stretched out, searching, until it felt the rough surface of a wall.

We're in a cave. The cave where he and his brother had trained with Roland?

"*You're beginning to understand now. They've set us up.*"

He'd been in Paris talking with Nico and Roland, and then....

"*They poisoned you.*"

I'm sure they had their reasons.

39

"They betrayed you. I'll kill them." The demon seethed with anger. It clenched and unclenched its fists, digging sharp fingernails into the flesh of its palms, reveling in the pain.

Betrayed me? No. That's not possible. Nico wouldn't do that. But already the seeds of doubt had begun to grow and send out roots. Had Nico and Roland planned this all along?

NICO TOOK a deep breath and freed his mind from his body. His thoughts flew outward into the countryside, seeking the source of his power. From the tiny droplets of water that clung to the blades of grass where animals grazed under the warm sun, to the stream that meandered through the nearby forest, he drew upon the power he discovered. As easy as breathing, he gathered the essence of the water and filled his heart and soul until he overflowed with strength.

"You betrayed us." Not Adrien's voice. It sounded brittle, with a knife's edge. Just as Roland anticipated, the demon had taken control. Nico hoped they'd done the right thing. He hoped Adrien would forgive him.

"I haven't betrayed him." Nico raised his hand and drew his sword. It illuminated the cave, creating shadows that danced over Adrien's face so his blue eyes seemed to glow as though they were a focal point for the anger that infused his soul. "Hatred will accomplish nothing."

The demon snarled in reply. No matter. The demon wasn't the prize Nico sought. He swung his sword in a wide arc and thousands of tiny daggers of ice dangled in the air, inches from Adrien's body. Awaiting Nico's order.

"You don't think I'm serious?" Nico said, his voice even, his emotions as tightly controlled as the ice.

"You won't harm him."

"You aren't Adrien. I owe you nothing. You're a parasite." Nico smiled and closed his eyes. The shards flew and stabbed Adrien's skin.

The demon roared in pain.

Nico aimed his sword at the top of the cave and the walls grew bright with frost that clung to the rocks. The demon's face contorted with rage as it wiped off the remnants of Nico's attack and smeared the blossoming points of blood that marked where each bit of ice had broken his skin.

"You won't kill me."

"I could. But will I? I suppose we'll find out today."

The demon flew at Nico and grabbed him by the throat.

"You cannot kill me with your bare hands." Nico dislodged the demon's hands. "Or have you forgotten?"

"I've forgotten nothing."

Nico threw the demon against the stone wall. It fell in a heap on the smooth floor. "You're nothing without Adrien."

"He could never kill you." The demon got to its feet and wiped the dirt from its face. "But I *will*."

Nico smiled and charged the demon, sword pointed in front of him. The demon drew its own sword, which materialized in a blaze of fire. A new power? Roland had warned him to be careful, that pushing the demon to its limits came with a risk. No matter. He would see this through.

Flames met ice, sending droplets of water and steam outward like a geyser. Nico slid a few inches, then more, until the demon backed him against the rough-hewn wall. He winced as a jagged piece of rock tore his shirt and scraped his shoulder.

The demon raised its sword, but Nico grabbed the blade. His skin stung where the blade sliced his palm, but Nico ignored it. Pain helped him focus. He shouted and pushed the demon away. It fell but quickly got back to its feet, sword at the ready.

"You're weak. Pathetic. Without Adrien, you're nothing."

The demon hissed and swung its weapon. Nico leapt upward as the blade stirred the air by his face. He landed on a rock near the cave ceiling and gazed downward.

"Do you believe if you kill me, you'll own his soul?"

From the reaction on the demon's contorted features, that was precisely what it hoped.

"The truth is far more interesting." Nico jumped and somersaulted in midair, swinging his weapon and landing a blow on the demon's thigh before he settled back onto the cave floor. "You see, demon," he continued as they crossed swords again and again, "if you kill me, you lose. He and I are bound together. We're stronger together. We don't need *you*."

"Then let's find out!" the demon shrieked and charged.

Nico moved out of the way to avoid the point of its sword when a shot of fire burst from the tip. It soared over Nico's shoulder and hit the wall, which exploded in a hail of rocks and dirt.

Nico rubbed his eyes and listened for his opponent's steps, then rolled on the floor as metal sang a path above his head. "Playing for keeps? But you'll lose. You won't kill me. You can't. He loves me too much."

The demon screamed as Nico's vision cleared. But instead of charging him again, the demon disappeared. An instant later, Nico felt it move behind him. It was too fast. Before he could react, the demon had him in a choke hold, elbow pressed to his Adam's apple.

"Will you yield?" The demon held its arm against Nico's neck, choking him.

"Not until you cede control to Adrien."

"Never." The demon's eyes flashed blue as it turned and stabbed its flaming sword through Nico's heart. The force of the blow was unexpected, the pain sending Nico to his knees. The demon withdrew the sword, triumphant.

"Well done," Nico whispered.

The demon roared its pleasure as it sliced through Nico's neck.

CHAPTER TEN
CHECKMATE

ADRIEN FORCED the demon aside, the thrill of the kill momentarily causing it to let down its guard. It fought to overpower him and retake control, but Adrien held his ground.

"Nico!" Adrien dropped to his knees over Nico's body. "No! God, Nico!"

Nico's face flickered, as though Adrien was seeing it through heat that rose from a fire. Three faces in one, each Nicolas, each with a slightly different expression frozen in time.

"Nico!" He gently cradled Nico's head in his bloody hands. The heat where the sword had cut was unexpected, burning his palm, searing it like Adrien's own pain seared his heart. "No! Nico!"

"He deserved it." The demon gloated in its victory.

"Nico! No. Please no." He threw his sword upward with deadly precision and moved beneath it. The weapon cut into his skin but did not penetrate deep enough to harm him. It clattered onto the ground. Tears mingled with laughter as he retrieved the weapon and ran a single finger over the razor's edge. It sliced a line through his skin, but it could not kill him. A hunter's weapon meant only to destroy vampires, Ianus could never take the life of its owner.

He searched desperately for Nico's sword. He screamed in anger and grief to realize it had vanished. Of course it would—a vampire's weapon was created from the vampire's soul. The sword would cease to exist when the vampire perished.

He reached into his belt and withdrew the small dagger he kept there. Would it suffice to remove his own head? He doubted it, but he'd try anyhow. He couldn't live knowing he'd killed Nico.

The demon roared and struggled for purchase as Adrien lifted the blade to his neck. Each time it tried assert itself, Adrien forced it back again. Over and over the demon flung itself against Adrien's mind, fighting to displace it, fighting for control. Adrien ceded no power.

You will not control me.

43

Hot tears fell over Adrien's cheeks as his thoughts cleared enough for him to understand what Nico had done. *He did this for me.*

"The bull is powerful. Fight it. Take it by the horns and argue with it. Perhaps it will lend you its power." Roland's voice sounded distant in Adrien's mind.

Adrien bent over Nico's head and touched Nico's cheek. Already Nico's skin felt as cold as stone. *Nico!*

Adrien stood and screamed. He closed his eyes and raised his arms skyward. He didn't believe in God, but he begged and pleaded for Nico's life. Nothing happened.

Twice he'd lost Nico. Twice the fault had been his. He'd been too weak to save Nicolas before, and this time he destroyed Nico with his own two hands.

"No!" he shouted. He couldn't think. He didn't want to feel. He wanted nothing more than to die here.

Before. The word reverberated in his thoughts, and the universe seemed to reassert itself. Before, he'd been able to turn back time. He'd saved Nicolas, hadn't he?

"Only for an instant," the demon reminded him, its laughter once again drowning out rational thought.

Before. The answer was simple, wasn't it?

"If you think I'll do your bidding, you're—"

You have no choice but to obey. You will take me back. Adrien shoved the demon aside, imagining himself pointing his weapon at the beast's throat. *You will obey.*

The demon roared, but this time Adrien forced it down again, his foot on its neck. He pressed harder and it whimpered in pain. *If you don't obey, we both die here. Now.*

The demon clawed at Adrien's mind, looking for a way out, but each time it made the smallest of openings, Adrien closed them before it could insert a single sharp talon. *You are me. You are mine. You are nothing without me. You are... nothing.*

The edges of Adrien's awareness began to blur, the cave walls becoming transparent, flickering in and out of existence and leaving behind a wall of white light that surrounded him like a box.

44

Unlike before, when Adrien had been an unwilling participant, this time the journey was completely of his own volition. The cave grew dark, and he floated in nothingness. No pain. No light. No life. *No time.*

Return!

The cave solidified once more. In front of him, Nico stood with his sword at the ready, brow furrowed, waiting for the demon to attack.

"You...." Nico released his sword and put a tentative hand to his neck. "I... died?"

"Thank God." Adrien dropped to his knees. "I'm so sorry," he whispered. His body shook. He couldn't move.

"Sorry?" The grin that spread across Nico's face left no room for doubt. He wasn't angry at all. His sword vanished. He opened his arms in invitation, but Adrien didn't move.

"No. I can't." How could Nico even want to touch him after what he'd done?

"You can and you *will.*"

"Please, kill me." He was pathetic. Unworthy. A traitor to his heart and soul.

"And allow you to wallow in your guilt?" Nico frowned and shook his head. "You didn't do this. I *permitted* you to do this."

"Wait." Adrien rubbed his eyes. Nico's words finally began to register. "You... you *let* me kill you? But I—"

"Do you think I went to all that effort for you to feel sorry for yourself?" Nico laughed.

"You think this is funny?" Adrien's hands still shook.

"I did this to set you free. *You* turned back time. Not the demon. You alone control the power. It's *your* power, Adrien. It's been yours all along."

"The hell, Nico!" Adrien struggled to control his anger. "If I failed—"

"You weren't going to fail." Nico pulled Adrien to his feet and embraced him. Nearly a full minute passed before Adrien let himself respond to the gesture by wrapping his arms around the living, breathing Nico. "There was never a question that you'd succeed."

Adrien lost the war with his emotions and sobbed against Nico's chest. Nico held him tighter as he caressed Adrien's hair and murmured words of comfort. Nico's touch, his warmth, his love acted like a catalyst for Adrien's grief. Too much loss. Too much heartache. *I'm so tired.*

"I won't let you go," Nico said in Adrien's mind. *"I'll never let you go."*

Lend me your strength. Please. I can't do this alone.

"I won't let you do this alone. Don't you understand that you never had that choice?" Nico pulled slightly away and kissed Adrien.

Adrien wiped his eyes. Instead of embarrassment, a quiet calm permeated his being. "Promise me you'll never pull something like that again."

Nico swept his thumbs over Adrien's wet cheeks and kissed him again. "I promise. From now on, we do this together."

Behind them, someone coughed. Adrien released Nico and turned to discover Roland grinning at them.

"Well done," Roland said.

Adrien glanced at Nico, then turned back to Roland and punched him.

Roland rubbed his jaw. "Feel better?"

"Much." Adrien's belly rumbled.

"Lunch?" Roland asked.

"I really am going strangle that man someday," Adrien told Nico as they followed Roland into the living quarters of the cave.

CHAPTER ELEVEN
CLARITY

"HOW LONG have we been here?" Adrien asked as they finished their meal of bread and stew an hour later. The young boy of thirteen or fourteen who had served them now sat at Roland's feet and ate.

"A few days," Nico told him. "We took your private plane and drove from Lyon."

He chewed thoughtfully and watched Adrien for a long moment. He could still see the demon swing his blade and feel the burn of the metal against the skin of his neck. There'd been no real pain. He knew he shouldn't remember the moment Adrien had killed him, but the memory was there nonetheless. He was too tired to think about what that meant.

Adrien's hands still trembled. Nico didn't regret his part in such a painful lesson, but he hoped Adrien would understand and forgive himself.

"Are you going to introduce them?" The boy frowned at Roland, who laughed.

"My apologies. Didier, meet Nicolas Rousseau and Adrien Gilbert. Adrien and Nico, meet Didier Fournier."

"Fournier?" Adrien reached over to shake the boy's hand.

Roland's eyes momentarily betrayed a mix of pride and pain. "He's Thomas's great-grandnephew."

Nico had met Thomas Fournier, Roland's longtime partner and lover, more than a century before. Thomas had been a powerful hunter in his own right, but he, like most hunters, had not been immortal. "You look very much like Thomas," he offered, unsure of what to say.

"I've been filling Nico in on this timestream," Roland said as he ladled more of the stew onto their plates. "And he's brought me up to speed on his. Pelletier isn't very creative. The tools he uses are always the same."

"The lost," Nico said in response to Adrien's frown. "You may have seen them in my memories. Demivampires. Pelletier used them to destroy our home in Lyon." Nico fought back a wave of anger and revulsion.

Adrien nodded. "Neither human nor vampire. Neither living nor dead. I've never seen one, except in your memories."

"You're lucky." Nico shuddered. He'd seen them kill vampire and hunter alike.

"He uses vampire blood to create them," Roland explained. "We aren't sure how he controls them, but it may have something to do with his hunter's blood. What we do know is that they're weak. Easy to kill."

"Then what is there to fear?" Adrien asked.

"In large numbers, they're difficult to fight. Together, they're strong enough to defeat the most powerful ancient vampire. Like a swarm of bees." Roland pulled a piece of bread from the baguette and chewed for a moment. "Pelletier is on the move, and word is that he's building an army of the creatures. The lost are his invitation to you, Adrien."

"CAN'T SLEEP?" Adrien asked Nico as he sat outside the cave watching the stars glitter above.

"Nicolas's note… it's dated two days from now."

"I've been thinking the same thing." Adrien rubbed his mouth. "Pelletier's headed for wherever the Nicolas of this timestream was supposed to be."

"I wish I knew."

"We'll find out soon enough. Pelletier knows we've come here. He's just biding his time." Adrien smiled at Nico. "He'll let us know where and when."

Nico looked away, unsure how to broach the topic. Maybe the time wasn't right. There were more important things to worry about.

"Pelletier's plans aren't the only thing on your mind, are they?"

Leave it to Adrien to see right through me. "There's something I'm not understanding." Nico met Adrien's gaze once more.

"The memories?"

Nico nodded.

Adrien put a hand on Nico's shoulder and sat beside him. His sigh was nearly inaudible. "You remember what happened in the cave this morning."

Nico hadn't wanted Adrien to shoulder that particular burden, but he wouldn't lie to him. "The moment of my death. Quite anticlimactic in the end. Peaceful, even."

"I wish—"

"No. This was my choice. Roland didn't approve of what I did. His plan never included my death, only baiting you into using your power to turn back time. He guessed if we angered the demon enough, kept it contained…. But none of that matters now." Nico slipped his arm around Adrien and pulled him close.

"What else do you remember?" Adrien's voice sounded tentative, as if he feared the answer.

"Nearly everything," Nico admitted. "The memories are like tiny gifts I can open. Like looking into the past in small pieces. I have to focus on them or they linger in the background. Some reveal themselves in response to my actions. Others I want to remember.

"I remember the first time I met you," Nico continued and kissed Adrien's hair. "In Lyon."

"At the dance?"

"I remember that too. But no, I'm thinking of when Jean first sent me to find you. When I planned to marry Rosina. I startled you as you walked the city in the early morning. You didn't realize I was there."

Adrien closed his eyes. "I wanted to hate you."

"Maybe you already knew me then." Were they doomed to dance around each other throughout time, never landing too long in one timestream, never truly being together?

"Do you remember what happened after Pelletier took you? At the wedding."

"No." Nico guessed it was better that way. "That Nicolas may be… unaware of his surroundings. I only remember that he took me—that I died and you turned back time for the first time. Nothing more." He didn't tell Adrien he knew that Nicolas was dead. Nico wouldn't tell him now, when he still seemed so fragile.

"Oh."

Nico kissed Adrien again. "You bear too much guilt. You had no control over Pelletier. There was nothing you could have done to save that particular version of me."

Adrien pulled away and stared at Nico as if trying to understand.

"You see where this is going, don't you?" Nico asked. "If I can remember that timestream…."

"The power of the Rousseaus has reawakened in your blood," Adrien finished. "The power you gave me."

Nico picked up a stone and tossed it into the air. He caught it and clasped it in his hand, then tossed it again. It clattered onto the rocks. "It's awakened because of you."

"Because of me?"

Nico inhaled and focused on the stone. *Back. Take me back.* Air stirred around his body. He opened his hand to reveal the stone he dropped before.

Adrien's lips parted and his eyes grew wide. "Did you just…?"

"Can you feel what I did?"

"I… yes."

"It feels familiar, doesn't it?" Nico saw understanding awaken in Adrien's eyes. "Like déjà vu."

"But I don't have the memories you do. My gift is more limited."

Nico shrugged. "Maybe not. But you sense the movement of time."

"I really didn't bring you here, did I? I thought I did, but now…."

Nico shook his head and smiled. "I think I chose to come with you. Through my own power. I have no idea what I did or how I knew to follow you. I only knew I didn't want you to leave without me."

"Shit."

Nico laughed, then glanced quickly to the cave entrance. *We're not alone.*

"Haven't been for some time either. Damned mother hen. Did he really think we wouldn't know he was listening in?" Adrien smirked. "I need to try a few more volleys to see if—"

"Tomorrow." Roland emerged from the shadows looking quite pleased with himself. "You need to rest now." He grinned and ran a hand through his hair.

Adrien pointedly ignored Roland. Nico repressed a chuckle but followed Adrien's lead. "Roland was always a know-it-all." Nico stood and pulled Adrien to his feet. "Even in my time."

"He's known all along that we aren't from this timestream, hasn't he?" Adrien looked over his shoulder and winked at Roland. Roland tutted as Adrien and Nico walked, hand in hand, back to the cave, laughing.

CHAPTER TWELVE
SHADOWS ON THE MOON

"...NOT LIKE that!" Adrien shouted as he spun to avoid Nico's blade.

Nico shook his head and jumped into the air. "Too slow." He landed gracefully behind Adrien and swung again, this time connecting with Adrien's thigh.

"Fuck!" Adrien rolled and pressed his hand to the wound. It would heal by itself in a few minutes, but this time he'd made up his mind.

Take me back, he ordered the demon. *A minute will do.*

The demon growled but obeyed. The familiar blue light that preceded a shift in the timestream had now become a barely perceptible flash, and Adrien no longer felt any adverse effects.

"Too slow," Nico said from midair. He moved to strike, but Adrien moved sideways and Nico's blade scraped the stone and sent sparks flying.

Nico frowned at Adrien. "You're getting faster. And you're getting better at moving through time."

"Thank you." Adrien bowed formally. "But there's something I don't understand." It had been bothering him since he and Nico had started sparring that morning.

"What's that?"

"You're far stronger than you ever let on. Faster too. And since we've never really fought together, the few times we've sparred together...."

"You want to know why I've held back when we've sparred?"

Adrien nodded.

"You weren't ready to understand." Nico shrugged. "More than anything, you wanted to protect me. And much as I didn't enjoy playing damsel in distress...."

"You figured it was easier. And you worried I'd give up if I realized how weak I was."

"You aren't weak. We're more than evenly matched."

This was true. At least it was now that Adrien had managed to tame the demon. Nico hadn't yet learned to use his own gift in battle, but Adrien was sure he would eventually. And when he did....

"When I do, together we'll be stronger than Pelletier."

The demon hissed at the thought of needing someone to help it. It was strong enough. It despised its submission. Adrien had, on occasion, allowed it to run free as he and Nico trained together—a reward of sorts for obeying its master. Adrien now understood he could channel its fury to accomplish what he alone could not.

"Dinner?" Roland peered into the cave. "The sun will be setting soon." He tossed two towels at Adrien, whose sword disappeared as he caught them. "But perhaps a bath first?" He screwed up his face in disgust and held his nose.

"Come on." Nico laughed. "We wouldn't want the old man to suffer, would we?"

They walked to the river and shed their sweaty clothes. As Nico stepped into the small pool that had formed among the reeds, Adrien admired his pale skin and the way the muscles of his swordsman's arms tensed and moved beneath.

"Are you going to join me, or are you just going to ogle?"

"Do I have to choose?" Adrien laughed and jumped into the water, dipping beneath the surface to rinse his face and hair.

"Not really." Nico pulled Adrien against him as he surfaced.

"I wish we had more time for this." Adrien sighed theatrically. "I know I shouldn't complain, but I—"

Nico silenced Adrien with his lips and pressed his tongue into the heat of Adrien's mouth. "We must make the time," he said after he'd released Adrien from his embrace.

Adrien tilted his head to the side until he felt the cool touch of Nico's tongue at his pulse point. Nico's sharp eyeteeth followed along the same path; then he gasped as Nico bit into his flesh and began to suck.

"Nico."

"A hundred years you waited for me. I'm not sure I can ever live up to that ideal man." Nico's thoughts swirled around Adrien's mind. Like this, joined by blood, it was almost as though the thoughts were Adrien's own.

I'm hardly ideal. I wallowed. If it hadn't been for Jean....

"It doesn't matter how you came to be what you are. You'll always inspire me." With his soul laid bare, Nico understood every emotion. Every doubt. Every part of him, good and bad. Weak or strong.

And you me.

Nico withdrew and rubbed his fingertips over Adrien's neck to seal the wound faster. From the expression on Nico's face, Adrien knew he wanted more than just blood.

"Later." Adrien nibbled his way up Nico's neck to suck on his earlobe. "And after that...." Once he'd been ashamed of his bloodlust. But that shame had vanished along with his hatred for vampires. Now he wanted Nico to see the red of his eyes and feel his body's need.

"Later." Nico drew a long breath and smiled.

THEY ATE their meal in silence, each alone with his thoughts. Afterward, Adrien lounged on the pillows while Nico read a book he'd found in Roland's collection.

I'm sure it's an interesting book, Adrien told Nico silently. *But I believe you promised me a later.*

Nico smiled and closed the book.

"Time for bed?" Roland said, the edges of his mouth turning ever so slightly upward.

"Time for bed," Adrien said as he and Nico rose. "Thank you for the hospitality."

"Of course." Roland stood and stretched.

Nico and Adrien had barely taken a step before Didier ran into the room, nearly bumping into them.

"Monsieur, monsieur!" he shouted, causing Roland to turn. "There's a message for you from Madame Lucien." He pulled a ragged envelope from his pocket and handed it to Roland, then put his hands on his thighs and tried to catch his breath.

Adrien put a hand on Nico's arm. *She's a friend of my family,* he explained while Roland opened the letter and quickly read it over. *An ally.*

Roland frowned and looked up.

"What is it?" Nico asked.

"What I feared," Roland said. "Our little respite is over. Much as I'd have liked more time for you both to prepare, it seems Verel Pelletier is ready to play."

Adrien fought the growing tension in his shoulders. He needed more time to control the demon, understand how to use its power.

"His forces will arrive in Lyon tomorrow." Roland glanced at Nico, then back at the paper. "Your brother will be there to meet him."

Chapter Thirteen
Dawn and Darkness

NICO AND Adrien drove Roland's ancient car through the night, arriving in Lyon just as the first rays of sun cut the darkness into ribbons of black, orange, and purple.

"If Pelletier's supposed to be dead in this timestream," Nico grimly mused to Adrien as they made their way along the winding roads that snaked over the countryside, "how does he continue to control the hunters?"

"Blood." Adrien gripped the steering wheel tightly. "Yours, most likely."

"Mine. The Nicolas he kidnapped from the wedding decades ago?"

Adrien nodded and pushed away the guilt that clawed at his heart. "Roland believes Pelletier makes Nicolas's blood available to his loyal followers. Just enough to keep them strong…."

"But not enough that they can challenge his dominance."

Adrien nodded. "He's figured out that Jean is working with Roland. But he's never resorted to something like demivampires before."

"He used them quite successfully in my world." Anger vibrated in Nico's voice.

"Tell me about them. The lost. How do you defeat them?"

"I don't know. We'd never heard of them before Pelletier used them to slaughter those who stood against him," Nico explained. "We tried attacking them in groups, but they were so numerous that we still lost too many. In the end, we abandoned the estate. You saw the result."

Nico appeared tense in the dim light of the car's display. "What they lack in power, they make up in sheer numbers. They have no thought except that of their master. Pelletier has learned how to direct them, but we don't know how."

And we know what Pelletier wants them to do. Adrien wished Nico didn't have to face the horror of these creatures again.

"I'll be fine," Nico said and touched Adrien's hand. "It won't be the same as then. We're stronger." *I'm stronger.*

Adrien clenched his jaw at Nico's unspoken thought. He would protect Nico, whatever the cost. He'd lost Nico—Nicolas—too many times. He wouldn't lose him again.

We fight together or we don't fight at all. The demon rumbled its disapproval but said nothing.

Nico nodded solemnly, his resolve no doubt born of a similar fear.

They left the car at the entrance to the manor house and made their way up the winding drive. Around them, Adrien sensed the presence of hunters and vampires alike, but none made a move to reveal themselves. They had just made it past the large forested area surrounding the mansion when a terrible cry cut through the early-morning calm.

"Adrien!" Nico grabbed Adrien's hand and they ran toward the mansion. "We have to get out of here. Now! Before they come."

They sped toward the house. Along with the inhuman screams, an undercurrent of sound thrummed like a river dancing over the rocks. Voices, none of which Adrien could clearly make out, seeking something. *Wanting* something. Desperate. Calling out to him. *Wanting* him.

"We can't hope to fight them off out here in the open." Nico led him toward the bushes that grew wild and covered what was left of the benches Adrien recalled. Near the front entrance, several figures gathered, hidden in shadow. Vampires. Some familiar. Others Adrien didn't immediately recognize. To avoid suspicion, Nico quickly released Adrien's hand.

Adrien shivered as the screams rose in pitch. Roland had once told him and François stories about creatures born of vampire blood, mindless soldiers used in ancient wars, but Adrien had only imagined them in his nightmares. "What do they want?"

"Want?" Nico frowned.

"I hear them. Or feel them. I'm not sure. I can't make out what they're saying, but—"

"Hear them?" Nico frowned. "That's impossible. They have no will of their own. No mind."

"But—"

A shot of blue fire arced across the lawn from the wall that led to the formal gardens, lighting up the sky before exploding in a hail of ice. The screams stopped and the shadowy figures scattered.

"Jean!" Nico shouted.

"Get inside!" Jean ordered as he moved past them and shot yet another volley toward the creatures. Several other people joined Jean, but Adrien couldn't clearly make them out from his vantage point.

"Let me help, I—"

"Nicolas," said another voice—Adrien recognized it as Blaise's. "We'll reinforce the barrier. Help the others protect the building. There are injured inside."

Adrien didn't hesitate. Where years ago he might have charged in, sword drawn, he instead pulled Nico toward the house. He knew nothing about this new enemy, and he wouldn't risk Nico's safety to find out more. They would act with caution, and they'd act together.

"Adrien! Nicolas!" Rosina yelled from the large front doors of the mansion.

They scrambled up the steps as the doors opened. A cracking like thunder echoed off the high walls. In Adrien's peripheral vision, an enormous tree fell and erupted into flames.

"I have to help them," Nico said as Adrien blocked his way. He wasn't going to let Nico out of his sight.

"Jean and Blaise are strengthening the wards," Rosina said as she, Charles, and François bolted the doors behind them. "Caroline is helping them as well."

"Wards? Like spells?" Adrien had never heard of such a thing. He found it difficult to think clearly with the voices chattering in his head. He breathed a sigh of relief as the doors to the mansion closed and the sound faded to a dull vibration.

"Not quite," Charles said. "But the Lambert blood seems to repel them for a time."

Why can I hear them?

Nico's expression darkened, but he didn't argue with Adrien.

"Pelletier wants you, Adrien," the demon whispered in his mind, *"and he knows you've accepted his challenge. What will you do now?"*

"What can we do to—?" Adrien's words were cut short as François waved to Charles and they opened the doors again. Blaise, Jean, and Caroline stepped inside looking tired but unharmed.

At least a dozen vampires watched them from the sitting room. Several others ran down the stairs with swords drawn, but sheathed them when Jean held up a hand. How many others were sheltered here? Hundreds, perhaps.

The ancients believed it was their duty to shelter weaker vampires, and the Lamberts were no exception.

"That should keep them at bay," Jean said as he helped bolt the doors. "But come sundown...."

Nico stared at Blaise, who stood by the doors, discussing something with Caroline in hushed tones. Perhaps realizing this might appear strange, Nico said to Jean, "Thank goodness you're all right."

"You should have stayed in Paris," Jean answered curtly. "I told you—"

"I'm to blame," Adrien said, hoping to draw attention from Nico's odd behavior. "I brought him here." So Roland was still persona non grata in this timeline. Adrien knew Roland well enough to guess there was a reason for that, although with the buzzing at the back of his brain, he couldn't focus on the explanation.

Jean narrowed his eyes at Adrien. "You? After your little demonstration in Paris? Giovanetti will suspect—"

"The fault is mine." Nico stepped between Jean and Adrien.

"I will speak with both of you in my study," Jean replied.

"Of course." Adrien nodded and glanced at Nico, whose eyes betrayed his concern. *This is Jean. A friend. An ally.* There was no reason to worry.

And yet as he and Nico turned and made their way through the manor, Adrien couldn't help but wonder if he and Nico had gotten in over their heads.

CHAPTER FOURTEEN
PAST IMPERFECT

ADRIEN CLOSED the study door behind them. "What will you tell Jean?"

"The truth, I suppose. Although I wonder why Roland neglected to tell him."

Adrien shrugged. "Put yourself in Jean's shoes. Would you believe the truth?"

"No." Nico sighed and glanced around the room. He hoped it was that simple. Although knowing Roland, there was probably something he and Adrien were missing. "I hardly believe it myself. But Roland...."

"The Roland of this timestream is said to have killed your family. I'm pretty sure Jean doesn't believe it, since I've seen them together, but Roland prefers to stay hidden." He rubbed his eyes and added, "I'm sorry I dragged you into this."

Nico touched Adrien's cheek. "You worry too much." Years before, he'd have been angry for Adrien's constant concern. He'd been raised to be strong and not to doubt his power.

Years before? Impossible. He'd only known Adrien for a few weeks. *You shared his blood. You saw what your life was like.* The explanation didn't quite ring true, but he was too tired—too overwhelmed—to think it through.

"That life was hell, Adrien," he said at last. He didn't want Adrien's pity. He needed his understanding. "However dangerous, this timestream, as you call it, offers hope." He kissed Adrien tenderly, hoping to express what he found so difficult to put into words.

Adrien wrapped his arms around him and Nico sighed. A burst of memory—something he had seen in Adrien's blood—flooded his mind. He saw himself through Adrien's eyes. Felt Adrien's pain and understood that he had been willing to sacrifice himself to protect Nicolas from Giovanetti. At the same time, he remembered the look on Adrien's face. His own despair. The hopelessness, the knowledge that what he'd done in marrying Giovanetti could never be undone.

"Nicolas." Adrien's eyes registered nothing but pain. He was pathetic. Broken. "Tell me you still love me and I'll leave."

"I won't lie to you," he told Adrien. But he would do just that. This had to be done. He needed to end this or Adrien would do something rash and everything he'd tried to do by marrying the bastard would be for nothing.

Adrien dropped his hands to his sides and released his sword. He walked toward Giovanetti. "I won't live without you, Nicolas."

Giovanetti pointed his sword at Adrien. "Then let me help you die, you bastard. Even an immortal can't survive without a head."

Nicolas felt for his blade. He must stop this. He couldn't allow Adrien to die. Not for his own sake. If Adrien lived, he too could live on.

Adrien closed his eyes and waited for Giovanetti's blow.

"No!" Roland shouted from the doorway.

"You?" Giovanetti glared at Roland, who grabbed Adrien and hit him over the head with the hilt of his sword. Adrien collapsed in a heap at Nicolas's feet.

Roland tossed Adrien over his shoulder. "This is getting to be a bad habit."

"Get him out of here," Nicolas told Roland.

"Nico?"

Nico gasped as he came back to himself. "What Jean spoke of… what happened in Paris with Giovanetti. I just remembered it."

"Remembered? Are you sure you didn't see it in my blood and just now remembered?"

Nico shook his head. "I've seen the memories in your blood. This… this was different. The memories were my own. I saw it through Nicolas's— with my own eyes."

"Your eyes?"

Nico nodded. "The entire scene, from *his*—my—perspective. You were prepared to die to keep Nicolas—to keep *me* safe."

Adrien stared at the floor and shook his head.

Nico smiled and kissed Adrien again. "I know why you did it," he whispered against Adrien's ear. "But that Nicolas…. No, *I* saw it for the ruse it was." He leaned his head against Adrien's shoulder as someone knocked on the door of the study.

Nico and Adrien pulled apart as Jean entered the room a moment later. "You agreed to remain in Paris," he repeated with steel in his voice. "We discussed this. If your husband were to discover—"

"Much as he'd like to believe otherwise, my husband does not control everything in my life." The words came easily. He didn't just imagine that he was the Nicolas who had married Antonio Giovanetti—he *was* that Nicolas. His anger for Antonio Giovanetti came easily, as did the powerful feeling of disgust at the thought of someone other than Adrien touching his body. But why was the memory of that touch his own?

Jean glared at Adrien. "After all you did to protect him with your little charade for Giovanetti's sake," he said with barely repressed anger, "you've once again put his life at risk. Your life may be worth little to you, Adrien, but I have no intention—"

"I did not ask Adrien to risk his life for me," Nico interjected before Adrien could reply. "But I understand why he did."

"If you understood, you should never have come here." Jean's expression was grim, his jaw tight. He looked older than Nico recalled. Tired.

"We didn't exactly choose to come," Adrien muttered.

"What?" Jean eyed Adrien warily.

"Roland told us you needed help," Adrien said. It wasn't the complete truth, but it was the simplest.

"Roland told *both* of you?" Jean's expression darkened, but it wasn't anger Nico sensed. It was something more like fear. Nico struggled to remember what he'd seen in Adrien's blood. In this timeline, Roland stood accused of the massacre of his parents and his brother Paul. Did Jean believe Roland was capable of something so terrible?

No. That's not it. It's something about me. "It's been a long day," Nico said aloud, hoping to distract Jean from Adrien's mistake. Jean was buying none of it. Nico felt as though Jean's dark blue eyes pierced right to his core. He fought the urge to squirm beneath the weight of Jean's intense scrutiny.

"You aren't Nicolas," Jean said at last.

He knows. But how? "I am Nic—"

"It's not only that you shouldn't be able to touch Adrien without pain because of your bond with Giovanetti. You're... different." Jean narrowed his eyes, then inhaled.

The scent of my blood is different. Of course!

"You are Nicolas," Jean continued. "And not."

"I am," Nico insisted even as he struggled to understand it himself. "It's difficult to explain, but I *am* the brother you know. I share his memories. I feel what he feels. It's as if by coming here, he and I became the same person, even if a few days ago, I was only Nico." He took Adrien's hand in his own. "But I'm not bound to that bastard Giovanetti. I'm sworn to Adrien alone."

Nico had never seen Jean so at a loss. "Impossible."

"I will always be your brother," Nico said with determination. "You've guided me. Sacrificed for me. We may not share the same blood, but you have been there for me." *Blood. Blood is the answer.* The proof Jean sought. "Blood never lies. Isn't that what you always told me?"

"I… yes."

Nico bowed low and extended his wrist. "Lord Lambert, I offer my blood as proof of our bond."

"Even if you don't believe Nico," Adrien said, "you need to know the truth."

Nico waited for Jean's bite, head still bent. Nearly a minute passed, the only sound in the room the ticking of the clock on the mantel. Then, finally, Jean lifted Nico by the elbow. "You need never defer to me. We have always been equals, in spite of what you believe."

Nico met Jean's inscrutable gaze without flinching. "You believe me. Even without—"

"I believe you, even if it's against my better judgment." He glanced at Adrien, whose lips quirked upward.

"Glad to hear it." Adrien grinned. "You usually take a hell of a lot longer to convince."

Jean frowned and for a long moment said nothing. "The way you come and go, it's a wonder I haven't completely lost my mind." He glanced at Adrien and shook his head. "Or that I haven't killed you."

"Your friendship's been the one constant in my life." Adrien smiled. "Much as I understand your frustration with me."

"I know you have Nicolas's best interests at heart, even so." Jean exhaled an audible breath.

"Your Nicolas asked for help," Adrien said. "I don't know how his message made it to me, but we're here and we want to make things right."

"Indeed. And you stepped through time and walked right into a battle." Jean tilted his head to one side.

Adrien chuckled. "It's a bit more complicated than that. But it doesn't really matter. What matters is that this timestream—where Nicolas is married to that bastard—this is my fault. If there's anything I can do to help fix it, I will."

Nico squeezed Adrien's hand. "You didn't mean to change this timestream."

Three different timestreams. Three possibilities. A world where Adrien had died young and Nico and Jean were among a handful of vampires to survive the massacre at the Council of Hunters. The world into which Adrien was born, where another Nicolas had vanished a century before, taken by Verel Pelletier. Dead, most likely, after suffering horribly. And *this* world, where Adrien had changed the future, where Roland was said to have killed the Rousseaus and Pelletier died a hero. In all of these worlds, Jean and Adrien had sacrificed their happiness to protect him.

"Regardless of why we're here, I want you to understand," Nico said, the memories spurring him on. "Please, take my blood. I want you to know the truth."

The sting of Jean's teeth as they pierced Nico's skin felt familiar and warm. Nico closed his eyes and heard Jean's thought: *"My brother."*

CHAPTER FIFTEEN
EVE OF DESTRUCTION

As ADRIEN walked into the study later that day, Jean sat facing the fire, his face pale even in the warmth of the light from the flames. "There was a time," Jean said in a low voice, "when I was quite sure you'd lost your mind."

Adrien laughed. It felt surprisingly good. "I've thought the same thing more times than I can count." He tried to push away the memory of the Council meeting when the demon had moved him through time and Jean telling him, "Pelletier died to save Nicolas's life."

"Nicolas came with you to this time and place, and yet you have no idea how?"

Adrien shook his head.

"Nor do you understand why he remembers this timestream as well as his own."

"Other than the stories of long-lost vampire abilities? None." Adrien took a seat next to Jean. Nico had gone to find Blaise. Adrien guessed he needed to create his own memories of the brother he'd never known. "I almost wish he didn't remember anything," he admitted after a long pause.

"Of which past?" Jean asked. "Of a past where all of the people he cares about are slaughtered? Or this past, where he sacrifices himself and marries a monster like Giovanetti?"

Or my past, where he's lost forever, where they bleed him dry to cling to power? The thought made Adrien shiver.

"I might ask the same of you." Adrien wondered if Jean regretted having tasted Nico's blood. "In all these pasts, you end up the same. Alone."

"Perhaps that is a fate I must accept."

"You're even more irritating than the Jean I know."

Jean glared at him. "I *am* the Jean you know. Or should I say, one of them?"

"You're right." Adrien laughed in spite of himself. "I spent more than a hundred years chasing after Nicolas. I can't even count how many times I came close to giving up. But every time, you were there. Kicking me in the…. That Jean is just like you. Irritating. Stubborn as hell."

Jean raised an eyebrow. "Then you should be thanking me."

"Thank you." Adrien smiled, and for once it didn't feel forced.

Jean stared at him, speechless.

"You and Roland are the only ones who know the truth of what Pelletier did the night Nicolas was born. In this timestream, everyone thinks Pelletier's a hero and Roland murdered the Rousseaus."

"The lie was necessary," Jean snapped. "To protect everyone."

"Maybe it was back then. But what good's your hero's lie now? Pelletier's alive. He's pulling the strings, and his marionettes are deadly. He's supplying Giovanetti and the others with blood like a drug dealer. He's behind this attack and these… things. Why not tell Blaise and the others the truth?"

Jean rubbed his mouth. "Roland asked me to say nothing about Verel's involvement. He prefers to work in the shadows."

"I doubt he meant you to keep it secret from the man you love."

"And what about you?" Jean countered. "You clearly blame yourself for Pelletier kidnapping the Nicolas from your own time."

"You… you know about that?" Adrien hadn't told *this* Jean about his past.

Jean nodded. "Ancients can read layers of memories in blood. You've shared your blood with Nico. Your memories, the most powerful ones, are there in *his* blood."

"I should have been able to stop it," Adrien said in an undertone.

"Do you still believe that? After everything you've seen? Or is it in your nature to want to suffer?"

"If I hadn't left the Nicolas you knew in the vineyard… alone…. If I'd been able to stay in this timeline, perhaps Nicolas wouldn't have married—"

"Bullshit."

Adrien stared at Jean. He'd never heard him swear before.

"You lecture me about martyrdom, yet you beat yourself up for having changed this timeline," Jean continued, unperturbed. "If you need someone to blame for that, you need look no further than Nicolas himself."

"But Pelletier—"

"The Nicolas I know—the Nicolas of this timeline—made his own choices. He's far older than you. Much as you and I blame ourselves for his suffering, in the end, his decisions are his alone. By blaming yourself for Nicolas's choices, you fail to acknowledge the man you say you love."

Jean's eyes glittered as he continued, "The Nicolas I know *chose* to marry Giovanetti in spite of my opposition… in spite of knowing what it would mean for his life. He believed it would protect you. The Nicolas you call Nico chose to follow you here from an even darker future. If anything, your gift has *saved* him. With you, he has a chance for happiness. And if he can master the power of his blood...."

Adrien released a slow breath. Jean was right. Nicolas was hardly weak. In each timeline, he'd made his own choices, starting with the first terrible choice to offer himself up as a bargaining chip for peace between the vampire clans.

"There's something to be learned here," Jean said after a long pause. "I've no doubt you'll figure it out."

"You're starting to sound like Roland," Adrien said with a chuckle.

Jean frowned. "Regardless of what I know, it's best not to mention Roland's name here. There are those who despise him and would raise their sword to someone who speaks kindly of him."

Yet another martyr. Adrien sighed.

"Roland, like Nicolas, made his own choices. We may not fully understand them, but who are we to say what he did was wrong?"

Adrien nodded. "I've missed this." In his own time, he and Jean had become friends over the long years they searched for Nicolas and Pelletier. How long had it been since he'd seen or spoken to that particular incarnation of Jean?

"Missed?"

"It doesn't matter now." Best to let it go. Move on. He might never return to his own timestream. What had he just told Jean about being honest with Blaise?

Jean studied him but said nothing.

"What do you know about those... things?" Adrien asked after a long moment.

"The lost?" Jean stood and walked over to the window, which, like all the others in the mansion, was shuttered and bolted. Jean pressed his hand to the heavy wood and briefly closed his eyes.

Adrien nodded.

"They're created by draining a human of blood but not giving enough blood to create a vampire. Neither human nor vampire. Mindless. They crave blood and will kill humans for it but are easily controlled."

"Zombies."

Jean chuckled. "It's possible they inspired that particular human myth. They resurface from time to time, usually when a young vampire mistakenly tries to create another of its kind. The ancients have been tasked with their destruction for millennia. Until now they've been a nuisance. Easily dispatched, like vermin. This time, though, Pelletier appears to have learned how to control them."

He'd guessed Pelletier used Nicolas's blood, but now he wondered. "Can they be created with the blood of an immortal?"

"An immortal?" Jean nodded solemnly. "Yes. I suppose so, since your blood is much like ours. And if Pelletier used his own blood to create them, it would explain why they've grown stronger."

Adrien breathed through a wave of hatred. "That might also explain why I can hear them."

"What?" Jean stared at Adrien, brow furrowed.

"I hear their voices." Adrien leaned back in the chair. "I can't make out what they're saying, but I know they're speaking."

"I've never heard of such a thing," Jean replied. "Still, we know very little of the lost. Nothing remains of the historical record apart from the few spells our ancestors used to create wards. After the Council of Hunters was established, those who created them were severely punished, and we've since seen them only rarely."

"What's your plan?"

"Plan?" Jean shook his head. "We'll fight them as best we can." He walked back to his chair and sat heavily.

"Have you called for help?"

"It's unlikely reinforcements will arrive in time. The Council has sent its best hunters to Russia to combat another outbreak of lost."

"The timing isn't a coincidence," Adrien said.

"Not likely." Jean rubbed his mouth and furrowed his brow.

"In spite of what you say—that Nicolas is capable of making his own decisions—you're worried about him."

"This surprises you?" Jean tilted his head to one side, and his lips curved ever so slightly upward.

"Hardly. I'm the same. And I know you'd rather I had nothing to do with him."

"There was a time when that was true. But I've since realized that you have his best interests at heart, even if you do have an uncanny knack for attracting danger. And if your coming here means he may no longer be bound to that bastard...."

"We can't stop him from fighting. But I promise I'll be at his side," Adrien said. "We're stronger together. Something it took me a long time to learn."

Jean smiled, his eyes lighting up with pleasure and something else Adrien couldn't quite discern.

"Why the look?" Adrien asked, chuckling.

"It takes strength to admit you can't do everything alone."

"You really *do* sound like Roland." Adrien stood and inclined his head.

Jean laughed outright. "I'll take that as a compliment."

THEY RETURNED early in the evening. They were told to come, although they had forgotten why. It didn't matter that they had forgotten; their prey was near—they could smell the blood of the others on the air. The others would hurt them. They would kill the others, for Him. The one who mattered.

"You know what you must do for me," their master said. "You must please me and, in return, you may feed on their blood."

Adrien woke with a gasp as pain lanced through his head.

"Are you all right?" Nico put a gentling hand on Adrien's shoulder.

Adrien looked around the room, at a loss to recall where he was. He felt strangely disconnected from his surroundings, as if he were still dreaming. "Nico?" He rubbed the bridge of his nose. The pain began to dissipate and his thoughts cleared a bit.

Nico wrapped strong arms around him, the bare skin of his chest pressed to Adrien's back. "I'm still here."

His Nico. Or was it Nicolas? The memories of three timelines blurred. "Nico," he said, as if by speaking the name he would be surer.

"Yes. Nico. But I'm Nicolas too. It's almost as if being here, in this time, helps encourage the memories to return."

"They're coming," Adrien said. "I feel them. Someone's guiding them."

Nico nodded. They both knew who that person was.

CHAPTER SIXTEEN
THE LOST

THE SOUND of someone knocking on their door roused Nico and Adrien from sleep.

"I'm so sorry to wake you," Lorelei, one of the vampire servants, said. "You're needed downstairs immediately. Lord Lambert says to tell you the main gate has been destroyed and the enemy is approaching the house."

They dressed quickly and ran downstairs to shouts and the sound of glass shattering. The front doors—what was left of them—hung partly off their hinges. The remainder of the wood burned red-hot in the darkness of night, flames licking at the interior.

Hunters.

"There are half a dozen of Pelletier's followers outside." François drew his sword and aimed at the space between the doors, releasing a stream of ice to extinguish the fire. "Jean and Blaise are fighting them. I counted at least twenty lost following behind, but I'm sure there are more we can't see. Caroline and Rosina are in the gardens behind the house, guarding the wall to keep them from coming closer."

"But what about the wards?" Adrien asked.

"The wards will only truly keep the lost at bay during the daytime. At night, they're far less effective." François looked as exhausted as Jean and the others. Vampires didn't need to sleep as humans did, but in a prolonged battle without rest, their bodies would eventually betray them too.

"How do you kill them?" Adrien asked. The voices in his mind had grown louder, but he focused instead on François.

"They're like vampires," François replied quickly. "They won't die unless you behead them."

"They're quite easy to kill one-on-one. Their strength is in their numbers," Charles added. "And if the hunters have more waiting…."

"We'll go around back and meet up with you later. Jean and Blaise will need help fighting the hunters." Nico headed for the rear of the building before anyone could object, Adrien following a few footsteps behind.

"There are hundreds of lost," Adrien told Nico as the vampires guarding the back doors opened them briefly to let them outside. "Surrounding the building."

Nico paled. "Hundreds? You can sense them that clearly?"

"The more I focus on them, the more I can feel each one of them. But there are so many, I can't make out what they're thinking. It's like a blur." Adrien wished he had more time to understand the creatures. The only thing that mattered now was that he and Nico protect those inside from harm.

The smell of death hung in the still night air. Not the pleasant smell Adrien associated with blood, but the scent of decay, cold and cloying.

"I can't sense them," Nico said. "But there are hunters in the trees beyond the gardens. Watching us."

"Giovanetti?"

Nico nodded. Adrien fought a wave of hatred and felt the demon inside him stir. *Not now. I'll call you when I need you.* The demon receded. Adrien guessed it would not remain docile forever, but for now, at least, it obeyed his commands.

They rounded the small stone building where the gardeners stored their tools. Adrien got his first look at their attackers as he stepped beyond the wall that surrounded the manor house. Pale, hairless creatures, some naked, some dressed in rags, waited at the edge of the woods. They looked every bit like movie zombies. Given their erratic movements and the way their eyes lacked focus, the last thing Adrien expected was the bursts of fire that issued from their hands as he and Nico stepped out from behind the shed.

Adrien swung his sword at the woman—if you could call it that—nearest to him. The creature's pitiful wail as his weapon connected with its shoulder made Adrien wonder if there wasn't some humanity remaining beneath the necrotic skin. He hesitated, and the creature reached for him.

Nico shouted and flew, slicing its arm off even as it reached to grab Adrien. It screamed and its face contorted with rage. "You mustn't let them touch you. Their touch is like poison—it will weaken even the most powerful vampires."

Adrien severed the creature's head from its torso in one blow. It fell silently to the ground and lay still. There was no blood.

"Adrien!"

Adrien looked turned to look for Nico. Where he'd expected to see him finishing off the last of the creatures, five or six dozen now surrounded them in a large circle. Adrien hadn't noticed the others approach. Hadn't heard them either. He guessed they'd hidden behind the buildings and made their move while he and Nico fought. They were faster than he'd realized.

Electricity charged the air, and the smell of rotting flesh made Adrien vomit and cough. He stumbled backward and gasped for breath, dizzy and disoriented. He leaned on his sword and tried to focus through the powerful sensations that held him hostage.

Nico, apparently unaffected, flew upward, stabbing at two of the creatures before landing atop the wall behind them. Adrien pulled himself together and charged several of the others, then swung his sword in an arc to relieve them of their heads.

Eight down. Sixty more to go. The lost headed toward the mansion, moving to close the gaps Adrien and Nico had made in the circle.

Adrien jumped and landed next to Nico. "What now?"

"We need to thin their ranks before they reach the house," Nico shouted over the creatures' screams.

"Stay there," Adrien answered. "I'll make a path and attack from the outside."

"I don't think—"

Adrien gritted his teeth and gripped his sword with both hands. He bounded off the wall, forcing back another wave of nausea, and managed to cleanly sever three heads before landing back in the center. Before they could advance to touch him, he leapt back to the wall, propelling himself off it once more like a gymnast might use a trampoline.

He shouted as he landed directly in front of a cluster, slashing wildly and connecting with their bodies. His sword vibrated with each attack, but the blade met little resistance. The creatures continued to approach. He managed to behead three more, but the rest milled about the wall, attempting to scale it.

"Adrien, watch out!" Nico shouted as Adrien dispatched two more.

One of the creatures jumped from its foothold halfway up the wall. *Too soon.* Adrien hadn't expected them to act so quickly. The lost shot a line of fire from its bony fingers, catching the leg of his pants. The sharp sting burned through the material and seared his skin.

Shit. Adrien landed on the soft grass and rolled, extinguishing the flames as Nico dispatched Adrien's attacker. "I'm fine," he called out to a very worried-looking Nico. He fought a wave of dizziness as he got to his feet, but it quickly passed and he began the work of destroying the lost closest to him. His ankle smarted as his movements stretched the newly forming skin, but he ignored the pain. Perhaps the creatures' touch wasn't as harmful to an immortal.

Adrien and Nico continued to fight side by side, until less than a dozen lost remained. The creatures on the ground looked around, seemingly confused, as if they'd only now realized how sharply their numbers had dwindled. The three or four that had nearly clawed their way to the top of the wall paused as well, as if waiting for something—or someone—to tell them what to do.

Nico didn't wait. He launched himself skyward again, swinging his weapon and knocking the remaining lost from their tenuous perches halfway up the wall gazing out over the property. "There are more in the forest. Many more." He shivered and looked toward the hills beyond. The first rays of sunlight illuminated the rolling hills.

Morning. When the wards were most effective. Time to rest and prepare for another night of fighting. The sense of dread that lingered at the periphery of Adrien's consciousness now burned too hot to ignore. He sensed something beyond the trees, dark and dangerous. Something he hadn't sensed before. "Something's coming," he said. "Something worse."

"Worse?" A muscle in Nico's cheek twitched. "Then we should get back to the house and prepare," Nico said before Adrien could put what he'd been feeling into words.

"Prepare?"

Nico frowned. "Yes. This is no longer just a skirmish. We must prepare for war."

CHAPTER SEVENTEEN
KING'S GAMBIT

IN THE bright morning light, the grounds looked far less menacing. Adrien and Nico made their way back to the main house, stepping over corpses of the lost that littered the lawn. As expected, with the advent of morning, the lost slowed their approach. Some turned and moved to the relative safety of the forest, whereas others milled about without obvious purpose, no longer an immediate threat.

Adrien released his sword and took a long breath. Nearby the bushes rustled, but the presence was a friendly one.

"You both fought well," Jean said as he wiped dirt and sweat from his brow. "It's time to rest now."

"What about reinforcements?" Nico asked as he too released his weapon.

Jean shook his head. "They were attacked. I doubt they'll make it here at all, and even if they do, their numbers will be small. We need to defeat Pelletier's forces ourselves."

They were outnumbered and surrounded. But what was the alternative? Adrien didn't want to even consider it. They would win this war and they'd survive. "It would help to have a better count of how many we're dealing with," he said.

"Adrien, that's too dang—"

"He's right." Jean turned to Nico.

"Then I'll go with him." Nico met Jean's gaze with steely resolve.

"No." Jean lifted Nico's arm. "You'll have this treated first." Adrien hadn't noticed the deep gash near Nico's elbow.

"It's nothing. I'll—"

"I'll go with him," Blaise said as he walked over to them.

Jean nodded. "You can join them after you've been treated."

"We'll be fine," Adrien added in response to Nico's look of concern. "You can join us later. You said it yourself—they're weaker now. I don't sense any movement, but if we meet up with any of them, we'll retreat immediately. Call for help if we need it."

Nico blew air from between tense lips. "Promise me you'll be careful."

"I promise." Adrien brushed his hand against Nico's, then watched as Nico followed Jean back to the house.

"Shall we?" Blaise asked.

"I'll scout the western side of the estate if you'll take the east. Meet back here in an hour?"

Blaise inclined his head and vanished a moment later.

Adrien glanced back at the house and took a deep breath. The voices of the lost had gone silent. Did they sleep, or were they, like vampires, simply more powerful at night?

He made his way along the edge of the formal gardens until he came to the fields that abutted the forest on the outskirts of the property. Unlike the area where they'd fought before, this part of the estate had been leased to local farmers. Wheat swayed in the gentle breeze, shimmering with dew. In the distance, cows grazed on rolling hills. Goats chased each other around a pen next to a ramshackle farmhouse. The stream that served as the boundary of the Lamberts' land was far away, but Adrien heard it as if it was nearby. He often forgot what it had been like to be human. He took his heightened senses for granted far too often.

He heard footsteps long before he sensed anyone nearby. He continued to walk, refusing to acknowledge the man whose presence he felt. The visitor would make himself known soon enough.

The demon stirred, infusing Adrien's body with its power. Adrien stretched, catlike, arms above his head. Unconcerned. He continued to follow the boundary of the Lamberts' land, taking his time, sensing the presence of the other unwelcome visitors—hunters and lost alike. All of them waited for one man.

"Decided you'd make an appearance," Adrien said. "What if the others see you? You're supposed to have died a hero in this timestream."

"You've grown." Pelletier stepped onto the path a few yards in front of Adrien.

"You're as condescending as ever." Pelletier wouldn't fight him here. That would be too easy, and there was no audience. He'd already settled on the rules of this dangerous game. Adrien had no doubt as to who the pawns were: the people he loved and cared for.

Pelletier chuckled, his lips set in a knowing smile.

"Let me kill him for you," the demon hissed.

Too easy. Too expected. *I've got this. I'll let you know when I need your help.*

Not surprisingly, Pelletier was alone. None of the others, not even Giovanetti, could challenge Adrien now, and Pelletier knew it.

Adrien kicked a stone off the trail and continued to walk. He met Pelletier's gaze as he neared, then stepped around him and kept going.

"We have unfinished business, you and I." Pelletier's voice was matter-of-fact, but the wave of power that struck Adrien in the back immobilized him and sent tiny sparks of pain lancing through his muscles.

Adrien did not resist. "I've made my choice." The demon thrummed in Adrien's mind, clawing at the weakest spot in Adrien's newly built wall. Adrien pushed away thoughts of Nico and, with them, the demon. *Rattling its cage.* How much more did Pelletier understand?

"You've turned a corner, I see. But you're still too weak to fight me."

Pelletier's words only intensified the demon's unrest. It threw itself against the barrier with renewed intensity.

This isn't the time to fight.

The demon quieted, but the word *weak* resonated in Adrien's mind. "What do you want?" he asked.

A shiver traveled up Adrien's spine as Pelletier walked around him, studying him. "To be honest," Pelletier said, "I'm not sure."

Adrien inhaled and allowed his anger to dissipate. The demon beat its fists against Adrien's resolve.

"You fascinate and disgust me in equal measure." Pelletier stopped, his face only inches from Adrien's. "With your gifts, I should be dead by now." He shook his head. "But here we stand, you and I...." He grabbed Adrien by the throat and squeezed.

"Are you going to let him squash you like a worm?" the demon hissed.

Adrien ignored this and closed his eyes.

"Not enough to interest you in fighting?" Pelletier said with feigned disappointment. "What more do I need? Perhaps I should start this little war by killing your vampire?"

Adrien clenched his jaw but did not respond.

"Ah, you really *have* changed, haven't you?" Pelletier squeezed tighter.

"Kill him," the demon urged. *"Show him how strong we are together."*

If he survived a fight with Pelletier, even defeated him, he'd be too injured to help them fight the other hunters and the lost. The risk to Nico and the others was too great.

"You've become timid," the demon growled. *"Since when have you run from a fight? You know you want to kill him."*

"Adrien!" Nico's voice replaced the demon's in Adrien's mind. *"Adrien, where are you?"*

Stay away! Adrien prayed Nico would listen.

"Interesting." Pelletier released his grip on Adrien's neck. Adrien opened his eyes again and gasped for breath. "Is your vampire that weak?"

Nico, stay—

"Not happening." Nico stood at Adrien's side an instant later. "We work together."

Pelletier stepped back a few feet and materialized his weapon. Before, he'd have waited. Toyed with Adrien.

"He knows how powerful we are now," the demon said gleefully.

Adrien guessed otherwise. Pelletier always believed himself stronger. Most likely he'd drawn his weapon because he thought putting Nico in harm's way would get more of a response.

But if together we can kill him.... Adrien caught Nico's gaze and drew his own weapon. Nico nodded almost imperceptibly and followed suit. For a long moment, the three of them waited as the wind rustled the leaves on the nearby trees.

Adrien took a quick glance around to size up the terrain. On one side of the pathway, the forest stood sentinel. On the other, a low rough-hewn stone wall marked the boundary between the Lambert estate and the adjoining farmland. Ahead of them, behind where Pelletier stood, the path crossed a small stream that exited the forest and cut its way through the pastures and dipped under the wall.

Adrien tightened his grip on his sword. *Plenty of room to maneuver.*

Pelletier smiled and sent a volley of black wisps that fluttered like the wings of a bird of prey as they flew at Nico.

Nico! Pelletier's weapon is—

"I've got this. I remember what his attack can do to vampire flesh." Nico moved so quickly, he seemed to disappear. Adrien spotted him a second later, standing atop the wall a few yards away.

Adrien didn't wait for Pelletier to set himself for another attack, but launched a fireball of blue energy barreling toward him. Pelletier dodged easily, but Adrien held his palm out and the ball of light sped around Pelletier several times, speeding up until it created a ring that circled his body. *Now!* He closed his hand and the light exploded into a brilliant shower of blue-and-white sparks.

Did I get him?

The smoke cleared. Pelletier appeared completely untouched. Adrien hadn't expected it would be that easy.

"What are you waiting for?" Pelletier leaned on his sword as though it was a walking stick. He hadn't even broken a sweat.

Adrien ignored this and focused on his attack. Power built from within his body, emanating outward and ringing his sword in a blue-black light. His weapon pointed skyward. When had he lifted it?

"Use me," the demon whispered.

One of the trees exploded, sending bits of wood and ash all around them. Adrien glanced at Nico, but Nico just stared back at him, lips parted, eyes wide.

"See what I'm capable of? Together we—"

You? You were the one who launched that attack? Adrien didn't need the demon's response to know the answer. The demon had been in control of his body.

Pelletier twirled his sword and sent a burst of black flame toward Nico, bringing Adrien back to the here and now. Nico dodged it easily, but the realization that he'd nearly forgotten Nico was there was all Adrien needed to shove the demon back to the depths.

"You'll regret this," it hissed. *"You need me to defeat him!"*

Pelletier chuckled. "You control it, but you haven't learned to use it yet."

Adrien gritted his teeth and ran his hand over the blade. His blood hissed on the metal. He needed to keep Nico safe, and without the demon's power, he'd lose this fight. He slowly opened the gateway between their thoughts. He only needed a little power to supplement his own. If he could control—

The demon burst through the barrier, pushing past Adrien and shoving his consciousness down into darkness. Adrien watched, momentarily helpless, as sparks flew from his fingertips and wound around the hilt of his sword. The metal glowed red-hot and the blade swung wildly as Adrien and the demon struggled for dominance.

A flash of blue fire soared upward, out of control, traveling until it met a gray cloud. Droplets of water fell over them. The demon growled its displeasure as Pelletier laughed and fired another volley toward Adrien.

Nico dove in front of Adrien and used his sword to deflect the attack. Light and flame arced in a dozen different directions, scorching both trees and grass as it flew. Smoke enveloped them, acrid and thick. He couldn't see Nico. Couldn't sense him nearby either.

"Nico!" Adrien shouted. "Nico!"

CHAPTER EIGHTEEN
THE MEASURE OF A MAN

NICO ROLLED to avoid another of Pelletier's shots as the smoke dissipated. *Adrien!* The presence he felt was familiar, but it was not Adrien's. The demon laughed, its eyes aglow with pleasure. It pointed its weapon at Pelletier and flames danced on the blade. It swung its sword wildly from side to side, and a ribbon of fire as wide as the blade was long snaked through the air.

Adrien's control over the demon was not yet absolute. "It will use every means in its power to take back what it believes it owns," Roland had warned only days before. "Adrien needs time to learn how to coexist with it."

Pelletier stepped aside. Behind him, a tree burst into flames and disappeared in a blur of smoke and flame. Nico stared openmouthed at the place where the tree had been moments before. *Such power. If Adrien could only control it....*

"Impressive. Though a bit wide with the aim." Pelletier smiled, then glanced at Nico. "Not much help to you either." He swung his sword, but this attack wasn't meant for Adrien.

Nico flew upward, but the flames chased him. He alighted on a high branch, then jumped to another. The tree exploded, Nico tumbling down with the blast. He righted himself as he fell, landing a few feet in front of Adrien.

The demon screamed and swung its sword again, its attacks missing Pelletier, who danced around with ease and appeared unperturbed, even amused.

Adrien! What the hell are you doing, letting that thing control you? Again, Nico avoided one of Pelletier's fiery attacks. They'd get nowhere like this. Pelletier had been toying with him. If he decided to get serious, he might wound Adrien badly enough that he wouldn't recover. *Adrien!*

The demon heard him, because it sneered at him, then went back to its wild attacks. Mindless battle, with no thought for strategy. *"Worthless!"*

Adrien, stop this! You can't control this. Not yet.

Adrien swayed and blinked. Pelletier fired off a shot at the same time as the demon. The attack pushed Pelletier backward, forcing him to lean against the stump of a tree charred from their battle. Something touched Nico's arm, and he hissed as pain spread up to his shoulder and down through his fingers.

At the same time, the demon raised its weapon to shield itself from the blow. Already weakened from deflecting the last of Pelletier's shots, though, it was too slow. Part of the attack deflected upward and hit one of the nearby trees, but a good portion of the energy in that deadly black beam sliced through the demon's—Adrien's—upper thigh.

"Shit!" The voice was Adrien's this time. He dropped to his knees and gasped for air.

"Adrien!" Nico sent a stream of ice into the air, where it split into tiny slivers like knives and sped toward Pelletier.

Nico helped Adrien up, his weapon still pointed at Pelletier. The wound on Nico's forearm hissed, and the skin around it blackened. He'd need treatment soon or the damage would spread.

Adrien steadied himself on Nico, then stepped in front of him.

"Adrien, I—"

Adrien smiled. "It's good," he said. "I've got this." His forehead beaded with perspiration as he aimed at Pelletier's chest.

Pelletier shook his head. "Another time." The ground beneath them shuddered and the wind blew, causing the charred leaves from the surrounding trees to rain down around them.

"No! Not yet. I'm ready for—"

Nico used his good hand to create a sphere of energy around them, protecting them from the fallout of Pelletier's final volley. A hail of red and silver flames sizzled as they touched the ground around them.

Pelletier's right. Adrien's not ready. None of us are.

Everything turned black.

"Nico!" Adrien screamed.

NICO FLOATED, rocked by a gentle wave. Fog surrounded him like a warm blanket. He touched the water and tasted it. An ocean of blood, sweet and satisfying. Adrien's soul opened to his lips.

"This was my fault. If I'd known you were injured—"

Stubborn as always, wanting to do things on your own, Nico said. *I told you we're stronger together.*

The fog lifted and he reached for Adrien. His eyes fluttered open.

"Took you long enough." Adrien's loving smile belied his words.

Nico drew a deep breath. Instinctively, he reached for his wounded shoulder. "How did you…?"

"Adrien's blood," Jean said from behind Adrien. "By the time Adrien brought you here, your entire arm had begun to wither. I tried to heal you first. When it didn't work… I feared we'd lose you."

Nico sat. He was about to get to his feet when Jean said, "You must rest."

"I feel fine." He felt surprisingly good, but then he always did when he drank Adrien's blood. "Really."

Jean glanced at Adrien, who shrugged.

Nico laughed.

"What's so amusing?" Jean asked.

"Only that much as I'm pleased both of you agree that I'm not a death's door," he replied, "I'm quite capable of deciding for myself if I'm recovered."

Adrien chuckled. *"And you call me stubborn."*

Nico shook his head, then remembered Adrien's injury. "Your leg. Are you all right?"

"Jean healed me," Adrien explained. "Seems Pelletier's attacks aren't as potent now that I'm immortal." No doubt Adrien too was thinking about the day just such an attack had nearly killed him. The day Nico had given him the gift.

Not me. The other Nicolas. Still, he remembered it as though he'd been there.

"Leave it to you two to get into a fight with a crew of armed hunters." Blaise stood in the doorway, grinning. "By the time I caught up with you, you were both unconscious and bleeding. What the hell happened?"

"Blaise carried you both back here," Jean put in. "He got there after the hunters who attacked you disappeared."

"Thank you." Nico forced a smile. He didn't understand why Jean would keep the truth about who was behind this war—or who had attacked them—from Blaise, but now wasn't the time to challenge the status quo.

"I'm just glad you're both all right." Blaise ran a hand through his hair, and for the first time, Nico noticed the dark circles beneath his eyes.

"You look terrible."

"I'm fine. Just a little tired." Blaise walked into the room and stood beside Jean.

Nico stood as a worried Adrien looked on. *I'm fine. Really I am.*

Adrien frowned and placed a hand on Nico's shoulder, then seemed to remember he shouldn't be able to so easily touch Nico and pulled his hand quickly away.

Blaise shot Jean a look of surprise. "Is there something you're not telling me?"

Jean pressed his lips together.

"Jean?" Blaise appeared less than pleased.

"We'll speak of it later," Jean said. "It is… a bit difficult to explain."

Blaise glared at Jean. "We'll speak of it now."

"We'll leave you two alone," Jean said quietly. But for the telltale twitch of his cheek, his face would have been unreadable.

Good. Blaise clearly had the strength to match Jean's own. Time was too short, too fickle. In Nico's own timeline, Jean had lost Blaise far too soon.

CHAPTER NINETEEN
RESPITE

NICO SLEPT most of the afternoon in Adrien's arms. He awoke as the first hint of sunset streaked the horizon and worked the fingers on the arm Pelletier had injured. Other than some residual stiffness, he'd fully healed. He'd be ready to fight again when the time came.

"Sleep well?" Adrien yawned.

"In your arms?" Nico smiled. "Always." He craved Adrien's body at least as much as his blood.

Adrien kissed him and sighed. "Someday," he said, his voice wistful, "we'll be able to stay in bed all day."

"It's hard to imagine you sleeping in, as much energy as you have."

"We could stay a bit longer and do something other than sleep," Adrien whispered against Nico's ear, causing Nico to shudder.

Nico ran his tongue over his eyeteeth, then kissed Adrien and licked at his neck.

"You're torturing me." Adrien groaned.

"Mmm." Nico rolled Adrien onto his back, straddling him. "And here I thought you were enjoying this."

Nico pushed Adrien's shirt up and laved a line from his chest downward. Adrien clasped Nico's ass and squeezed. "Much better than sleeping, don't you think?" he teased as Nico pulled his shirt over his head.

"The vampire part of you may not need to sleep," Nico said with a wicked grin. "But the human in you—"

"Is doing just fine, thank you." Adrien dug his fingernails into Nico's buttocks until Nico hissed with pleasure.

"And you humans call vampires evil." Nico leaned over and bit Adrien's neck, just enough to sting.

"I want to fuck you," Adrien growled, clearly at the limit of his patience. "We've done enough talking for one night."

Nico laughed and began to slide Adrien's jeans over his hips. An explosion followed by the sound of shattering glass had both of them jumping out of bed and pulling their clothes back on.

"Torture." Adrien groaned and shook his head. "Next time I'm just going to tie you down to the bed and fuck you into the sheets."

"You won't need to." Nico chuckled. "If I don't get a few waking moments alone with you, I'll die from lack of Adrien." At least they'd gotten some rest before the next round of hostilities. This fight, he guessed, would prove far more challenging. Pelletier had to know others would come to help them. He'd use the opportunity to eliminate any hunters who opposed him, and having more join the fight would be just the kind of battle he'd savor.

Ten minutes later Nico and Adrien joined the others at the edge of the forest. There, they found Charles, Blaise, and François doing their best to push back a group of lost that had scaled the wall and were advancing through the formal gardens.

"We'll fight in pairs," Blaise told them as he dispatched one of the creatures. "It's too dangerous to venture out alone."

"You're injured." Nico reached for Blaise's shoulder and ran his hand over the charred and bloodied fabric of his shirt. The smell of burnt flesh stung his nostrils. The wound wasn't fatal, but he'd need treatment soon.

Blaise smiled, then tensed his jaw. "I'll be fine. Not to worry."

Charles met Nico's eyes and shook his head almost imperceptibly, frowning in obvious displeasure. Adrien glanced around. "Where's Jean?"

"He went to scout the fields. We were supposed to rendezvous here." Blaise looked toward the rolling hills that bordered the northwest corner of the estate.

"He's alone?" Nico's heart leapt to his throat.

"We'll find him," Adrien told him. "If we don't return after reinforcements arrive, come find us."

"No," Blaise said. "I'll come with—"

"You're injured." Charles touched Blaise's wound, and blue light emanated from his fingertips. "Let me heal you. You can join them later."

"But—"

"Please, Blaise. Let Charles heal you," Nico said. "My brother wouldn't want you fighting like this. Adrien and I will make sure Jean's safe."

Blaise hesitated, then finally nodded. "Promise me you won't fight alone."

"I won't let Nicolas out of my sight," Adrien said. "We'll stay together."

CHAPTER TWENTY
TOO SOON TO DIE

THE DOZEN lost who surrounded Jean were no match for him, but they'd succeeded in keeping him at bay for the past hour. Now, as the sky darkened, he felt uneasy. Ten more of the creatures lingered at the edge of the field, waiting.

Waiting for what?

The answer came in the form of movement in the trees beyond the field. Something new. Not the lost. Something more dangerous. Neither human nor animal. Yet their familiar scent left him with little doubt.

These creatures had been created at least in part with Nicolas's blood. But there was more. Blood just as familiar, but just as rare. *The blood of an immortal.*

Leaves crackled on the ground behind him. Jean spun around to face a creature taller than the lost, its eyes bloodred and without irises. Its equine body was completely hairless and pale as death, like the lost.

Evolution.

The thing hissed at Jean, its nostrils flaring. Its cracked lips revealed sharp yellow teeth. Then it did something unthinkable: it looked at him with intelligent eyes and laughed.

A sentient pawn. Far more dangerous than the others.

Jean shot a blooming trail of ice that hit the creature directly in the chest. Bloodless cuts appeared over its body, but it merely hissed and licked its lips. Saliva ran down its chin.

The creature raised its front legs, uncurling long fingers from beneath what Jean had thought were hooves. Lines of yellow-orange fire snaked from its fingertips and flew toward Jean, who dodged.

The beast raised its hands again, and this time Jean deflected with his sword. The twisted ropes of energy flew upward and wrapped around the lowest branches of the tree overhead, which began to crack and fall.

Judging from the sound of footsteps behind him and the scent of blood, several more of the creatures had joined them in the clearing. Jean swung his weapon in a wide arc with both hands, pivoting to send the energy toward the newcomers. A swath of silvery ice attached itself to the two closest creatures, covering their bodies. They writhed and clawed at their skin, seeking to free themselves, but to no avail. Jean raised his left hand, then turned his wrist and pulled the invisible strings on the shards embedded in the creatures. They howled in pain. Jean swung his sword low and decapitated them both in one swift movement.

At least they can be killed like the others.

Jean shot another blast of ice and was just about to duplicate the attack as he'd done before when both of the creatures burst into flames. The ice melted, but the creatures' bodies did not appear affected. Flames emanated from their skin as Jean attacked a second time. Again the flames melted the ice, thwarting the attack.

He tried the same technique on the creatures who had just arrived, expecting them to fall victim to his initial attack. But as with their brethren, they easily repelled the daggers of ice and remained ablaze, their flames acting as a shield.

Had they learned from his first attack? But how? They hadn't seen him attack the first two creatures.

A common consciousness in a sentient being? It might explain what Adrien thought he'd heard. *I must warn the others.*

By now, nearly twenty of the creatures had joined the fray. Jean glanced around to assess the best path for his retreat. Beyond the fields was the house, with its formal gardens, stone fountains, and benches. The fountains could be used for cover, the benches for a better vantage point. Blaise, Charles, and the others fought to maintain a perimeter around the house. If he drew the creatures toward the wards, the vampires might pin them there and more easily defeat them. As weak as the wards were at night, he prayed they would hold at least long enough to give them the advantage.

He retreated slowly, keeping the creatures far enough away that he could fend off their attacks. He didn't know what damage the glowing ropes might do to him, and he had no intention of finding out.

The creatures did not seem to be in any hurry. They matched his pace and kept their distance. They did not attack him but watched him with curiosity. They were judging his actions. Evaluating him.

When he was about a hundred yards from one of the largest fountains, he removed his jacket and let it fall to the ground. He would need as much free movement as possible if he was going to fight so many at once.

One of the creatures walked ahead of the others. It stopped, head cocked to one side. *"Why do you run? You cannot win."* The creature spoke in Jean's mind.

"For whom do you fight?" Jean asked in an effort to mask his surprise.

"We fight for the one who matters."

"Who is the one who matters?" He'd buy the others as much time as possible. If he could hold them here—

The creature responded with a hail of gold ropes that snaked through the air toward him. The fountains were still too far away. He had no choice but to engage his attackers where he stood. He swung his sword, severing the ropes before they could touch him, then spinning around to meet attacks from some of the other creatures who gathered behind him.

Managing to cut most of the ropes with one swing, he braced himself for more. Two glowing ropes wound around his ankles, causing him to fall face forward into the dirt. He'd miscalculated. He'd thought the creatures at the back of the group couldn't reach him with their attacks. *A fatal mistake.*

Pain snaked through his body to his chest, horrible and sharp. He imagined it carving a path through bone and muscle, past his heart, to his brain.

The world exploded.

JEAN AWOKE to a room filled with blinding light. The same creatures he'd been fighting moments before now surrounded him. The largest approached, arms outstretched. Jean tried to move, but his muscles wouldn't obey.

"Your blood is old." The creature grabbed Jean's head and held it in a viselike grip.

This isn't real. Jean imagined himself standing on the dirt path. Tried to imagine the taste of blood in his mouth and the smell of the leaves.

"You will serve us well in death," the creature said.

Jean struggled to reclaim reality, but whatever force bound him to this dreamlike place was far more powerful than he had anticipated. He couldn't speak. He couldn't move. All he could do was wait for the inevitable.

Death. Years before, he'd have embraced it. But now ....

The creature's teeth ripped into his neck as it began to feed. Jean saw himself as one of them. He felt their hunger, their desire for blood. He desired what they did. He wanted to protect the one who mattered. He saw the one who mattered through their eyes. He would do anything for the hunter, even sacrifice himself. The one who mattered had given them life, power, given them consciousness and the ability to choose for themselves. The one who mattered would show them the way.

Jean struggled against the comforting warmth of their thoughts. But in their thoughts, something became clear. A way forward. An understanding of how they might win.

Peaceful oblivion beckoned.

No.

He needed to survive. There was something he needed to do. Something he needed to tell the others. Someone he needed to protect.

Blaise.

Someone laughed. "It has regrets," said a voice in his mind.

Blaise. Forgive me.

As pain spread from where the creature still sucked his neck, Jean fought to regain control. There was something he must tell the others. Something important. Urgent. Something that might save them all. Something about blood. About Adrien's blood. But no matter how he fought, his body refused to respond. The creature would suck him dry, and then he would be one of them....

NICO AND Adrien left the fields for the forest, making their way slowly through the dense trees. They'd expected to see lost at every turn, but instead they met with nothing but the sounds of birds and the occasional scampering squirrel.

Nico had been sure Jean was here—he'd caught the scent of Jean's blood on several occasions since they'd left the manor house. But as ten, then fifteen minutes passed and still they saw nothing of Jean or the lost, he began to wonder if something about the creatures was interfering with his sense of smell.

Adrien glanced at him, lips tensed. *"Something's not right."*

Nico tightened his fingers around the hilt of his weapon. *He's here. I'm sure of it.*

Adrien nodded.

They walked a few minutes more, swords at the ready. They had nearly reached the trail that followed the stream when a branch snapped somewhere behind them. Nico turned, weapon at the ready, his heart racing. Pelletier wouldn't let them off as easily this time. But *this* time, he'd be ready.

Leaves rustled, accompanied by footsteps. At Nico's side, Adrien too stood ready to attack.

A minute, then another, passed. Then a figure flew out from between the trees, launching itself into the air, moving so quickly Nico barely recognized the shape of a man.

"Adrien, no!" Nico shouted just as Adrien touched the blade of his weapon with his hand. "It's—!"

"Blaise." Adrien lowered his weapon and shook his head. "You scared the shit out of me."

"My apologies." Blaise pressed his lips together. "I felt you both. And Jean."

Nico took a few deep breaths, calming his racing heart. "He's close."

"Let's go," Adrien said. Had he sensed Jean's distress too?

They followed the trail along the water until it veered back toward the mansion. "This way." Nico pointed toward where the trees thinned, the edge of a large field at the center of the forest.

He saw Jean the moment they stepped into the clearing. He lay on the grass, several creatures crouching over him. Not the lost. Something different. Less human, and yet—

"Watch out!" Adrien shouted.

Nico ducked as something like liquid sunshine flew over him. It wrapped around a nearby tree trunk. The tree snapped like kindling.

What the—?

"Jean!" Blaise shouted.

Nico moved to cover Blaise as he charged into the center of the lost. Adrien followed, sending a wide arc of power toward the creatures, who had just begun to react. It was almost as if they were slowly awakening from some sort of stupor. One, then another, moved to face them. *As though one by one they came to understand the danger.*

Blaise swung his sword, striking the creature that fed on Jean's limp body. It shrieked and released Jean. Still in the throes of ecstasy from feeding, it was too slow to respond as Blaise swung his weapon parallel to the ground. The creature collapsed in a heap, its head rolling onto the grass. Blood spattered Blaise's feet. *Jean's* blood.

As Adrien and Nico fought the remaining creatures, Blaise gently gathered Jean into his arms and flew upward, into the nearby trees. They'd be safe there, at least for a short while.

Time to get the hell out of here!

Adrien inclined his head and he and Nico both swung wide. The creatures in the front of the group staggered backward, knocking several of their brethren onto the ground. They quickly recovered, but they moved slowly. By the time Nico and Adrien made their way into the forest, the lost were nowhere to be seen.

Blaise had already begun to run toward the house. Nico and Adrien stopped from time to time to make sure none of the creatures followed them. They reached the fountains a few minutes later, all of them panting, eyes focused on the forest, waiting for what they knew would come.

"How is he?" Nico glanced back at Blaise, who was gently laying Jean on a stone bench.

"Weak." Blaise frowned and put his hand to Jean's cheek.

Jean looked like death, his skin so white that Nico feared they were too late. Blaise ran his wrist across the blade of his sword and allowed the blood to drip onto Jean's colorless lips.

Nico backed up so that he stood beside Jean and Blaise. Adrien squeezed his shoulder.

"Jean! You must drink." A muscle twitched in Blaise's cheek as he smeared blood over Jean's lips.

Jean didn't move. Blaise released his weapon and pulled Jean into a seated position. His wrist had already begun to heal, so he tore at the skin there with his eyeteeth, then pressed his wrist to Jean's mouth. "Jean. Please."

Jean's eyes fluttered open and he moaned.

"You must have blood," Blaise repeated.

Jean slowly began to drink.

"We need to get him inside," Adrien said, his focus still on the trees.

The creatures were coming. Nico felt it too. They were vulnerable here. Even as weak as the wards were at night, inside, they would at least give them some protection.

Jean moaned again. He reached up and grabbed Blaise by the arms, his body shaking with the effort. "Blaise…."

"Shhh. You're weak. You must—"

"No." Jean gripped Blaise tighter. "There's something…. Adrien…. I must… must speak with…."

"Let's get you inside," Adrien said. "You can rest, and afterward you can tell—"

"No… I must…."

Blaise scooped Jean into his arms. "Time to retreat."

"I'll stay here and make sure they don't follow," Nico said.

"*We'll* stay here," Adrien corrected and turned to Blaise. "Let me know when he's conscious."

Blaise nodded and disappeared a moment later. Nico drew a long breath. *Too close.* If the creatures had succeeded in draining Jean of his blood….

CHAPTER TWENTY-ONE
REFLECTIONS IN BLOOD

CHARLES SLASHED wildly as the lost advanced from the forest in waves. François fought nearby, his movements so fast they were barely visible. The air around them reeked of death and decay. They were outnumbered. None of them had expected this many. The lost were challenging enough—whatever new atrocities Pelletier and his followers had created were even more terrifying. Even if they defeated the legions of lost and their brethren, the hunters who manipulated them weren't far behind.

We should retreat, François! They would regroup and use their powers to fortify the wards until the other hunters and vampires could join the fight. *I'll lend you cover.*

"But—"

I'll follow once you've reached the main gate. The others are back at the mansion. So far the wards around the front of the house appeared to be holding.

François hesitated, then nodded and extricated himself from the middle of a half dozen of the creatures by slashing his way through several and backing away. The clanging of metal a minute later announced the closing of the gates. Charles sighed with relief. But instead of following François, Charles fought his way toward the forest, beating the lost back to where they'd come from.

"Charles!"

Charles ignored François's desperate call and hoped Jean and the others would convince François not to rejoin the fight. He didn't intend to die here, but he'd make sure François survived regardless of the cost.

He'd nearly made it to the gate when someone familiar appeared behind a particularly large group of lost. Antonio Giovanetti raised his hand and the creatures stopped moving. Jean and the others had guessed Pelletier had given his men some control over the lost, but seeing how easily they did so made him shiver.

"Charles. So good to see you."

"Doing your master's bidding as always, I see." Charles glanced around. Nearly a hundred creatures stood immobilized. Waiting.

Giovanetti chuckled. "Verel Pelletier is a champion. Our cause is just."

"And what do you get out of this?" Charles pressed, stalling. If he could take them by surprise, he might still make it out of this with his head attached to his body.

"We seek only what justice demands." Several other hunters stepped out of the trees from behind Giovanetti, weapons at the ready. "We've lived too long in the shadow of your kind."

"So you create these abominations from the very humans you're sworn to protect. An interesting view of justice."

"It doesn't matter that you fail to understand." Giovanetti drew his weapon. "I have my orders. There can be no survivors."

Charles swung his sword high, sending a shower of ice shards flying at his attackers. Giovanetti raised his hand and the ice fell to the ground as drops of water.

He's stronger than before. Jean was right—they'd experimented on the vampires they'd kidnapped. Giovanetti and the other hunters had somehow learned to use vampire blood and Pelletier's immortal blood to augment their power.

Charles tried to attack again, but his body refused to move. His arms fell to his sides and his weapon vanished. Giovanetti raised his hand and beckoned the lost forward.

I've lived far longer than I deserved. How paradoxical that death had come for him now, when he'd finally found happiness with François. When his life was, at last, truly worth living. *I've been more than fortunate.*

For centuries, he'd hidden his guilt. He hid himself away from both vampires and humans. He kept his heart safely locked away.

Until he met François.

François, who loved him unconditionally. Who sought the transformation. Who had suffered greatly for him, because of him. And yet sometime, when he'd least expected it, Charles had finally come to believe that François wanted him. Loved him, in spite of his many flaws.

Giovanetti and the others retreated into the woods as the lost surrounded Charles. They were so close now, he could see nothing but the blank expressions on their faces.

François, you saved my soul.

Charles smiled and allowed himself to fall into emptiness.

CHAPTER TWENTY-TWO
THROUGH THE FOG

"WHAT THE hell are you doing?" Adrien demanded as Blaise made his way through a hail of red and black volleys, one arm around Jean's waist and Jean leaning against his shoulder. "You were supposed to be recuperating."

"He insisted on speaking with you." Blaise gently set Jean down so that he leaned against a crumbling marble pillar. "If I hadn't carried him, he'd have crawled."

Adrien glanced at Nico and crouched beside Jean. "And you call *me* stubborn?"

Jean glared at him, his skin so pale that but for the fresh scent of Blaise's blood on his lips, Adrien would have worried for Jean's life.

"I'll be fine in a few hours." Jean's voice was thin, his words laced with pain.

"What's so important that you risked *both* your lives to tell me?" Adrien held his sword up to deflect an attack launched from behind the stone wall.

"They are sentient, slavelike creatures. Created to obey a hunter's command."

"Pelletier's command?" This was hardly a revelation. "Of course they do."

"Not just his." Jean coughed and a thin line of blood traced its way over his lips. He was far more seriously wounded than he let on. Blaise must have known this, because a muscle in his jaw twitched as he steadied Jean with a hand to his back. "I believe they will respond to the command of any hunter whose blood they recognize."

"Recognize?"

"Earlier... in the woods... I realized something," Jean whispered. "They're bound by blood. Created from it. And these new creatures... they're all connected by it. They communicate through it."

"Blood?" Adrien shot a look at Nico, who blanched. No doubt he too was thinking of the Nicolas Pelletier had kidnapped from the wedding.

"Nicolas's blood, yes." Jean nodded. "But until now… no one has been able to control them. Something is… different."

"Jean," Blaise said, "we can discuss this later, when you're safe."

"No. You must…. I have to explain. Now." Jean gripped Blaise's forearm so tightly Blaise winced. "The key to control… it isn't Nicolas's blood. It's *Pelletier's*. The blood… he's… given his followers."

"Pelletier's *immortal* blood." Adrien ran a hand over his lips as the import of Jean's words finally hit home.

"So an immortal can control them?" Blaise asked.

"It's a guess," Jean admitted. "But if it works…."

Nico, who'd been watching them as he fought back another wave of lost, grabbed Adrien's arm. "You can't be thinking of allowing them to taste *your* blood." He met Adrien's gaze, and Adrien heard the unspoken thought: *"Especially not when you still can't fully control the demon."* Then, aloud, "If it's my blood that created them, why not let me try?"

"I do not believe they will heed the will of a vampire," Jean put in. "Too risky, given *we* are their prey."

Adrien nodded. "If I can control them without risking the lives of hunters and vampires alike, then of course I'd—"

"You have no idea what they might do to you. Look what they've done to my brother," Nico snapped. "You value your life so little."

Adrien understood Nico's fear, but he feared more for Nico and the others.

"We'll watch over him," Blaise said. "If they don't release him, we'll free him ourselves."

"Adrien." Nico frowned.

"Please, Nico, let me try." Adrien waited for Nico's argument, but none came. He turned to Jean. "There's one thing I ask. Something I need from you, Jean." Jean raised a skeptical eyebrow, and Adrien laughed. "I've asked much of you over the years, but this time, I want to give you something." He held out his wrist. "Take my blood. If I'm injured… if something happens to me, Nicolas and the others will need your help to fight these things. The loss of blood won't weaken me, but it will give you strength."

Jean nodded, his face impassive. Already he looked far better than he had when Blaise had carried him. He brought Adrien's wrist to his lips with a shaky hand and drank.

ADRIEN STOOD at the edge of the clearing. Nicolas and Blaise waited behind him, their weapons trained on the trees, ready to strike. The sky had grown lighter, but thick clouds blocked the sun. The lost waited, their pale skin visible through the trees, the rotting stench of them making Adrien's stomach roil.

They'd agreed that Adrien would face the lost in the morning, when they were weakest. Still, Adrien sensed the fear in Nico's heart as he stepped front and center, hands by his sides. Unarmed.

"I'm waiting." Adrien stood before them.

After a while, several of the larger creatures approached, flanked by several dozen lost. Their raspy breathing echoed in the silence as they drew nearer. Soon others joined the first. Without understanding how, Adrien sensed that each was hungry for his blood, driven by the scent of him, *wanting* to devour him.

They stopped abruptly a few feet away.

"You do not fear us?" asked a voice in Adrien's mind.

Adrien stood his ground. "I have nothing to fear from you."

"You smell like him," they said.

"Him?"

"The master."

Adrien bit the skin at his wrist and held it out. Droplets of blood fell onto the grass, and some of the lost moved closer still.

The creature closest to Adrien raised its hands and two ropes of gold light flew toward Adrien, winding around his body. Adrien felt stabbing pain in his chest but did not flinch or fall. Something grabbed his wrist. Pain lanced through his arm, and the world around him melted away.

SHADOWY, AMORPHOUS shapes ringed Adrien. The intense light in the room burned his eyes. The shapes moved like humans, but he guessed they were the lost. He blinked and tried to focus on their faces, but they remained blurry. Adrien rubbed his eyes and his vision finally cleared. Each creature wore a human face. The face of the human they'd been before Pelletier had resurrected them as his slave. More surprising still, Adrien realized that the larger creatures weren't human at all.

Hunters! Of course. He'd sensed the difference before, but he hadn't understood. Pelletier wouldn't hesitate to experiment on his own kind.

"You do not smell like the others," the hunter creature who held Adrien said.

The creature's emotions coursed through Adrien's mind like molten metal, searing his soul, forcing themselves into the deepest recesses of his mind. All the others feared them, but this other did not. Never before had it met someone like Adrien. No one but the master.

Adrien was drowning, and still the creature pressed him to open his thoughts, violating his consciousness, trying to discover what truth he hid. He was transported back to the day of the wedding, watching Nicolas die at Pelletier's hands, then watching him disappear. The image changed into a more recent memory, Nico dying by his blade as he fought to control his demon. This memory morphed into a vision of Nicolas with Giovanetti at his side, touching Nicolas, claiming him as his own while Adrien looked on, powerless as he groped Nicolas—

Adrien screamed in anger and pain. Get the hell out of my mind! *Tears streamed over his cheeks and he sobbed as the creature looked farther still to the memory of his mother tossed like a piece of trash into the mud, dying for him.*

Maman! *He bent over her broken body, felt the heat of the sword in his hand, the pleasure of the kill as he beheaded the bastard who did this to her.*

And still the creature insinuated itself into his thoughts.

Adrien struggled not to fall into the pain. I won't let you do this. *He needed to think. To keep the thing out of his mind. Keep it focused on something—*

That's it. Focus. *If he could distract the thing, he could kick it the hell out of his mind. Change the focus of his thoughts and control the conversation.*

The master? Who is the master? Your creator? *He didn't need the creature to explain, but the question had the desired effect: the creature ceased its attack on his mind.*

"Creator," the creature repeated, considering its meaning. Several other creatures repeated the word. Adrien sensed their confusion and... curiosity? *"Yes. There is only one creator. The master gives us purpose. He is everything."*

"But you have other masters," Adrien continued.

"No. But there are others who command us."

"I am also your master." Adrien focused his thoughts on this concept.

"You lie," it said. The golden bands of light constricted around Adrien's chest. He struggled to breathe. The creature sniffed Adrien's neck as Adrien fought to remain conscious. A second later the creature grabbed him by the head and dug its teeth into his flesh. A sharp pain, then numbness. The creature began to drink.

"You can feel it, can't you?" Adrien felt the demon stir, but forced it away. He would not fight them. *"I am your master."*

"You lie," it repeated.

The bonds around Adrien tightened again. Tiny specks of silver clouded his vision. Had Jean been wrong?

Adrien focused his thoughts and pushed his doubts from his mind. *"You will acknowledge me."*

The pressure on his chest grew. His body screamed for oxygen. He saw bits and pieces of the creatures' memories. He felt their intense hunger, their need for direction, their desperate search for purpose. The master knew all this, and he gave them what they desired; he fulfilled their needs and gave them a reason to exist.

"Release me." He'd run out of time. He would soon succumb. Jean had been mistaken. An immortal's blood wasn't enough to control them. It wasn't enough to control the demon either.

He heard the demon's laughter as he ceased his struggle. And then it came to him, although he wasn't sure if the thought was the demon's or his own. The blood itself wasn't the power that would allow him to control the lost—only the monster that lurked in the depths of his soul could. The horrible wretched demon within him was his salvation!

He closed his eyes and focused on the erratic beat of his heart and called to the demon. Lend me your power! *he commanded silently. The demon obeyed without comment, and a moment later the bonds encircling him eased and he could breathe again. There would be a price to pay for the demon's power, no doubt. But for now....*

"I am your master," Adrien repeated.

"Master." The creature gasped and released its hold on Adrien. It pulled away, eyes wide with fear. The golden ropes that bound Adrien vanished.

He stood once more in the clearing. The creatures remained frozen, as if bound there by invisible strings.

Adrien, Adrien, Adrien, Adrien.... The demon's voice echoed in his brain as it clawed its way upward, seeking control of Adrien's body. His head hurt.

Adrien resisted and the demon quieted.

"Where is the master?" Adrien demanded.

"He is not here," came the answer in his mind. *"His general commands in his stead."*

"Show me where he hides." An image of Giovanetti in the woods flashed through Adrien's thoughts. But which woods? The entire mansion was surrounded by them. "Show me more!"

This time Adrien saw a man bent over a body. Around them, more lost advanced from all sides. Flashes of light illuminated the man's face. *François!*

"You will not harm the others," Adrien commanded the creatures who watched him.

"But the general—"

"He isn't your master, is he?"

"No."

Adrien hoped Pelletier was far away. In a struggle to control the creatures, he guessed Pelletier would prevail. "Charles and François need help," he told Blaise. "Get back to the house. We'll meet there as soon as we can."

Blaise nodded and ran back toward the mansion.

"Nico," Adrien said after Blaise disappeared beyond the fountains. "Fight with me?"

"Of course."

Adrien turned back to the lost, who were still immobilized. He drew a long breath and materialized his sword. "Is this wrong?"

"What do you believe?" Nico countered as he drew his own weapon.

"There's no choice. They want to be released."

"Then let's do this," Nico said as pointed his blade at them.

THEY RAN toward the forest a few minutes later. Later, they would give the creatures a proper burial, but for now the needs of the living took precedence.

"How are Charles and François?" Nico asked as they ran.

"François managed to free Charles from the lost before they bled him dry, but he's gravely injured." Adrien had seen this in the creatures' minds. "But we don't have much time. François is with him, trying to protect him, but he won't be able to hold out long. And Giovanetti is nearby." *Waiting for me.*

"And the lost?"

"I don't know. I don't know how close I need to be to control them." Adrien stopped and pointed between the trees, where a group of lost stood poised to attack. "François and Charles are there," he told Nico, "just past that stand of trees. Help them. I'll join you as soon as I can."

"I don't think—"

"I'll be fine. Please, they need you."

Nico hesitated a moment longer, then walked quickly toward Charles and François. Adrien drew his sword and walked toward the creatures, weapon pointed in front of him. The creatures turned toward him. Beyond them, a group of hunters approached, swords drawn—Giovanetti and several men Adrien didn't recognize.

Leave this place, Adrien commanded. The lost stopped moving and turned toward him. *Leave now!* They looked at Giovanetti, then turned and disappeared into the trees.

"I should have guessed." Giovanetti watched the lost withdraw, jaw tensed and anger burning in his gaze. "Verel warned you would interfere. But this? How did you—?"

"What do you want?" Adrien stood his ground. "You can't expect the Council will turn a blind eye."

"I *am* the Council. The mandate is clear." Giovanetti reached into the pocket of his jacket and held up a stack of papers with obvious relish. He tossed the cartes onto the ground. "Death sentences. All sanctioned by the Council. All quite legal."

Adrien picked up one of the cartes and turned it over. The name Blaise Rousseau was inscribed in gold ink. "What has Blaise Rousseau done to warrant execution?"

"He's a vampire. Nothing more is needed," Giovanetti replied.

"Then the order is…?" Adrien expected the answer, but it shocked him nevertheless.

"Extermination."

"And the humans you've killed to create these abominations? Humans we're sworn to protect?"

"Extermination," Giovanetti repeated. "Whatever the cost."

"The cost is too high." Adrien swung his sword in an arc and sent showers of red flame skyward. Giovanetti easily sidestepped the attack but did not counter.

"I'm told you've grown powerful," Giovanetti said. "But perhaps the news was premature. Leave now and I'll let you live."

Adrien lifted his hand and sent a stream of blue flame shooting toward Giovanetti, who easily blocked the attack. The branches in the tree above him caught fire and fell to the ground as ash.

"It seems I have your answer." Giovanetti leaped into the air and sent a volley of fire and light at Adrien.

Adrien raised his arm to parry, but the light changed shape as it moved, forming hundreds of tiny blades that hovered in midair and glinted in the sunlight. A new technique? So Pelletier had been doing more than just waiting for him to take up the fight. His anger flared at the thought of Pelletier's experiments. Had he obtained another ancient's blood to add to his arsenal?

Adrien called upon the demon and his body warmed. Orange light flickered at the periphery of his vision—the demon's power, shielding him as one by one, the blades gathered speed and flew at him. As they touched the energy field that protected him, drops of silver fell to the ground like rain.

Giovanetti reset himself, his jaw tight. He swung his blade again, sending several more waves of blades flying toward Adrien, each meeting the same barrier. By now a pool of silver encircled Adrien.

"It won't work," Adrien said. "Take your men and leave."

Giovanetti reached toward Adrien with his left hand, turning his wrist so that his palm faced upward. A slight breeze blew across Adrien's face, but nothing happened. Adrien was about to send another volley Giovanetti's way when, faster than his eyes could follow, a column of silver rose from the ground, entirely surrounding him. The liquid metal conformed to his body and began to harden, squeezing him so that he was unable to see and making it nearly impossible to breathe.

The demon laughed. *"Fool."*

"ADRIEN!" NICO yelled and sent a hail of ice flying at Giovanetti. With his free hand, he felt the cold metal that coated Adrien, who stood frozen in midstrike.

101

"Get François and Charles to safety. I can handle this," Adrien said in Nico's mind.

Nico glanced back to see François supporting a barely conscious Charles on his shoulder. Soon other lost would follow, replacing those he and François had destroyed.

"Trust me. Get them back to the house. I'll join you there."

Nico hesitated a moment too long. Giovanetti placed his left palm on the top ring of his metal crossguard. The ring began to spin, creating a crown of silver light as it moved. The circle spun faster and faster, growing until it was nearly as tall as Giovanetti himself. Then, with a high-pitched whistle, the ring suddenly split into many different rings and flew upward. With a slash of Giovanetti's sword, the air around the circles grew thick and dark, surrounding Nico. The forest vanished, replaced by impenetrable darkness.

An illusion attack? They were rare among hunters, but Nico had read about them in the ancient vampire texts. Mind manipulation. The lost who had tried to control Adrien had done the same. Whose blood had Pelletier stolen to impart this particular ability to his followers? Nico shuddered at the thought that there were others like his alter ego.

"Nicolas, take my hand." Nico still couldn't see, but he recognized Jean's voice and felt his powerful presence. "Hold on," Jean called to him.

Something pulled him to the ground, and he heard the sound of metal sing through the air. Giovanetti's sword. Nico felt this too. He guessed it had missed them both by just a few inches. He tried to call out to Jean, but he couldn't speak. Giovanetti reached into his thoughts, but Nico resisted. The power to hide his mind from others was something Pelletier had given Giovanetti—a power stolen from Nicolas's blood.

"You'll yield to me as you've always done, Nicolas," Giovanetti said. "You're weak."

Nico forced back the memory of Giovanetti's hand on his ass, groping him, forcing him to submit. Another Nicolas. The one who'd sacrificed himself to keep Adrien safe. As real now as it was then.

"That's it," Giovanetti said and licked his lips. "And after we're done here, I'll take you and fuck you until you scream. You like it when it hurts, don't you, my little vampire cu—"

Nico pushed back hard, channeling all his strength and will into the effort. Giovanetti, unprepared for the counterattack, had no defense. Nico slipped inside Giovanetti's mind and peered into the hidden reaches of his being.

"You fucking bastard. Before you die," Nico hissed in Giovanetti's mind, *"I want you to feel what* he *felt when you touched him."*

Giovanetti screamed and reality reasserted itself. His weapon vanished and his eyes grew wide.

"Get down!" Nico shouted to Jean and the others. Ice erupted from his sword as he swung. The resulting explosion sent Nico flying backward as tiny bits of ice glittered for a second in the air, then dissipated.

Nico came to in the center of a large crater, looking up at the canopy of trees. He sat and dusted himself off. Nearby, Charles leaned on François's shoulder. Charles nodded weakly, and relief coursed through Nico.

"Impressive." Jean offered Nico a hand and pulled him to his feet. Pain lanced through Nico's arms and legs. He looked down to see several blades embedded there. Blood slowly oozed from the wounds.

"Giovanetti?" Nico asked as he pulled a blade from his thigh.

"Dead." Jean gestured to a severed head that lay upon some leaves. "Your aim is true."

"Dead," Nico repeated. In another time and place, Antonio Giovanetti's death would have been cause to celebrate. But the memories of how his counterpart from this timeline had suffered at the bastard's hands lingered.

Jean touched Nico's wound and Nico flinched. His flesh warmed, but the cut did not begin to close as he'd expected. "Hunters' weapons," Nico said with a sigh. He pulled out the other pieces of metal.

Over Jean's shoulder, the metal that held Adrien captive melted like the ice. It hissed and dissolved, disappearing into the dirt. Adrien stared at Nico. "What happened here?"

Nico smiled. *This* was his reality. "Welcome back," he said and collapsed into Jean's arms.

CHAPTER TWENTY-THREE
THROUGH THE FLAMES

FIRE ROSE from the grounds of the Chateau Lambert, smoke joining with the early-morning mist to blanket everything in gray. Rain fell from the dark clouds that hung low on the horizon. In the distance, a faint rainbow peered out over the rolling hills. A promise yet unfulfilled.

They stood side by side, hunter and vampire alike, watching the funeral pyre as it burned. Adrien sighed when Nico squeezed his hand. He'd ordered the lost to come to the edge of the forest, where they'd stood silently as he and the others destroyed them. *Like lambs to the slaughter.*

How many innocents had found their final resting place here? And for what?

"You did what you had to do," Nico said. "There was no place for them in the world of the living. You released their souls."

Adrien nodded. They'd scoured the grounds but found no trace of Pelletier or the surviving hunters. He wondered vaguely if Pelletier had left him to destroy the creatures, knowing their deaths would weigh heavily upon his soul.

"The sin was always Pelletier's," Nico told him. *"He'll pay for what he's done. It's only a matter of time."*

Time. An enemy and a friend.

"Things are different. You've won far more than this battle." Nico smiled at him, his eyes wide and dark with emotion. *"We will choose the future. Together."*

JEAN STOOD amidst the ruins of his ancestral home. All around him lay the vestiges of the fierce battle they'd fought: broken glass and pottery, dirt and blood.

Rain fell in earnest now, pouring through the gaping holes in the roof and onto the marble floor of what had once been the conservatory. He turned at the sound of light footsteps on the wet floor.

"We'll rebuild it," Blaise said.

Jean nodded, trying not to read more into the words.

"I'm sorry. I know this was your family's—"

"It's nothing," Jean replied. "A dwelling place. Nothing more."

"Of course." Blaise turned to leave.

"I...." Words failed him yet again. Why was it so difficult to move forward from where they'd ended up? He wanted Blaise. Loved him. Cherished him.

"Yes?"

"Thank you," Jean said. "For saving my life."

"You're welcome." Blaise waited a moment, as if expecting Jean to say something else, but when Jean said nothing more, he inclined his head and walked out.

Jean rubbed the bridge of his nose and gazed beyond the remains of a wall to the formal gardens. Statues lay blackened and crumbling, the fountains silent.

"Let him go again?" Adrien stood outside in the rain, looking in through what was left of a shattered window.

"It's none of your concern." He was too tired to argue with Adrien.

"You're right." Adrien climbed through the window and, finding a mostly intact chair, sat facing Jean. "It's none of my business, but—"

"But you make it your business." He sighed and shook his head. His vampire body didn't need sleep to survive, but at that moment he wanted nothing more than to close his eyes and escape into dreams.

Adrien chuckled. "I've known you in three timelines, and you're just as obstinate in each."

"Three." Water pooled on the marble floor in front of him, his face reflected there grim. "One would think three lifetimes would give you more perspective. Instead, you repeat the obvious."

"I've seen things...." All traces of humor fled from Adrien's face. What horror of the past had he remembered? Jean wasn't sure he wanted to know. "It doesn't matter now. What matters is that life is short. Before you know it, the present is the past and the words you wish you'd said are just words."

Jean waited, but Adrien said nothing more. Instead, he offered Jean a smile steeped in pain and loss, then turned and left Jean alone once more.

Chapter Twenty-Four
A Shared Truth

JEAN PAUSED in front of Blaise's bedroom door and took a long breath. He'd headed back to his own room at the other end of the only wing of the mansion that had not been devastated by the fighting, but he'd ended up here instead.

Nothing's changed. He'd told himself that so many times, it felt like a mantra. Yet in one night, everything had changed. At least if he was being truthful with himself. He'd nearly died today. And in the moment when he'd realized death was imminent, he'd thought only of Blaise.

"Are you going to stand outside the door all day?" Blaise asked silently.

Of course Blaise sensed him nearby. They had shared too much through the centuries for Jean to hide. Or to hide his true feelings.

Jean opened the door and hoped the heat in his cheeks wasn't obvious. He prided himself on staying calm, even in the most challenging situations. But with Blaise, his self-control was a fragile thing.

Blaise sat on the floor by a smoldering fire, knees drawn against his chest, all pretense of nobility gone. For a moment Jean was transported back to the Cathédrale Notre Dame de Paris nearly three hundred years before and a very young Blaise, who'd sketched his portrait.

How many times had he told himself that keeping his distance from Blaise was for his own good? When he'd taken Nicolas in, protected him from the hunters, he'd believed he had no choice. But after the war between the clans ended, there'd been no excuse. He'd told himself that a relationship with Blaise would put both Blaise and Nicolas at risk.

I lied to myself.

He walked quietly into the room and closed the door. Blaise looked up at him, his smile not reaching his eyes. "You should be resting."

"You as well."

Blaise began to get to his feet, but Jean stopped him. "May I?" he said and gestured to the floor.

Blaise nodded, eyes wide.

"I've surprised you," Jean said.

Blaise smiled and patted the floor. "There's plenty of room."

Jean sat and made a few awkward attempts to arrange his long legs, first in front of him, then finally folding them. "You're far better at this than I."

Blaise laughed. "You get used to it once you relax."

"I can't say relaxation is my strong suit," Jean replied.

"Neither is humor. But so far, you're doing quite well."

Jean smiled, and for the longest time they sat in silence, watching the coals glow as the air between them and the fire bent with the intense heat.

"I don't mean to be rude," Blaise said finally, "but why are you here?"

A fair question, and one Jean wasn't sure how to answer. He settled on the simplest explanation. "I came to see how you were."

Blaise raised an eyebrow and chuckled. "You never were a good liar either. Still aren't."

Jean tensed and got to his feet. He wanted to run as far from here as possible. His heart raced and blood pounded in his ears.

"Jean, please don't go. That wasn't fair of me. I'm sorry."

"The fault was mine." Jean forced his body to relax, and his fear eased. This was Blaise, he reminded himself. The man he'd hoped to spend the rest of his life with. *The man I still wish I could spend the rest of my life with.* "I have no difficulty calling out those who lie to me. Nor should you. You're right. That's not why I came here." He sat once more.

Blaise frowned. "Is something wrong?"

Jean laughed. "Does my candor worry you?"

"To be honest, it makes me a little nervous," Blaise answered. "It's, ah… unusual."

Jean sighed and rubbed the bridge of his nose. "My usual tactics have gotten me nowhere."

"Fair enough." Blaise eyed him warily. "Does that mean you're ready to tell me the truth of why you came to see me tonight?"

"Yes." Again, Jean hesitated. Why was this so difficult? "There are many truths," he finally managed. "But the first is that I do not wish to be a stranger to you."

"For that, you have no one to blame but yourself." Blaise clenched his jaw and focused his gaze on the fire.

"It's strange," Jean began, doing his best not to betray his discomfort.

"Sitting here with me?"

"No." Jean shook his head. "Being with you is the most natural thing I can imagine." He clasped his hands in an effort to stop them from shaking.

"You're trembling." Blaise took Jean's hands in his own, warming them. "Has something happened?"

"Yes…. No." He fought to maintain his fragile control.

Blaise laughed softly. "You're more of an enigma tonight than usual."

"I am? How ironic. For once, I see things clearly, yet I'm finding it far more difficult to explain."

"You might start at the beginning," Blaise said. "That's often best."

"Indeed." Jean breathed deeply and willed the tension from his body. "The ancient ability is alive in Nicolas's blood."

Blaise, who'd appeared relaxed before, now sat ramrod straight. "Ancient ability?"

Jean nodded. "The ability to travel through time."

"The Rousseau gift?" Blaise shook his head in disbelief. "When I was young, I heard stories. Legends, really."

"The gift is real. I'm told your great-grandfather possessed the same gift. And when Nicolas gave Adrien immortality, with it, Adrien gained the same power."

"Nicolas gave…? Impossible."

"Think about it, Blaise. What do you sense? What do you see? You've seen Adrien and Nicolas together. Is it so impossible?"

"I…." Blaise frowned and rubbed the bridge of his nose. "I've seen them touch each other. But instead of pain, Nicolas clearly craved that touch."

"The Nicolas we know is bound by blood to Giovanetti. If he were to touch Adrien, he would suffer…." The thought made Jean shudder. *And yet I did nothing to stop him from marrying the bastard.*

Blaise pressed his lips together and touched Jean's arm. Jean's heart ached at the silent gesture of support. No one but Blaise understood the depth of his grief and his guilt, except perhaps Adrien.

"He isn't the Nicolas we know," Jean said under his breath.

"Not Nicolas? But…."

"That Nicolas is from another time, just as Adrien is."

Jean expected Blaise to laugh or dismiss his words, but instead he knitted his brow and glared at him. "You've known this for some time, haven't you? Since they arrived."

"I... suspected as much."

"You're lying again. You knew, and you kept it from me." Blaise sighed. "You still don't trust me, do you?"

"It's not that I don't trust you, it's...." Jean glanced away. What difference did it matter how he justified the lie? "I'm sorry."

"Look at me, Jean," Blaise demanded. "You came here looking for... what? Absolution? Forgiveness? What the hell am I supposed to think?"

"I have no excuse." What did he have to lose in admitting the truth? His pride? "I regretted keeping the truth from you when Nicolas was born, yet I did the same thing this time. I was wrong."

Blaise closed his eyes briefly, then met Jean's gaze. For the first time, Jean noticed the dark circles beneath his eyes. How long had it been since he fed?

"I'm sorry," Jean said, his voice cracking beneath the weight of his grief.

"You make it so damn difficult to be angry with you. I know you thought you were protecting me. It's how you're made."

"I can't seem to do anything right when it comes to you," Jean replied. He ached to touch Blaise. To hold him. He'd spent two centuries trying to convince himself he'd be fine on his own. He'd accepted the fact that Blaise would move on and find someone worthy of his love. *But in the end, we're both still alone. Unhappy.*

"Long ago, you did do the right things," Blaise replied. "But something happened."

"Yes." He'd fallen in love with Blaise.

"You're a stubborn bastard." Blaise closed his eyes briefly.

"You're not the only person who's told me that recently."

Blaise laughed. "I guess some things really *have* changed."

"Perhaps." He didn't dare get his hopes up. He was happy just knowing that Blaise forgave him. The rest....

Blaise reached out and touched Jean's cheek. Jean strangled a sigh. "But there's another truth you learned tonight, isn't there? The real reason you came."

Jean covered Blaise's hand with his own. "I remember standing on the balcony the day we were to pledge ourselves in marriage. I remember how fortunate I felt to have found you."

"And yet here we are. Dancing around the truth, as we always do."

Jean sighed. "I've had more than enough chances to fix things between us. You forgave me for not telling you that Nicolas was your brother, even though I didn't deserve it." He took a few deep breaths and met Blaise's gaze.

"You were afraid for me."

Jean nodded. "That's true. But I was *more* afraid of what would happen if I lost you."

"Lost me? I don't understand. All those years, you pushed me away. You never had me to lose, Jean."

Jean couldn't meet Blaise's gaze. The pain he'd banished to the deepest recesses of his soul overflowed its damaged vessel. His grief threatened to swallow him. "When Stéphane died," he said, his voice breaking, "I felt his soul pass from his body. His grief for the loss of your mother nearly strangled my heart."

Blaise wiped Jean's tears with his thumbs. "Please," he whispered, "tell me why you've hurt me for so long."

What was left of his self-control shattered. He opened himself completely to the emotions he'd hid for centuries. The pain overwhelmed him, but he forced himself to speak, the words coming out in fits and starts as he struggled not to break down and weep. "I couldn't think…. The night your parents died, I ran to find Paul. I carried Nicolas in my arms…. I couldn't think. I didn't want to feel…. I… I only knew I needed to find Paul. He and I… we would protect you. But Pelletier had gotten there first. When Paul died, the only thing I could think of… the only thing I knew was that I… I couldn't bear it if I lost you too…. I believed you were safer… without me. If Pelletier came for Nicolas, I'd die defending him, but I… I couldn't ask you to do that. I couldn't imagine…."

"So Pelletier *was* the behind the attack?" Blaise didn't seem angry, more relieved to hear this.

"Yes."

Blaise gathered Jean into his arms and held him. "When you shared your blood with me before Nicolas and Rosina's wedding, I sensed very little of your emotions. You hid what you didn't want me to see."

"I didn't want you to know about Roland."

"No. You didn't want me to feel that pain," Blaise gently corrected.

"Yes." He'd gotten quite good at hiding his pain over the centuries. "I knew how much grief I'd caused you already."

"You're the most stubborn man." The warmth of Blaise's embrace belied his harsh words.

"You asked for my truth," Jean said, his cheek pressed against Blaise's shoulder.

"Indeed I did. Although you're the only one who had yet to realize it."

Of course Blaise had known. As had Adrien.

"I also have a truth," Blaise said as Jean's tears abated.

"You?"

"I still love you as much as I did the day we were to be married. More, perhaps. Back then I was barely more than a child." Blaise ran his fingers through Jean's hair, the gesture so tender Jean moaned in reply.

"After all I've done, you still love me?"

Blaise smiled. "If you're done running from me, perhaps it's time you spend the rest of your life at my side.

"Y-you... you would still have me?" He hadn't dared believe Blaise's forgiveness would run so deep.

"For someone who's lived so long, you understand so little." Blaise lifted his chin and found his lips. The kiss deepened, warm and promising like the sunrise that illuminated the sky. When they pulled apart, Blaise smiled at him. "Unless your feelings for me have changed?"

"I've always loved you," Jean said without hesitation. "From the first time I saw you in the stables, and more each day since."

"I don't want to wait," Blaise said and ran a finger over Jean's lips. "Let's speak our vows today."

"Here?"

"What better place than here? What better time?" Blaise rose and offered Jean a hand up.

"But you deserve so much more than this."

"More than this?" Blaise laughed. "If you mean the kind of wedding we nearly had, I want none of it."

"But—"

"What good did all that pomp and circumstance do me? The one thing I wanted more than anything—what I *still* want—is to spend the rest with you. Don't you see?" Blaise leaned in and brushed his lips against Jean's. "We'll exchange our vows in the company of those we love and cherish. Tonight," he added with the hint of a grin.

"Tonight?"

"Do you object?" Blaise's eyes sparkled with challenge.

"No. Of course not." Jean's chest tightened and warmed with the realization that Blaise meant the offer in all seriousness.

"Then pledge yourself to me now and forever, Jean Lambert."

Jean smiled through his tears. "I will," he whispered.

CHAPTER TWENTY-FIVE
DAWN

ADRIEN STOOD with the back of his hand just touching Nico's as Blaise and Jean exchanged vows in what was left of the ballroom. Stars danced above and a gentle wind wound its way around the participants. They stood in a circle under a moonlight sky.

The lost were destroyed and the surviving hunters had fled, but each of them understood this peace was only a lull in the battle yet to be won. Still, for the first time in more than a hundred years, Adrien had hope for the future. At least *this* future—the future he'd unwittingly created.

"Blaise Rousseau," Charles Duvalier said, "I wish you a long life."

Blaise bowed. At his side, Rosina beamed and stood tall. The hint of dark circles beneath her eyes betrayed the exhaustion they all felt, but her smile was genuine and loving.

"Jean Lambert," Charles continued, "I wish you a long life."

Jean bowed. Adrien had never seen him so happy. It was as if he'd shed the darkness of his past overnight.

"I've never had many friends," Jean said when he'd given Adrien the news earlier that day. "But I consider you one. Will you stand up for me?"

Adrien had accepted, of course. And as he stood to Jean's right, Nico met his gaze and inclined his head ever so slightly. Adrien's joy was tempered by his own longing for a future with Nico. And though they had not spoken of it, Adrien was sure Nico felt the same.

"Someday," Nico silently confirmed. *"I promise you."*

Jean and Blaise pressed their hands together and their lips met.

The room erupted into shouts of "Long life!"

There would be no grand celebration to follow this bonding. Pelletier and his men might have lost this particular battle, but the threat remained.

ADRIEN YAWNED as he and Nico climbed the staircase to their rooms an hour later. Nico went to draw the shades, but Adrien stopped him. Outside, the sunrise bathed the grounds in pink light. In the barren fields beyond the woods, smoke rose in wisps, an echo of the bonfire they'd lit to dispose of the dead.

How many humans had Pelletier and his men killed and resurrected to use as weapons? When they'd fought the lost, Adrien had managed to keep the thought from his mind. They'd been tools. Things. Less than human. Until Adrien heard them clearly.

"You returned their dignity," Nico said as he wrapped his arms around Adrien's waist. "You gave them back their humanity by treating them as human."

Adrien rested his head on Nico's shoulder and tried to silence the echoes of their voices. He'd never forget the undercurrent of pain and yearning.

Nico brushed Adrien's cheek with his thumbs, then traced Adrien's lips. Adrien knew what Nico had thought when they'd watched Blaise and Jean speak their vows. Nico's longing mirrored his own. Yet neither of them spoke of their hopes for their own future.

"Don't think," Nico told him silently. *"I've got a better idea. Unfinished business."*

Adrien sighed as Nico ran lithe fingers through his hair and began to feather kisses over his jaw and neck. Gooseflesh rose over Adrien's arms in response to the gossamer touch. They'd shared each other's body and blood only a few days before, but it felt like an eternity.

Nico slowly unbuttoned Adrien's shirt and allowed it to flutter to the ground. He traced lips and tongue over one of Adrien's nipples, then gave the other its due. What tension remained in Adrien's body evaporated as Nico bit and licked each bud.

Before when they'd made love, Nico had taken full advantage of his sharp eyeteeth. This time he tenderly explored Adrien's chest. He unbuttoned Adrien's jeans and slipped a hand beneath the waistband. He squeezed the bare skin beneath, not enough to cause painful pleasure, but lovingly exploring Adrien's ass as the heat of his mouth on a sensitive nipple caused Adrien to shiver.

Adrien closed his eyes and the world outside faded. Nothing mattered but this.

"What are you thinking about?" Nico whispered against Adrien's abdomen.

"You can't tell?"

"I want to hear you say it," Nico said, a smile in his voice.

"You. Always you. Only you."

Nico pushed Adrien's pants to the floor, then stepped back and admired his handiwork. "I like you like this." He walked behind Adrien and kissed the back of his neck, laving the skin and causing gooseflesh to rise over Adrien's body.

Adrien gasped as Nico scraped his sharp eyeteeth beneath his ear, then rubbed his hand over Adrien's abdomen and found his hard cock a moment later. Adrien's bloodlust warred with his physical need, but he embraced them both.

"Please," he begged.

Nico worked Adrien's cock with his hands as he bit and began to suck on Adrien's neck. Delicious pain mingled with the pleasant floating sensation that always accompanied Nico's bite.

"You always think too much," Nico teased as he pushed Adrien onto the bed and shed his own clothes.

Make me forget everything but you.

Nico's pale skin reminded Adrien of the moon rising over the forest, cool and ethereal. He straddled Adrien and pricked his fingertip, then ran it over Adrien's lips. The taste wasn't enough to glimpse Nico's innermost thoughts, but Adrien sucked on Nico's finger and canted his hips upward in reply.

Nico smiled down at him, then leaned over and licked a line over Adrien's jaw, over the place where he'd bitten him, and onto his shoulder. Adrien imagined Nico's teeth piercing his skin again, the thought making his cock pulse.

"Always impatient," Nico silently chastised. *"Later, I promise."*

Adrien pulled Nico toward him and kissed him roughly. He reveled in the warmth of Nico's body against his own as he dug his fingers into Nico's ass. The vampiric nature he'd inherited with Nico's gift of immortality warred with the human within. Nico's self-control had always been better, although judging by what he'd seen over the centuries, Adrien guessed this was more a result of years of discipline than something innate.

At first, bloodlust had both frightened and fascinated Adrien. Now, as Nico forced Adrien to balance on a knife's edge of restraint, Adrien repressed his hunger. Denial, and later—

"You're still thinking too much," Nico thought and smiled happily down at him. *"I'm clearly not doing my job very well."*

Adrien laughed and kissed Nico. *You're doing your job* too *well.*

"No, but for now, I intend to claim all your thoughts." He reached between them and grasped Adrien's cock, his gaze still locked on Adrien's. *Nico.*

"Much better. But there's no need to deny your bloodlust either. Let me show you." Nico nipped at his finger and pressed it between Adrien's lips. Blood dripped onto Adrien's tongue, and Nico worked his hand up and down to Adrien's moans.

The room flickered in and out of reality as tiny bits of Nico's memories danced in Adrien's mind. The combination of Nico's ministrations and the telltale buzz of bloodlust worked together to heighten the physical touch.

Nico withdrew his finger and pressed it into his own mouth, his lids heavy with his pleasure. He reached beside the bed and palmed a bottle of oil, which he spilled onto his palms before rubbing them together to heat. He pressed a slick finger into Adrien, who opened to him and allowed Nico to press a second inside.

Adrien gasped as Nico pressed against his gland, working it until Adrien keened and begged. "More," Adrien whispered. Nico gently rubbed as he continued to stretch Adrien's body, readying it for what was to come.

"Nico," Adrien said. *Always you.*

The pressure of Nico's cock at his entrance had Adrien falling back on the bed, his legs open, welcoming. The pain of entry was nearly as delicious as the pain of Nico's bite, and as Nico seated himself fully inside, Adrien's hunger grew.

"Drink, beloved." Nico leaned over so that his neck was near Adrien's lips. *"Let my blood give you strength and pleasure."*

The salty taste of Nico's blood combined with the rhythmic pulsing of Nico's cock as Nico moved back and forth. Adrien hung on to Nico, moving with him as he sucked, careful to take only enough blood to keep him floating through Nico's soul as Nico brought his body to the edge.

"Tell me you love me," Nico said, his words less like a command, more like a prayer.

Forever, Adrien replied. *I love you always.* He spilled onto his belly, his release as warm as the blood that danced in his mouth and spread throughout his body.

"I love you, Adrien. Always. Forever." Nico cried out as he came, his body trembling and tensing. *"Always."*

They fell asleep in each other's arms, the steady beat of Nico's heart vibrating against Adrien's chest and the heat from their spent bodies cocooning them.

CHAPTER TWENTY-SIX
A POINT IN TIME

THE MAN who lay on a scattering of dirty straw looked nothing like the Nicolas Adrien remembered. His hair was a matted tangle, his skin so pale his veins traced visible lines over his body. The legs pulled against his chest were nothing but bone beneath the thin rags he wore. But for the slight rise and fall of his chest to mark his rattling breaths, Adrien would have thought he was dead. A living ghost.

"Nicolas?" Adrien shivered as he knelt on the damp stone floor. When he received no response, he reached out and feathered gentle fingers over Nicolas's cheek. "Nicolas? It's Adrien."

Nicolas whimpered. "Please... you must.... Please...."

"I'll take you home."

"Can't." Nicolas's voice was barely a whisper. "You... please... you must.... Please... kill... me...." He turned and met Adrien's gaze with unseeing eyes. "Please... Adrien... it's the only... way."

Adrien woke to Nico's arms wrapped around him. He forced himself to breathe through the terror and grief. His heart slowed and the dream began to fade. He needed air. He needed to think or he'd lose his mind.

He untangled his limbs, taking care not to wake Nico, and walked naked to the open window. He took a breath of cool air, inhaling the sweet fragrance of the trees and grass. Outside, a thin glaze of fog lay on top of the grass. He shivered and glanced back at where Nico slept.

He padded back to the bed and sat. He listened to Nico's breaths, letting everything else disappear and, with it, his fear. The guilt, however, remained, gnawing at his gut.

Nicolas.

He searched for Nicolas for more than a hundred years, but since he'd met Nico, he'd become complacent. Now that he'd finally mastered the demon, he had the means to return and save the Nicolas he'd lost at the wedding. So why was he still here?

"Adrien?" Nico yawned and looked up at him from the bed. "Are you all right?"

"I'm fine." He offered Nico what he hoped was a reassuring smile and climbed back into bed.

Nico pressed his shoulder against Adrien's. "Bad dream?"

"When I was a little boy, my father used to tell me to turn my pillow over when I had a nightmare." He'd had so many of them, each the same—watching his mother lying facedown in the mud as the rain stung his face.

"Did it work?"

"Sometimes." He sighed and pulled Nico closer. "This is much better than the pillow."

"It is?"

"Yes."

"Good." Nico met his gaze and grinned. Still, there was something in his eyes Adrien couldn't quite comprehend. Wistful, perhaps.

"I love you," he murmured.

"I know." Nico rolled onto his side and kissed Adrien.

Adrien fell asleep a short time later and this time, he didn't dream.

ADRIEN SLIPPED out of the bed just before sunrise and headed down to the gardens. If things went the way he planned, he'd be back before Nico woke. Before any of them realized he was gone.

"Take me back," he ordered the demon.

The demon sniggered but obeyed. The first hint of color on the horizon dissolved as the world around him spun into nothingness.

ADRIEN STRUGGLED to remain on his feet as his vision cleared. People moved all around him inside the Rousseau castle, laughing and talking. A strong hand on his shoulder steadied him.

"Adrien?" Rémy frowned.

Damned demon. Sending him directly into the thick of the action without warning? *I know what you're doing.* He pushed it downward and closed his mind to it. This was his own fault. He'd become complacent, to trust it not to take advantage of the situation.

"I'm fine," he told Rémy. "Just a bit tired."

Rémy laughed and nodded. "Roland finally got the best of you, eh?"

"That would be an understatement."

They continued through the crowd of guests, headed for the conservatory. Charles and François would be nearby, as well as Caroline and Victor. Adrien glanced around but didn't see any of them. Soon enough, they'd make their stand.

This time will be different.

They reached the conservatory and made their way to the simple platform where Nicolas and Rosina would exchange their vows. Some of the guests murmured in surprise, but no one moved to stop them. A brass quintet played Mozart as people milled about, most holding a glass of wine or champagne. From his vantage point, he finally spotted the other members of his group, all in their designated locations. Thunder rumbled in the distance like an omen as rain fell over the glass ceiling and walls.

Adrien saw no sign of Pelletier, his men, or Reynaud, but he felt Nicolas's presence. He closed his mind to Nicolas, not wanting him to sense something different in his heart. In a short time, everything would change for them both. Adrien steeled his heart. He knew the secret Jean would reveal, the joy he felt to hope that he and Nicolas might truly have a future together. He also knew the pain that would follow if he didn't defeat Pelletier.

The sky turned darker as night banished the last light. Shimmering candlelight danced like stars as the room filled to capacity.

Rémy leaned in and said, "Vampire weddings are quite simple. Both bride and groom enter the place of marriage hand in hand. The clan leader officiates and the couple exchange short vows. The marriage is consummated by the sharing of blood before witnesses. Far more time is spent celebrating afterward than at the ceremony itself."

Before Adrien could respond, Jean entered the room, followed a minute later by Blaise. Jean still looked tired, but the Jean Adrien knew in the future appeared far older. The loss of Nicolas had haunted him just as much.

Jean glanced his way and Adrien inclined his head, gripping the hilt of his sword with far more resolve than he had before. A hundred years ago, he'd wished Nicolas would change his mind. He'd admired his strength of conviction, knowing Nicolas would go through with the marriage for the good of his people. The stakes had been high back then. But now....

Clarion horns replaced the gentle string melody, cutting through the din to herald Nicolas and Rosina's arrival. The guests grew silent, the sea of people parting as the betrothed entered hand in hand and made their way to the platform. Adrien had forgotten how beautiful Rosina had looked in her blue silk dress with silver embroidery, her dark hair swept off her neck. Diamonds dripped from her ears and wrists, but her throat was bare.

Still, this time, as before, it was Nicolas who held Adrien's attention. Dressed in a perfectly fitted suit, his hair secured with a silver clasp to reveal the smooth skin of his nape, Nicolas strode with purpose, his head held high, his eyes focused. Adrien's bloodlust rose unbidden, and he drew a long breath in an effort to maintain his self-control.

Nicolas turned and met Adrien's gaze. Adrien repressed a shudder. Nicolas, too, shielded his thoughts, although his gentle smile and the shadows of longing and sadness in his eyes made Adrien's heart ache.

I will make this right.

Rosina gathered her long train in her hand and smiled at Nicolas as one might a beloved brother. He returned her smile, and together they climbed the platform before turning to face the guests.

Reynaud Rousseau entered next, flanked by several guards. Pelletier, Giovanetti, and Bremen followed close behind. The wave of anger and hatred that rose in Adrien took him by surprise. The demon roiled and fought against its bonds, eager to fight. Ianus vibrated, its blade responding to its master, its hilt warming beneath Adrien's hand.

Ianus! Of course. In the first fight against Pelletier, when he'd lost Nicolas, he'd wielded his mother's sword. But there was no doubt that the sword now at his side was his own. The realization thrilled Adrien. He could do this. He would stop Pelletier this time and save Nicolas from a lifetime of pain and suffering.

"Let's do it. Now!" the demon shouted.

Not yet.

More hunters swept into the room, taking their place near Adrien's allies. Adrien forced the tension from his body but remained alert and ready for the battle to come. Thunder roared, closer still, a flash of lightning briefly illuminating the sky.

Reynaud climbed the first step and stopped in front of Nicolas and Rosina. He bowed to them, then turned to face the room. The crowd assembled bowed and curtsied, some shouting, "Lord Rousseau!" Reynaud nodded solemnly, then turned back to Nicolas and Rosina.

"Nicolas Lambert," Reynaud said loudly enough for all to hear, "I wish you a long life."

Nicolas inclined his head.

"Rosina Rousseau," Reynaud continued, "I wish you a long life."

Rosina nodded.

"Today we celebrate not only the union of Lady Rousseau and Lord Lambert," Reynaud said, "we also unite two clans who have been at war for centuries. With this marriage, there will be peace between our clans."

Next Reynaud turned to acknowledge Jean. "Jean Lambert, I ask your permission that these two be married."

Jean stepped forward so he stood only a few feet away from Reynaud. Reynaud blinked and paled beneath Jean's intense gaze.

"Monsieur," Jean said, his deep voice resonating throughout the room, "as we stand here before our kin in peace and reconciliation, I ask that you do now what you have failed to do for more than two centuries."

The guests murmured and turned to one another with looks of surprise. Reynaud glanced quickly toward Pelletier, who ignored him completely, his expression unchanged.

"I don't understand, my lord. We are here to unite our clans and bring lasting peace to our people." Reynaud shifted his weight from one foot to the other, and tiny beads of sweat appeared on his brow.

"It is not that particular wrong I seek to right," Jean replied serenely. Blaise, who had been standing on the other side of the podium, now crossed in front of the guests and stood at Jean's side.

Nicolas and Rosina exchanged quick glances. Even knowing what was to come, Adrien stood transfixed.

Reynaud frowned. "This is the time to put aside the past and move toward the fut—"

"There will be no marriage." Jean walked over to Nicolas and Rosina, Blaise at his side. The crowd's chatter grew louder. Adrien schooled his expression, knowing Pelletier and the others watched him.

The demon screamed and pounded against Adrien's mind. *"I will fight for you! Let me kill the bastards!"*

You will have your chance. For now, we wait.

"Jean," Nicolas said, "have I done something to displease you?"

Jean shook his head. "You have done all I have asked of you and more. I could not be more proud, Nicolas."

"Lord Lambert, you have pledged your brother's hand in marriage." Reynaud's voice shook. "Is your promise so easily broken?"

"I have allowed this farce to continue," Jean said evenly. "It's time to exorcise the ghosts of our pasts. It's time to heal a festering wound inflicted centuries ago."

Pelletier, who had been standing off to the side watching the proceedings with interest, now walked over to Reynaud and Jean. "Every action has its consequences," he told Jean.

Jean nodded but held his ground. "Indeed. I have withheld the truth for far too long. But you will not harm him." Jean glanced at Adrien and nodded. Adrien moved to Jean's side and drew his weapon.

"Tell him your *precious* truth, then. It matters little now." A ghost of a smile lit Pelletier's face as he glanced toward Adrien. His eyes danced with challenge.

Adrien tensed and struggled to maintain his composure as the demon hissed with pleasure.

"Truth? What truth?" Nicolas's words brought Adrien back to himself.

"The truth of what happened to your parents two hundred years ago." Jean's voice waved almost imperceptibly.

"My parents? They died in battle when I was very young," Nicolas said. "But why—"

"*Your* parents were killed by Verel Pelletier," Jean explained. "He killed your brother as well."

The whispered murmurs from the guests rose to a din as Reynaud again shifted uncomfortably on his feet.

"My brother?" Nicolas asked. "But *you* are my only brother."

"In my heart, Nicolas, you will always be my brother." Jean lowered his voice so that only those nearby could hear. "I couldn't have loved you more." Then, turning so that he would be heard by all present, he continued, "But the truth is that you are a Rousseau, and brother to Blaise and Rosina."

The room erupted in loud chatter. Adrien moved between Pelletier and Nicolas. Caroline, François, Rémy, and Victor had drawn their weapons and taken up positions between Pelletier's men and the platform.

Nicolas appeared even paler than before, as though he might crumble under the weight of Jean's revelation. He rallied and regained his composure. "I'm a... Rousseau?"

"Lord Lambert," said Reynaud pleadingly, "I beg of you—"

"You didn't kill Stéphane or Anaïs, nor did you assist in Paul's death." Jean's expression was unforgiving. "Still, you must live with the consequences of permitting this lie to be perpetuated. As must I. You knew the truth centuries ago, Reynaud, yet you chose to do nothing."

Reynaud remained silent, but he looked to Pelletier.

"Jean, how is this possible?" Nicolas tensed his jaw but met Jean's gaze head-on.

"Pelletier stole the gift of immortality from your older brother and left him to die." Jean said this without affect, but he clenched his fists at his sides.

"Stole...?" Nicolas gasped and shook his head.

By now the guests crowded around so that they might better hear. François and Charles moved closer to Pelletier's men. Adrien's heart beat wildly in his chest. He scanned the room with new focus. He needed to draw on all his experience if he was going to change what would come.

A flash of lightning preceded a sharp crack of thunder that struck nearby.

Jean nodded. "Pelletier's men killed your father as he shielded you with his body."

Blaise still stood by Jean's side, his expression fiercely loyal. Loving. He already knew the truth. Adrien had seen this in Jean's blood. He'd never understood how Jean had kept his distance from Blaise after losing Nicolas. That loss should have brought them together. Perhaps by saving Nicolas, Adrien could repair the rift between them.

"For two centuries now, I have kept this a secret." Jean's face remained impassive. "I told myself I did so to protect you, Nicolas. But I've come to realize that although I genuinely feared for your safety, I also feared I might lose you should the truth come to light. I should have revealed the truth of your birthright long ago. I beg your forgiveness."

The room became suddenly silent. Jean fell to his knees before Nicolas, his head bowed low.

"No," Nicolas whispered, his dark eyes now filled with tears. "Please don't." He stepped from the dais and laid a gentle hand on Jean's shoulder.

"You owe me nothing, especially not an apology. That I am not your brother by blood and that I am brother to Rosina and Blaise… I don't deny this is quite a shock."

Jean remained on his knees in supplication.

"But I understand one thing above all others." Nicolas put his hand to Jean's chin and gently raised his head until their eyes met. "You will always be my brother. You have loved me as your own, and you have protected me with your life. There is nothing to forgive." He helped Jean to his feet, then embraced him warmly.

Throughout all of this, Pelletier watched patiently. *He knew this would happen.* Adrien was sure of it. He made no move to deny Jean's accusations, nor did he seem to care that all those present might know such a terrible truth.

He's waited for this. And if Adrien was right, he'd come back to the past to relive this moment. Adrien gripped his sword tighter, allowing the power to build, waiting, knowing this was the moment. The demon sensed this too, but Adrien pushed him back once more.

Not yet. Pelletier couldn't know for sure that Adrien, too, had come to the past. He wouldn't tip his hand until the moment was right.

"You bastard!" Rosina charged down from the platform toward Pelletier. Her sword materialized in her hand and her eyes flashed black with hatred.

Pelletier held his ground.

"Rosina, no!" Reynaud shouted.

She aimed her sword at Pelletier, who appeared mildly amused but entirely unconcerned. "Draw your weapon."

"No." Pelletier waved his hand like someone batting away a fly. The flash of power that flew from his fingers sent Rosina flying against the wall some ten yards away. She landed with a hard thud and lay still.

"Rosina!" Nicolas ran over to her and put his hand on her chest. He breathed deeply as he met Adrien's gaze. "She's alive." Nicolas gathered her into his lap and glared at Pelletier.

At the same time Nicolas went to Rosina's aid, Jean and Blaise closed ranks to protect him. As he had done before, Adrien placed himself between Pelletier and those gathered around Rosina. Several people screamed as a burst of energy from the back of the room hit the glass ceiling and sent shards flying in all directions. Charles and François engaged several hunters as the wedding guests scattered, most running from the room. The few who remained stood near the doors, too curious to leave but clearly unsure if it was wise to remain.

Reynaud walked quickly toward where Rosina lay, still cradled in Nicolas's lap. Adrien watched in stunned horror as Pelletier shook his head and sent a bolt of black fire at Reynaud's back. Reynaud fell forward onto the tiled floor and lay still.

Adrien met Jean's gaze for just an instant. As Jean moved toward Reynaud, Adrien aimed a burst of blue-and-red fire at Pelletier to cover him. Jean moved so fast, Adrien could barely follow him as he retrieved Reynaud's limp body from the center of the room and set him down near the wall. Pelletier neatly deflected Adrien's attack with his bare hand, but not before Blaise crossed behind him and stood guard over Jean and Reynaud. Jean ran his hands over the wound on Reynaud's back, his fingers glowing white as he worked to heal him.

Adrien glanced to where François fought Bremen. François moved with surprising confidence as Charles looked on with obvious concern. Adrien grinned as he reset himself for another attack. François would be fine.

"Let me—"

Not yet. Adrien launched another volley at Pelletier, knowing he would deflect this one just as easily. *He's not sure who he's fighting, and we aren't going to tip our hand.*

Someone screamed as a beam of energy from a hunter's sword hit the doorway to the kitchens, causing the onlookers to retreat to safety.

Adrien and Pelletier circled each other as the remaining guests fled the room. Rain poured in from a large hole in the ceiling, splashing Adrien as it landed on the already slippery tile floor. The cool water on his face felt good and helped maintain his focus.

"You thought the blood of innocent vampires would make you stronger," François said as he and Bremen faced each other, circling, their weapons only a few feet apart.

"But I *am* stronger." The edges of Bremen's mouth turned upward as he and François exchanged another round.

"Not as strong as I." François glanced in Adrien's direction, and Adrien inclined his head. "I am the blood of a hunter, the blood of a vampire, and the blood of an immortal." François touched the edge of his weapon to his left palm. He raised his hunter's sword and swung the blade. With a movement both grotesque and strangely graceful, François severed Bremen's head from his shoulders.

The look of surprise on Pelletier's face was a victory in and of itself. With renewed determination, Adrien pointed his sword at Pelletier, who had yet to draw his weapon. A loud hum filled the room as Adrien sent waves of light soaring. The resulting vibrations shook loose some of the broken glass overhead and knocked over the marble statues that still stood amidst the chaos. Gripping his weapon with both hands and channeling his strength through the tip, Adrien focused his thoughts on the blade. Waves of gold and blue spiraled around the weapon in tight circles, growing in size until Adrien drew the weapon back, then brought it down so that the rings flew toward Pelletier.

Pelletier moved quickly out of the line of fire. The rings of gold and blue soared unimpeded toward the windows, obliterating what was left of them with such power that the entire side of the conservatory was now open to the elements, and droplets of rain blew into the room. The iron supports that had once held the glass ceiling in place began to collapse. Both Adrien and Pelletier jumped backward to avoid a web of twisted metal as it fell with a resounding crash onto the marble floor.

"Interesting." Pelletier appeared far more amused than concerned by Adrien's display of power. And Pelletier had yet to draw his weapon.

With a quick flick of his wrist, Adrien ran the blade across his left forearm, cutting deeply into the skin. Blood ran down his arm toward his palm and began to pool. He gathered the blood in his hand and then ran the blade across his palm, coating it in the viscous red liquid.

"Now?" the demon begged.

Not yet. It must be the same as before.

Adrien's fingertips tingled with the mixture of heat and power from the sword. He breathed in deeply, holding back the power that beckoned. He needed to lure Pelletier in, let his overconfidence grow.

Pelletier did not move.

"Die, you bastard." Adrien shot an arc of blue-and-gold fire toward Pelletier that grew wider as it left the blade, combining with the lightning overhead and obscuring the place where Pelletier stood. Vampires and hunters alike stopped fighting and covered their ears, so painful was the high-pitched hum that accompanied the flames.

Fire swirled around Pelletier, forming a sphere of gold and blue that completely engulfed him and grew so dense it appeared nearly solid. Adrien felt Pelletier within the sphere, fighting to maintain the integrity of his body, which threatened to dissolve under the weight of the circular mass.

Before, the attack had taken every bit of strength Adrien could summon. This time, however, Adrien used only enough energy to maintain the attack. He allowed himself to fall prey to Pelletier's power, causing his heart to slow, hesitate, and skip beats.

Where before the fear of death had been all-consuming as he'd fought to stay alert, this time he ignored the stabbing pain as his heart stuttered, beating a syncopated rhythm against his chest.

Not yet.

Two beats… then another. Another beat, out of time, erratic.

Not yet.

A single beat now, then a long pause, then another, feeble beat, and the pain began to fade.

Not yet.

Adrien's heart stopped. He struggled to stay on his feet. No pain, but a feeling of floating. Peacefulness. Release.

Not yet.

He squeezed Ianus's hilt and allowed its power to flow into him. His heart beat once. Then a second time, stronger than the first. Three beats, four, five…. His heartbeat steadied. He inhaled deeply as flashes of silver light filled his vision. His head spun, but he didn't care.

"You may actually be stronger than I." Pelletier smiled. "But you still have much to learn."

Ianus shattered into a hundred pieces.

Chapter Twenty-Seven
The Unexpected Guest

ADRIEN STEELED himself for Pelletier's attack, unarmed. The demon screamed and fought against its imprisonment. Adrien ignored it.

Not yet.

A sword materialized in Pelletier's right hand, the blade of the weapon twisting and swirling like molten metal on the jeweled hilt. Pelletier swung his blade in a circular motion from just a few feet away. The air grew thick and hot.

Adrien moved quickly out of the line of fire, the blade barely missing its mark.

Pelletier again swung his sword at Adrien. "Adrien!" Nicolas screamed.

Molten black metal flew at Adrien's chest, hardening into glittering steel like the razor-sharp teeth of a snake seeking its prey.

Now!

The demon shouted as its power pulsed through Adrien's body. Ianus materialized in Adrien's hand, solid and familiar. Adrien turned the weapon sideways and held the blade in front of him. The attack bounced off the smooth surface and flew upward, disappearing into the night.

"No!" Nicolas shouted again, closer than before.

Time slowed. Adrien focused on the space in front of Nicolas, materializing there just before Pelletier's blade could strike, and batting the blade away.

Pelletier's eyes grew wide with recognition, and he laughed. "Come back to play?"

Adrien wouldn't give him the satisfaction. "Get back!" he told Nicolas, who retreated to where Jean and Blaise were standing.

"I hoped you'd find me here." Pelletier moved to meet Adrien's blade, and sparks showered the room.

The demon growled its approval as Adrien jumped and swung his sword. Pelletier countered, once again matching Adrien's movements. Adrien landed a few feet away and shot a stream of fire. Pelletier met this attack as he had the others, by countering with his own. Black flames surrounded Adrien's attack. Ash rained down on them as the attacks exploded. The rest of Pelletier's followers fled in the resulting chaos.

Pelletier didn't hesitate. He attacked once more. This time Adrien dodged by materializing a few feet away.

Pelletier shook his head. "All that power, and you do nothing but avoid me?" He struck before Adrien could answer, and again Adrien moved out of the way. "Pathetic."

Adrien glanced at Nicolas, who had materialized his own sword and stood shoulder to shoulder with Jean, ready to join the fray. Adrien wouldn't let that happen. He would finish this fight himself.

Give me your strength.

His arms burned with power; his fingers tingled with the heat of it. This time the volley that issued from his sword glowed blue and red as both flames and ice shot skyward. Adrien moved the sword back and forth, and the energy wrapped around Pelletier's shoulders. Adrien willed the energy to circle about Pelletier, again creating a sphere. Flames licked at the frozen crystals, which melted and reformed as they moved about.

Inside, Pelletier struggled against his restraints. He managed to raise his sword to cut the bonds, but just as quickly, they reformed and continued their twisted path.

More. I need more!

The demon responded. Fire erupted from Adrien's fingers as he continued to manipulate the attack into a ball that spun faster and faster and tightened so that it began to take the shape of Pelletier's body.

Adrien sensed Pelletier growing weaker as the swirling power intensified. Pelletier reached out to try to manipulate Adrien's body as he'd done before, but Adrien brushed away the attack with ease. Another minute, perhaps two, and Pelletier would be crushed beneath the bonds of flame and ice.

Adrien allowed the demon to surface and fight alongside him, their minds intertwined as power flowed between them. Where before the demon had been erratic and undisciplined, now it obeyed Adrien's commands, feeding him the power he needed to maintain the attack. Together, they fought as one, and the demon's strength became Adrien's. There was no wall between them now. Had there ever truly been one?

Roland's words echoed in Adrien's mind: *"There is no bull."*

The demon vanished, its power now completely Adrien's own. The surge that accompanied the realization that he'd still not completely understood sent flames flying toward the thickening strands of energy that bound Pelletier. Inside, Pelletier was dying, his efforts to fight the overwhelming wave of fire and ice diminishing with his flagging strength.

At last, Pelletier's consciousness faded and vanished. Adrien allowed the power to recede. A cloud of steam rose where Pelletier had stood, slowly dissipating in the rain.

We've won! Adrien turned to Nicolas, who beamed at him. "He's gone." Adrien dematerialized his sword. "He's really gone."

The world shifted.

No. It's not possible!

"Adrien!" Nicolas shouted.

Pelletier swung his weapon. There was no time to react as Pelletier's blade moved parallel to the floor, aimed at his neck.

I've let you down again, Nicolas.

Time stopped. An eerie silence descended over the room. Jean, Blaise, Charles, and François's faces were frozen in expressions of shock and horror. Droplets of rain were suspended in midair. Lightning illuminated the room like sunshine.

Adrien tried to speak, but he couldn't move. The entire scene played out like a dream. Was this death? A moment suspended in time when he could do nothing but accept that he'd failed once again?

In the midst of the stillness, something—*someone*—moved. Swiftly. Without hesitation.

But how…?

Nicolas swung his weapon, striking Pelletier.

For a long moment, nothing happened. Then reality came roaring back, flooding Adrien's senses like color returning to a world of black and white. The room erupted into shouts, punctuated the dull thud of Pelletier's head as it hit the tile floor.

Adrien stared at Nicolas as his sluggish brain began to comprehend what he'd just witnessed. "Nico?"

Nico smiled.

Chapter Twenty-Eight
Forever Can Wait

AFTER REASSURING himself that Rosina would be all right and making the lamest of excuses to Jean and Blaise, Nico pulled Adrien into one of the sitting rooms and closed the door behind them.

"Don't you *ever* do that again." He grabbed a very surprised Adrien and held him tight. "If I'd lost you…."

"I'm sorry." Adrien pulled away to reveal tear-streaked cheeks and an expression of genuine regret. "I couldn't stand it anymore… seeing him suffer… knowing I had to do something to stop this."

"I know." He kissed Adrien. "And you did stop it."

"*We* did." Adrien pressed his lips together. "Without you…."

"You won't make the same mistake again." Nico sighed and shook his head.

"*This isn't the end of his fight*," Roland had told him months before, when Adrien finally faced his demon. "*He still needs to learn that he can't win this alone.*"

Nico brushed his fingers over Adrien's cheek. "The demon… it's gone, isn't it?"

"You felt it too?"

"Roland told me this would happen. You just needed to realize it on your own. The bull and all." He chuckled and kissed Adrien again.

"You're not angry with me?"

"I was," he admitted. When he'd woken to find Adrien gone, he'd felt both anger and panic.

"I really am sorry." Adrien sighed and shook his head. "I hurt you."

"I know you didn't mean to." Nico drew a long breath. "Neither of us spoke about the future. To be honest, I really didn't want to talk about it." What future did he belong in? What right did he have to stay here, in Adrien's timestream? The thought of returning to his own terrified him.

"You have every right." Adrien pressed his hand to Nico's chest, over his heart. "There is only one Nicolas, and he deserves some happiness."

Nico put his hand over Adrien's. "Marry me." He'd wanted to say the words forever, but the moment had never been right.

"Marry you?" Adrien stared at him.

"If you'd prefer, we can pledge—"

"No, I didn't mean... or, what I meant wasn't that marriage...." Adrien's shoulders fell. At that moment, he looked like the young man he'd been when they'd first met in Lyon.

"I shouldn't have brought it up now, before we'd had a chance to—"

"Yes." Adrien blinked back tears. "Of course. Yes and yes." He took Nico's hands and met his gaze. "I've wanted you since the trip to England to find Charles. I didn't believe it was possible."

"You were as reckless then as you are now." Nico kissed Adrien, wrapping his arms around those powerful shoulders. The kiss deepened, the taste of Adrien's mouth sweet, their tongues dancing, wanting more. Everything in Nico's being resonated when he touched Adrien.

Their lips parted. "You're Nico. You're Nicolas. The only man I've ever loved. The only person I can imagine a future with."

"Are you sure? We haven't even spoken of where—of *when*—we will live."

Adrien brushed his lips with his own. "It doesn't matter. We don't need to decide that now. We don't ever have to decide it."

Nico wanted to believe that. Still, he couldn't stop thinking about how unfinished things felt. *Did we stop him?*

"Nico."

Nico forced a smile. "I know. I try to hide my thoughts, but—"

"I want to know what you're thinking." Adrien kissed Nico's hands.

"I'm thinking I'd like to share our good news." He'd think about the implications of what they'd done later.

"YOU'RE VERY quiet tonight," Nico said as they strolled hand in hand through the gardens after dinner several nights later.

"I didn't want to interrupt, not when Rosina was having too much fun telling stories about Blaise pretending to be a stable boy when he first met Jean." Adrien smiled. "It's good to see her back to her usual self."

"I don't think I've ever seen Jean blush."

"I thought Jean's face would crack." Adrien laughed. "In all the years I've known him, he's barely smiled."

Rosina had done her best to keep the mood light at dinner, and Jean had played along with Rosina's gentle teasing. No one mentioned Reynaud by name. That morning, Blaise told Nico the clan would soon meet to decide their uncle's fate.

"Jean would never admit it, but he felt terrible about using me to force Reynaud's hand. It will take time before he believes there was nothing for me to forgive." Nico sighed. "Seeing him let down his guard, even a little, makes me happy."

"Do you think he and Blaise will reconcile in this timestream?"

"I'm sure of it. Some things are meant to happen." Nico pulled Adrien close and met his gaze. "Give them a little time. Blaise is still pretty angry that Jean kept the truth from him about the day I was born. But Jean's still here, isn't he?" Nico had managed to get Jean to agree to stay until the end of the month. He hoped by then Jean and Blaise would have time to work things out.

"You think it's fate?"

"Do you doubt it?"

Adrien shrugged. "I don't know what to believe anymore." He leaned in and whispered against Nico's ear, "The only thing that matters is that you're here."

Nico kissed Adrien's cheek. "Something's bothering you."

"It's nothing. Really."

"Hearing that makes me nervous. You have a knack for doing crazy things when you say nothing's bothering you." Nico pointed to the high stone wall. "Join me?"

"Sure."

They sat for several minutes, looking out at the distant lights of Paris. "I've missed this view," Nico finally said.

Adrien tensed his jaw but said nothing.

"That's it, isn't it?" Nico put a gentling hand on Adrien's shoulder.

Adrien let out an audible breath. "I should be happy, shouldn't I? The man I've loved for more than a century asked me to marry him. I have everything I've ever wanted."

"Do you really?"

"I do. I—"

"You've gotten a lot better at hiding your thoughts." Nico placed his hand atop Adrien's. "But I can still see what's in your heart."

Adrien turned to face Nico. "Then you know I love you more than life."

Nico smiled in spite of himself. "Of course I do. But I also know there's much more in your heart."

Adrien chuckled, but the pain in his gaze made Nico's chest ache. "I really do have everything I've always wanted."

"But?"

"But it isn't really over, is it?"

Nico hardly dared speak the words. "You worry the Pelletier from the past will find a way to come here." The thought had simmered at the back of his mind ever since he'd killed Pelletier.

"He could change all of this in an instant." Adrien looked away and ran a hand through his hair. "Everything we've done."

"Before you say anything more, there's something you need to know." Nico knew where this was going.

Adrien turned so he faced Nico, his face set in a frown. "I'm not sure I want to hear it."

"You need to. Before we speak of what might be...." He inhaled slowly in an effort to quiet his racing heart.

Adrien nodded but said nothing.

"I'm forgetting things."

"You're...?"

Nico took a moment to gather his thoughts, then said, "You know that I've remembered most everything now. The Nicolas who married Giovanetti... the Nicolas of this timestream whom Pelletier...." He repressed a shudder. "But those memories... of what Pelletier did to me... of that horrible cell... I'm forgetting them."

"I don't understand."

"What we did here. Killing Pelletier, it's changed the future. *Our* future. That Nicolas—the one who suffered at Pelletier's hands, whom he bled dry—he no longer exists."

Adrien's eyes grew wide with understanding. "The only way to make sure this ends is to stop it where it began."

"Yes."

"But if we do that... if we kill Pelletier before he steals the gift from your brother...."

Nico's mouth was suddenly dry. "If we do that, the you and I who exist here and now... we disappear, Adrien. And everything that has happened between us... it's gone. Forever."

CHAPTER TWENTY-NINE
THE SACRIFICE

HE'D KNOWN what Nico was going to say, and still the words took his breath away. "Nico."

Nico smiled sadly. "There really isn't a choice, is there?"

"What you said about fate…." He wanted to believe, but the thought that if they succeeded, they might never find their way to each other settled onto his chest like a heavy weight. He laughed bitterly and shook his head. "I was an idiot. I acted without thinking. I thought that coming here, saving you from what would happen… I believe it would fix things. But it hasn't fixed anything, has it?"

Nico leaned in and brushed his lips against Adrien's. Adrien closed his eyes and tried to focus on that gossamer touch. He wanted to remember it. Write it indelibly on his heart. *I don't want to lose you.*

"You won't."

"Will I even know what I'm missing if you're wrong?" Adrien said aloud.

"You're ready to end this. In many ways, it's just like before."

"Maybe I should have stayed in that future with you." In his mind's eye, Adrien could still see Pelletier's text message: *If you choose to stay here, I won't get in your way. Keep your sweet vampire. Live your perfect life.*

"You weren't happy." Nico smiled again, but his eyes filled with tears. "You couldn't be, not knowing that Pelletier would continue to hurt the people you loved."

"I can't do this to you, Nico, I—"

"I make my own choices." Nico frowned and lifted his chin. "And this is my choice as well."

Adrien didn't know how to respond, so he just nodded.

The silence stretched like an eternity, broken only by the plaintive call of an owl. Finally Adrien said, "We do this together."

Nico laughed, but he wiped the corner of his eye. "Oh?"

"We're better together." Adrien strangled a sigh. He alone could not bring about an end to Pelletier's horrors, but the realization left him feeling uncomfortable. Weak. Fearful his heart might not survive losing Nico and angry with himself for the selfish thought. "My power is only an echo of what you're capable of, Nico. The only way we can be sure to make this happen is if we do it together. I'm not that big a fool to think otherwise."

"I love your faults as much as your charms," Nico said with a grin.

"Liar."

"Mmmm. I might be a liar," Nico agreed. "But I've realized I don't particularly *want* to change you."

"I think there may be a compliment hiding in there. Somewhere."

"Could be." Nico squeezed Adrien's hand.

Adrien nodded. "We'll leave this morning." *Together.*

Nico smiled, but tension simmered in his dark eyes. "Together," he repeated aloud.

THEY WALKED hand in hand through the formal gardens at sunrise. The climbing roses had erupted in a riot of color as they snaked over the ancient stone walls. They could have traveled to their destination from the comfort of their rooms, but Nico understood why Adrien sought the comforting beauty of this place and the connection to the earth. They might be able to change time and redirect past and future, but the ground beneath their feet felt immutable. Reassuring.

Adrien stopped at the edge of the forest and drew a long breath. He offered his hands to Nico, who clasped them and closed his eyes.

The knowledge of where they were headed both thrilled and terrified Nico. The day everything changed. Before Pelletier became an immortal. The day Jean was to have been married to Blaise. *The day Pelletier and his men murdered my brother and parents.*

Adrien squeezed Nico's hand. *"It's not selfish to want someone you love to live."*

Nico closed his eyes and imagined the world around them changing. Nothing happened. When he opened his eyes, they were still standing in the garden. He closed his eyes once more and tried to picture the Rousseau castle centuries before. Something stirred in his soul, like a pinprick of light. He reached out to it and tried grasp it, but it remained beyond his reach.

"Let me help you." Power vibrated in Adrien's hands. Unlike before, it bent to Adrien's will, lending him strength instead of struggling beneath him. Nico, too, ceased to force his own power, instead following the light like a bird on a current of air.

Their combined powers blew them forward, down a spiraling tunnel, until they reached the light. Around them, everything faded to a peaceful, warm glow. Nico held Adrien's hands tighter as they fell into time. *Together.*

CHAPTER THIRTY
WHERE IT ALL BEGAN

Paris, France—August 1803 (Original Timestream)

THE HAZE of nothingness cleared as the ground beneath Nico's feet reasserted itself. He grasped Adrien's hand to reassure himself that they'd both made the jump in time. There was no reason to worry, was there? Neither he nor Adrien existed in this place. But still he asked, *Do you remember?*

Adrien smiled back at him and nodded. *"I remember everything. And you?"*

Nico nodded and allowed the memory of the first time he and Adrien had met, before Adrien had become immortal, to resurface. Jean had asked him to invite Adrien to dinner. At the time, he hadn't understood why Jean would want this young hunter to escort him to Paris. Nicolas was far stronger, capable of defending himself. Yet Jean had insisted that Adrien, who'd been barely of age at the time, act as his bodyguard.

"You really should be more careful," Nicolas said as they nearly collided on the deserted Lyon street.

"My apologies, monsieur." Adrien's hand instinctively rested on the hilt of his sword.

"I've been looking for you, monsieur Gilbert."

"You know who I am?" Adrien's eyes widened in surprise. Had he never met an ancient before? Probably not, given the tiny town he'd grown up in.

"I know many things, monsieur," Nicolas said. *"I know why you are here. I know whom you seek."*

"Who are you?"

"I am Nicolas," he replied. *"Nicolas Lambert."*

"Nico? Are you all right?" Adrien's voice brought Nico's focus back.

Nico nodded. Still, something felt different than before. It was as if a thin veil of time had been peeled back to reveal his memories. Things seemed somehow clearer, as if the jump back in time had opened his eyes. This should have frightened him, but instead he felt as though a heavy weight had been lifted from his shoulders.

"I…," he began, not wanting Adrien to worry and not knowing how much to say. "I wasn't sure what to expect. But I feel fine."

The sweet smell of grass and flowers wafted on the light breeze. Nico repressed a sigh as he took in the familiar grounds. The memories of Rousseau castle weren't really his, but he knew this place.

Adrien squeezed Nico's hand again, bringing his thoughts back to the task at hand. Nico gave in to the overwhelming urge to kiss Adrien.

"Why did you do that?" Adrien asked after the kiss ended, his lopsided smile making Nico wish they were anywhere but here.

"Do I need a reason?" Nico laughed in an effort to hide his unease. What would Adrien do if he knew Nico had regained *all* the memories of the Nicolas from Adrien's time and more?

He cowered in the corner of the basement. He'd tried to mark the days by scratching a line into the damp stones each time they came to bleed him. But the visits ran together as he became weaker, blurring like an oil painting where the strokes viewed up close seemed unconnected. Days and weeks turned into years, the only proof of the passage of time the telltale lines on the faces of his captors and the fading color of their hair.

He'd not allowed himself the pleasure of tears. He'd not shown them his pain, even when they'd beaten and humiliated him. He would not give them the satisfaction. He was an ancient vampire, too proud to admit they'd broken him.

Eventually he retreated into his own thoughts within the shell of his immortal body. If he couldn't die, he'd leave the nightmare of his reality and lose himself in dreams of the past. Dreams of Adrien and what might have been. Hoping for death….

That Nicolas had found what he'd hoped for. Nico's memories of the Nicolas Adrien had first loved, the Nicolas he'd lost to Pelletier, ended abruptly. Nico hoped he'd found peace in death.

"Nico?" Worry etched Adrien's handsome face.

"It's nothing. It's just strange… being here… now." Not a lie. Not the truth. But he couldn't lie to himself. The other Nicolas's memories were his *own*. He experienced these memories as surely as he experienced this current reality. *I am Nico. I am Nicolas. I am all the Nicolases Adrien has known, and some he will never know.*

"I know you better than that." Adrien smiled and squeezed Nico's hand.

"I am… uneasy. I can't explain it more than that. At least not now. But I promise when I fully understand this gift, I'll explain." The fear that had taken up residence in Nico's gut roiled as the enormity of what they needed to do hit him once again. A nagging fear. Something terrible he almost remembered. Or perhaps it was a nightmare. Nico pushed the thought away. "What do you have in mind?" He knew Adrien would see through his feeble attempt to change the topic.

Adrien tilted his head to one side, lips pressed together as if considering something. "We pose as wedding guests."

"Guests? Of whom?"

Adrien shrugged and gestured to the line of people approaching the castle. "There are enough people here that nobody will question us. And if they do, I'll tell them I'm a distant relative of my father. As long as he's lived, I doubt they'll even think twice. I'm sure you can say the same for your family."

"And then?"

"We follow the plan." Adrien's smiled faded. "Judging by the sun, it's three, maybe four in the afternoon. Pelletier attacks at sunset, just before the ceremony. Jean believes Pelletier lured your parents by creating chaos outside the kitchens. Anaïs and Stéphane went to their defense, but Pelletier's men surrounded them."

Nico was grateful this was a memory he *didn't* have. He knew only too well how this day had ended: in the death of both his parents and his older brother. *My birthday.* "That gives us a little time. An hour or two."

"A time and a place," Adrien corrected with a smile.

Nico nodded, thankful now that Jean had refused to share this particular memory with him. His parents were stronger than any of the hunters or vampires who fought with Pelletier, but they'd been outnumbered, and Nico's mother had been pregnant with him.

"Are you sure you're ready for this?" Adrien asked. "If we fail—"

"I'm ready." They wouldn't fail. Too much was riding on this. Not just his family's future, but the future all of the vampires, hunters, and humans Pelletier would kill.

"We need to find some clothing." Adrien chuckled. "Much as I prefer you in jeans and a T-shirt, we look a little out of place."

In spite of himself, Nico smiled. "There's a laundry near the well behind the kitchens. Or at least there was one there, when your Nicolas spent time here before the wedding to Rosina."

A half hour later, dressed in garments they hoped no one in the castle would recognize, they joined the other guests and made their way through the enormous wooden doors at the front of the castle. Inside, the rooms were draped in the traditional blue and silver of the Rousseau Clan. Large vases filled with flowers lined the hallways, and the sounds of clinking glasses and laughter as guests indulged in wine and spirits filled the rafters.

What would it feel like to disappear? Nico swallowed hard and pushed the thought from his mind.

"Nico?"

"Yes?"

"Are you all right?" Adrien asked.

"I… I'm fine," Nico lied. Past and present seemed to collide in his thoughts, mingling and distorting his perception of time.

"You look pale." Adrien frowned.

"It's just strange, being here." Nico focused once more on his surroundings and offered Adrien a reassuring smile.

"So pleased you could join us."

Nico turned to face a tall man with green eyes and dark hair. Dressed in a blue suit with silver embroidery at the cuffs, he smiled and offered his hand. His resemblance to Blaise was so strong that for an instant, Nico was sure it *was* Blaise. He nearly gasped when he finally realized this was his father.

"Have we met before?" Stéphane Rousseau asked.

"I…. No. I don't believe so," Nico said as he shook his father's hand. "Armin Rousseau." He hoped his discomfort wasn't etched across his face. If his father challenged him….

Stéphane hesitated an instant, his gaze like a knife cutting into Nico's defenses, forcing the truth to surface. Nico held his breath and waited for his father to signal the guards, but instead Stéphane smiled. "Armin. Good to meet you." Then he turned to Adrien and said, "And you must be a Gilbert."

Adrien's eyes grew wide, but he laughed and said, "That I am. Claude Gilbert. But how…?"

"Your eyes," Stéphane answered, his smile widening as he shook Adrien's hand. "I've never seen any quite like them."

"It's an honor to celebrate with your family," Adrien said.

"The pleasure is ours." Stéphane's lips parted as if he wanted to say something more, but a large group of guests interrupted. "Perhaps later we can speak about your family." Stéphane inclined his head and turned to greet the newcomers.

Nico and Adrien bowed.

"Follow me," Nico said and led Adrien down a hallway and into a small sitting room. He closed the doors behind them and settled onto a couch by the window. He lifted a shaky hand to his face and rubbed his mouth.

"Are you all right?" Adrien sat next to him and wrapped an arm around Nico's shoulders.

Nico nodded. "As all right as I think I can be." He closed his eyes momentarily, remembering his father's strong grip and the smooth skin of his hand. The way he'd felt vulnerable, pierced to the soul by his father's eyes. "I should be happy to have finally met him, but…."

"But it's painful."

"Yes." Nico leaned against Adrien. "And wonderful." And something else he couldn't describe.

"He suspected something," Adrien said. "I'm sure of it."

"You felt it too?"

Adrien nodded, his eyes kind, understanding. "Your father sensed the Rousseau blood in your veins."

"Probably." This explained why his father hadn't challenged him. Still, the encounter left Nico unsettled.

Adrien leaned in and kissed Nico's cheek. "You will grow up knowing your father."

And Jean? Nico didn't want to think about what Pelletier's death might mean to their relationship.

Adrien turned Nico's head and this time kissed him on the lips—a chaste, loving kiss that helped settle Nico's restless heart. "Whatever happens," Adrien said against Nico's ear, "I will always love you."

Nico sighed and the last of the tension fled his body. He hoped Adrien was right. To hope for more was to tempt fate.

Chapter Thirty-One
Dead Reckoning

"Are you ready?" Adrien stood and offered Nico his hand.

Nico had never felt as unsteady, even in the face of the annihilation of the Council of Hunters. "I'm ready." He took Adrien's hand and kissed it.

Throughout all the memories, one thread remained constant: Adrien's love. In every timestream, Adrien had been there to offer him strength.

Adrien smiled, but Nico sensed fear. He wouldn't show it. He'd want to be strong for them both. That was Adrien's way.

"Whatever happens," Nico said, "even if we fail, I *will* find you again."

Adrien wore a faraway expression, as if remembering something. But he nodded and claimed Nico's lips with such passion that Nico nearly lost his balance. Nico responded to the kiss without any thought but that he wanted to remember this. He wanted to imprint the kiss on his heart and soul.

"We follow the plan, then," he said after Adrien released him.

Adrien nodded.

Nico opened the door and slipped into the sea of guests in the hallway. He glanced back and Adrien smiled at him. *We can do this*, he thought. *Together.*

Nico reached the courtyard a few minutes later. He'd shaken enough hands for a lifetime. Some of the people he'd never heard of. Others he'd known but would die at Pelletier's hands in the massacre a century later.

He brushed off these gloomy thoughts and focused once again on the task at hand. The hardest task, perhaps, and the one he'd looked forward to the most. He drew a long breath and opened the door to the stables.

"Lovely mare," Nico said as he approached the man who unbuckled the saddle, then handed it to one of the servants.

"She is that." Paul Rousseau turned and smiled. He reminded Nico of Rosina, with his dark hair and green eyes.

Nico offered his hand. Paul wiped his own on his britches, glanced at it, then grinned up at Nico and said, "It's not exactly clean."

"I don't mind." Nico chuckled. "Besides, it's a familiar and happy smell."

They shook briefly. Paul's eyes widened at the touch, as though he recognized something in Nico. "Paul Rousseau. I don't believe we've met."

"Armin Rousseau," Nico offered. "Fifth cousin. Maybe fourth? I'm afraid I've lost count."

"Good enough for me." Paul pushed an errant lock from his eyes and smudged his nose with a bit of dirt.

Nico laughed and wiped it away without thinking. The gesture left him feeling both bereft and satisfied. How many men were given the gift of meeting the older brother they never knew? In just an hour or so, Pelletier would kill Paul, and Nico would never have the chance to get to know him.

This time will be different.

"May I?" Nico picked up a brush from a nearby table.

"Please." Paul took a cloth and began to wipe the horse's neck and shoulders. "You really do like horses, then?"

"My brother taught me to ride before I could walk." He offered Paul a smile. "Or so he tells me. I don't remember."

"My little sister will be a better rider than I." Paul's bright eyes reflected his deep love for Rosina. The expression made Nico's heart ache. He pushed away the emotion. It wouldn't do to dwell on things.

"Rosina. She's quite the firebrand."

"Oh? You've met her, then?"

Nico nodded. "She's a beauty too. And kind."

"Kind?" Paul laughed. "Yes, I suppose so. Although to be honest, lately she's tried my patience with her antics."

Nico repressed a sigh. "I don't doubt it."

Paul paused and looked up at Nico.

Damn. He'd said too much.

"So, Armin," Paul said, obviously wary. "I sense this meeting is not purely chance."

Nico inhaled slowly. "Much as I wish. No. It's not." He and Adrien had agreed they would tell as much of the truth as they dared. "I'm here because I believe your life is in danger."

"*My* life?"

"There are rumors of a growing rift in the Council of Hunters. Those who don't wish our races to remain allies."

"Yes." Paul frowned. "I've heard the same. My father and I spoke of it only last night." He put down the rag he'd used to clean the horse, picked up a brush, and joined Nico.

"There is one hunter in particular who wishes power. I fear he will do his best to disrupt the union of our family with the Lamberts."

"A marriage that puts to rest the longtime strife between our clans would not be in the best interests of those who wish to see hunters and vampires working at cross purposes," Paul agreed. "But why now? What proof do you have that this hunter seeks to prevent my brother's marriage?"

"None save my word," Nico admitted. "But you know I speak the truth."

Paul eyed him, his brow furrowed. "I sense no deceit. But I also sense there is something you don't wish me to know."

"Yes." What more could Nico offer but the truth?

Paul continued to brush the horse in silence. Nico expected he would be rejected and asked to leave. But instead, Paul stopped and met Nico's eyes with an intensity that Nico felt in his blood. "I believe you, though I'm not sure why."

"Will you help me?" Nico asked.

Paul nodded. "Tell me what I must do."

CHAPTER THIRTY-TWO
TIME AND AGAIN

NICO LEFT Paul a few minutes later, headed toward the kitchens. The first floor had, even in his time at the mansion, been used by guests of the family. It was here that visitors might withdraw to rest after a long journey, where nannies might care for children while parents played games in the conservatory or took their meals in the formal dining room.

He passed several women who laughed as their maids chastised them for taking off their beaded slippers and running barefoot through the hallway. They glanced at him, curtsied, then disappeared into one of the sitting rooms and closed the door behind them. He walked on toward the end of the hallway, following the sound of a piano playing a familiar melody: Mozart's Fantasy in D Minor, a dark, brooding piece Jean had taught him when he'd been quite young.

He reached the music room a moment later to find the door ajar. He peered inside, but from his vantage point, the open piano obscured the identity of the musician.

"Come in, please." Stéphane spoke over a sequence of repeated arpeggios.

"I always found that section to be quite challenging," Nico said as he entered the room. "I can still recall the expression on my teacher's face when I stopped playing and looked to him as if he might guide my fingers to the correct keys." He had tested Jean's patience more times than he could count, as little as he'd practiced for their lessons.

"Many a young pianist has suffered the same fate." Stéphane's warm expression made Nico's heart ache.

"My teacher was kinder than I deserved. I was far more interested in reading than in practicing." Jean had given him everything and sacrificed so much to keep him safe. In every past Nico recalled, Jean had been there for him.

The music ended and Stéphane rested his hands on the keys. "Armin, was it? Have we met before?"

"I.... No. I don't believe we have."

Stéphane rose from the piano bench and studied Nico. "Yet I know you."

Nico forced a smile. "I'm not sure I understand."

"You're a friend of my son."

"Paul." Nico relaxed a bit. "Yes." Paul, whose blood would give Pelletier the power to destroy countless lives. The brother he'd never met, whom he'd never seen, even in Jean's blood. Jean had hidden this from him as he'd hidden so much of Nico's past. Only recently had Nico understood how much losing Paul had affected Jean.

"You aren't a friend of Paul's," Stéphane said after the silence stretched uncomfortably.

Nico pressed his lips together and shook his head. "I…. No." Of course his father would know he'd lied about. "I—"

"You needn't keep up the pretense with me."

Nico inhaled a long breath in an effort to steady the pounding of his heart. "I can't… I wish I could, but—"

"I have three sons." Stéphane smiled and gazed at Nico with an expression of love that took Nico's breath away. "There is one I have yet to meet," he continued, undaunted. "But I would know him anywhere."

Impossible. "I don't know what you mean."

"I think you do."

"I really should leave." Nico moved toward the door.

"My grandfather possessed the Rousseau gift," Stéphane said softly. "We all thought it died with him."

"I don't understand."

"I was never able to bend time to my will," Stéphane continued. "But I can sense when things are not as they should be. Like a piece of a puzzle that doesn't quite fit. It's a strange sensation. I experienced it only twice before. Both times were my grandfather's doing." He chuckled and looked past Nico, as if he could see the old man there.

Stéphane came closer, then reached out and touched Nico's cheek. His smile deepened with the touch, his eyes filling with tears. "You've grown strong, my Nicolas."

"I'm not—"

"Paul has no friend named Armin." Stéphane shook his head. "Nor do I have a relative by that name."

"I'm sorry," Nico whispered. He hadn't considered what effects his appearance here in the past might have.

"I would know my own son no matter where—or when—I saw him." He slowly removed his hand from Nico's face. "The color of his eyes. The angle of his jaw. The scent of his blood. Still, my instinct tells me your presence does not bode well for this day."

Nico blinked back tears, powerless to stop them.

"I was right." Stéphane's smiled faded. "You aren't here because you're curious."

Nico exhaled a long breath. "If only that were the reason…. Father."

"From the moment I saw you, I knew you, but I'd never met you before." Stéphane sighed. "The way you looked at me. The curiosity there. The need…. The only explanation is that you've come here for a reason. That it is no coincidence that you are here today, of all days."

"No."

"Is there something I can do to help?"

"I… I don't know. The hunters have developed new weapons." Nico wasn't sure how much he should tell Stéphane. What if his actions today *caused* his parents' deaths?

"Then the rumors of a new faction within the Council of Hunters are true."

Nico nodded. "We're here to stop it. To end things once and for all."

"You and this hunter. This *immortal* to whom you gave the gift. Is he Jacques's son? He looks so much like him."

Nico smiled and nodded. "My beloved."

The edges of Stéphane's mouth danced upward. "You needn't tell me more. I understand enough of this power that I know there are things better left unsaid. I am the only one who knew of my grandfather's abilities. He told me only because he believed a child of mine might inherit this power, and he wanted me to be prepared. What can I do to help you?"

Nico considered the offer. "Be on your guard. They will come after you and Mother. It's me they want. My blood. They will try to take me from her." He decided not to tell Stéphane about Paul. He and Adrien would protect his brother from Pelletier.

Stéphane's self-control flickered, his eyes momentarily burning with anger. He said only "I will keep you and your mother safe."

"They will try to draw you out. If you hear something—if anyone tries to attack the servants—you must hide."

Stéphane shook his head. "You know as well as I that I cannot do that. As the head of our clan, I'm sworn to protect *all* who are here. Servants, guests, and kin."

Nico had expected the answer. "Someday we'll speak of this day. And I'll tell you about my journey."

"I look forward to it."

Nico bowed and walked over to the door.

"You will succeed."

"Thank you."

Stéphane began to play again. "Be well, Nicolas." He didn't look up from the keys. "We will see each other again soon."

Nico slipped out of the room. Outside, the sun had already reached the tops of the trees. He needed to find Pelletier, and soon. *I will see you again, Father. I swear it.*

CHAPTER THIRTY-THREE
WHAT'S OLD

ADRIEN MOVED quickly around the house, shaking hands and making small talk. Throughout it all, he reached out with his mind for the presence of the man he'd come to kill. If Pelletier was already here, however, he hid himself well. Jean had never known if Pelletier had been lying in wait for Nicolas's parents or if, as a member of the Council, he'd been invited. No one other than Jean remembered seeing the man.

He has to be here. The thought repeated endlessly, each time more desperate. *There's no time left.* In less than an hour, the ceremony would begin.

"So good to meet you," a woman—Adrien had already forgotten her name—said. She held his hand far longer than customary. He smiled, murmured something polite, then extricated his hand before turning and leaving.

He glanced around another room, what he guessed was Stéphane's study, then, finding no one there, exited and closed the doors. A moment later he slipped inside an empty sitting room toward the back of the house. He drew closer to the fireplace and rubbed his hands together. He'd wait until the crowd of newly arrived guests made their way toward the conservatory. Once they were past the main entryway, he would slip upstairs and search the house for Pelletier's men.

"I didn't expect to see you here. I thought you were in Russia on some secret mission for the Council." Roland smiled at him from the doorway.

"I'm not sure I—" Adrien hadn't heard the door open.

"My apologies. For a moment I was sure you were Jacques." Adrien had never seen Roland so flustered. Had he been looking for Pelletier as well?

Adrien held out his hand, hoping his own surprise didn't show. "Claude Gilbert. Jacques and I are distant cousins."

"Indeed." Roland titled his head to one side and studied Adrien with a cockeyed grin. "The resemblance is uncanny. Then you're from Paris?"

His father had moved from Toulouse after he'd married Adrien's mother, hadn't he? Or was it her family who'd come from there? "Toulouse,"

Adrien said with more confidence than he felt. He needed to get moving and find Pelletier. If he didn't—

"Really?" Roland's perpetual smile faded. "And here I thought all his family lived in the Auvergne."

Shit. Adrien glanced out the window. The sun was beginning to descend over the gardens. "Excuse me. But I really best be go—"

"Stay a bit longer." Roland pressed his sword against Adrien's neck. The metal felt cool, almost pleasant. "And tell me a bit about yourself. Starting with the truth, that is, and perhaps I'll be less inclined to believe you're here to disrupt the festivities."

"What would you have me tell you?"

"You might start with how you became an immortal," Roland said.

Of course Roland would have guessed. Adrien hesitated a moment longer. "As if you'd believe that particular story."

"Not at all. I enjoy a good story."

"No kidding," Adrien said under his breath.

"What was that?"

Adrien tamped down the usual irritation he felt when Roland questioned him about something. "Nothing."

"I'm not inclined to let things go that easily," Roland said with infuriating calm. "Not when there are people I care about whose lives could be at risk.

"I'm not here to hurt them. And judging by the way you're holding your sword, you don't think I will either."

"Indeed." Roland grinned. "And how have you come to that conclusion?"

"The only way to kill me is to take my head." He sighed and added, "Not that cutting my throat won't hurt like hell. But to be honest, I'm not in the mood to fight you today."

Roland released him. "Even more interesting." He retrieved his drink and sat in one of the chairs near the window.

"That's it?"

Roland raised an eyebrow. "Have we fought each other before?"

"Why would you think that?" Adrien repressed a laugh. How many times had he been at the mercy of *Roland's* circuitous answers?

"You seem amused, monsieur…?"

"Gilbert. Adrien Gilbert." The name would mean nothing to a Roland who'd never met him before.

"Adrien. We know each other, then?"

"Perhaps." When he said nothing more, Roland frowned.

"You won't tell me when we met."

"You'll find out eventually." If and when they met again, Adrien had no doubt that Roland would remember this day.

Roland chuckled and released his sword. Adrien rubbed his neck.

Roland stood and walked past him, over to the table where a decanter and several glasses had been set out for the guests. "Care for a drink?" he asked after pouring a bit of liquid.

Another game, since only another immortal would fully understand the effect of alcohol on an immortal body. "Just a little, thank you."

Roland poured a second glass and handed it to Adrien. Adrien took a small sip of the heady cognac he'd normally have been tempted to savor. He needed his wits about him not only for the fight to come, but in order to deal with Roland.

"So why are you here?"

"I'm here to attend a wedding." Adrien eyed his half-empty glass longingly.

"A dull answer," Roland replied.

"Why are *you* here?" Adrien countered.

Roland raised an eyebrow and set his empty glass down. "Why should I tell you?"

"Because we want the same thing."

"How can you be sure?" Roland's cunning smile had returned.

"You're stronger than I am. If you believed me a threat, you'd have killed me by now. And as you've said," Adrien added with a nod, "I know you well."

"Touché."

He'd wasted enough time chatting. Best to cut to the chase. "You know what Pelletier's planning."

"Verel?" Roland raised his eyebrows.

"He's gathered his followers. He wants the child. And if he gets what he wants—"

"Whose child would that be?"

More games. He'd play along. He needed Roland's help if they were to protect the Rousseaus and keep Pelletier from stealing the gift. "Anaïs's child." *Nicolas.*

Judging by the hint of a grin on his lips, Roland already knew.

"Then the Rousseau gift…?"

"It's not a legend," Adrien said.

Roland remained silent.

"Please, if you believe me, help me stop this. If I could show you…. There's no time. We have to kill Pelletier." *So much depends on it.*

Roland shrugged and sat once again. He swirled the alcohol in his glass, observing it create caramel legs inside, then finally took a long sip. "I'll help you," he finally said.

"Thank you." Adrien hesitated, then asked, "But how can you be sure you can trust me?"

"I can think of no good reason why you'd tell me what you've told me," Roland said matter-of-factly. "Unless, of course, you're an idiot."

You've called me that on at least a few occasions.

"Verel arrived about a half hour ago. I saw three others with him, but I'm sure there are more. He's been gathering followers for several years now. He's clever, and he avoids suspicion." Roland massaged the back of his neck. "He just recently learned the truth about me."

"He wants immortality. And why not take care of two birds with one stone?"

Roland nodded. "By preventing a marriage, he hopes to rekindle the war between the clans. What could be better?"

At that moment, the door to the room opened and another man slipped inside. "I followed them to the kitchens. They have something planned, but I don't know how we—" He stopped when he saw Adrien. "Excuse me." The man glanced at Roland.

"He's one of us," Roland said.

Adrien stared at the newcomer. He should have expected he might run into him, but—

"Jacques," Roland said, "I'd like you to meet Claude. Claude… Clement. He's the son of an old friend of mine. Claude, this is Jacques Gilbert."

"A pleasure."

"The… the pleasure is mine." Adrien shook his father's hand.

Chapter Thirty-Four
Together Before the Fall

"An immortal?" Jacques glared at Adrien, who swallowed hard.

"What's going on?" Jacques demanded. "And who the hell is he really?"

"It's all right, Roland," Adrien said. "I'll tell him who I—"

A woman in the hallway outside the room laughed and peered inside. "So sorry. I didn't mean to interrupt."

"You're hardly interrupting," Jacques said without missing a beat and kissed the woman's hand. "A beautiful woman like—"

"I'm afraid we have some urgent business to attend to," Adrien put in, garnering a look of disappointment from his father and a sigh from Roland. Jacques wouldn't meet Adrien's mother for more than a half century, but he'd clearly been quite the ladies' man in his day.

The woman smiled and left, closing the door behind her.

"This isn't a game. Pelletier and his followers are here," Adrien said. "I suggest we split up and find Anaïs and Stéphane. By now they'll probably be outside the kitchens. They're the ones Pelletier's after."

"The kitchens?" Jacques stopped and blocked Adrien's way, his sword pointed at Adrien's neck. "And how would you know what Verel intends to do?"

"Claude isn't the enemy." Roland pushed the blade away. "You have my word."

Adrien took a deep breath. "Pelletier wants the child, and if he takes what he wants, we'll suffer for it."

"Child?" Jacques lowered his weapon. "What child?"

Roland met Adrien's eyes. "The son Anaïs is carrying."

Jacques looked to Roland. "Later," Roland said, "when there's time, I'll explain."

Jacques hesitated a moment, then nodded.

"We'll keep searching for Verel," Roland said. "If you find him or see anything out of the ordinary, call for me. And best of luck."

Adrien nodded and slipped out of the room, moving carefully with the crowd of well-wishers. He made his way slowly down the hallway where he and Nico had last seen Stéphane. He stopped from time to time to speak to other guests, even tasting some of the food the servants offered.

"Have you seen the lord of the house?" he asked one of them as he helped himself to a glass of champagne a few minutes later.

"There was a bit of a disturbance near the kitchens a short time ago," the young woman told him as he pretended to sip his drink. "Lady Rousseau asked for his assistance. I haven't seen him since."

"Disturbance?"

"One of the cows wandered into the gardens." She giggled. "Probably that little sprite Rosina making trouble again. Master Paul says it's because she's taken a fancy to Lord Lambert."

"Jean?"

"He's a handsome man." She blushed crimson.

"Thank you." He set his drink back on her tray. She blushed again and continued on her way.

A cow? *The perfect ruse to lure Stéphane and Anaïs away from their guests.* Adrien's heart beat faster as he went to find Roland.

"…and I found the fox hiding in one of the barns," an elderly vampire was telling Roland when Adrien finally caught up with him.

"Indeed." Roland chuckled, then glanced at Adrien, who nodded and inclined his head toward the hallway.

"I'm so sorry, Lord Covington," Roland told the vampire as he exited the room. "I really must be going. It seems an old friend of mine has arrived and is asking for me. It's been a pleasure."

Roland closed the sitting room door. "You couldn't have chosen a better time to interrupt." He sighed. "The last time Ralph Covington cornered me, it took me hours to escape."

"Hopefully you'll remember that in the future," Adrien muttered under his breath. Roland raised an eyebrow, but Adrien just pointed him toward the kitchens.

"Did you find them?" Roland asked.

"No, something better. A cow," he answered.

"A cow?"

"Loose in the gardens behind the kitchens. Perfect distraction, don't you think?"

"I'll find Jacques and meet you there as soon as I can."

Adrien took off at a brisk walk and arrived at the kitchens to the sound of clanking pots and servants coming and going.

"Sir," one of the servants said, "I'm afraid you're going the wrong way. The party is—"

"I'm looking for Lady Rousseau," Adrien said. "Did she come this way?"

"Yes." The servant looked a bit confused but added, "Lord Rousseau followed her into the gardens a moment ago. Something about a cow being—"

Adrien didn't wait to hear the rest. He dodged servants with trays of food and drink, wove between several cooks bent over large pots, and barely avoided colliding with a scullery maid as she wiped up something on the floor. He opened the door onto the gardens and dashed out, drawing his sword as he ran. Anaïs and Stéphane stood in the middle of the courtyard between the herb and vegetable gardens, looking around.

"I don't see a cow," Stéphane was saying. "They said—"

"Get down!" Adrien shouted just in time to deflect a shot of red fire from behind one of the storage buildings.

Stéphane grabbed Anaïs and moved behind another building as another volley hit the ground where they had been standing only moments before. Adrien launched a line of fire toward the attackers and ran across the courtyard, joining Anaïs and Stéphane a moment later.

CHAPTER THIRTY-FIVE
STORM CLOUDS

NICO RAN across the field from the stables at the sound of the first volley. By the time he arrived, one of the storehouses was already engulfed in flames. Servants scattered and shouted, some drawing weapons and others fleeing to the relative safety of the large stone wall that bordered the courtyard on one side. On the other side of the small fountain, Roland fought side by side with Adrien's father. They'd made some progress—one of the hunters lay dead near the burning building—but at least two dozen more hunters were visible, some atop the wall behind the buildings and others taking cover by the fountain.

"Adrien!" Nico shouted as he materialized his sword and raced toward Adrien and his parents.

"Please take her somewhere safe." Stéphane launched a stream of ice toward the attackers.

"I won't go without you," Anaïs snapped. "I'm more than capable of defending myself and our home. Haven't I always fought at your side?"

Stéphane took Anaïs's hand. "You're more than strong enough," he said, his voice tender despite the chaos. "But there's a life you must protect above all others." He placed his hand on her belly. "Armin will make sure you're *both* safe."

Nico offered his hand. "My lady. I'll protect you with my life."

Anaïs frowned and looked to her husband.

"Please, beloved. This time, allow me to fight for all of us. Our child is too precious to risk." Stéphane glanced at Nico and smiled.

"If you're killed," Anaïs told Stéphane as she took Nico's hand, "I will never forgive you."

Stéphane grinned. "I'll find you after this is done."

"I'll be waiting,"

"This way," Nico said as Adrien and Stéphane sent off several blasts in unison, creating a cover of fire and ice. All the while, Anaïs appeared to take her measure of him, but if she suspected what Stéphane had immediately known, she said nothing.

"Where are we going?" Anaïs asked as they neared the side of the house, by the high privet hedge.

"The old dungeons," Nico replied. "With the wards—"

"First we find Rosina," she said.

"But—" He and Adrien had discussed Rosina, of course, but since she'd been nowhere near the fighting, at least in Jean's memories, they'd decided she'd be safe.

"She's far too young to be on her own, and far too hot-headed. If she decides to fight…. We have to find her first," Anaïs insisted.

"Of course, my lady. Do you know where we might find her?"

"Last I saw her, she was headed to the stables. She was not… pleased, shall we say, with my son's decision to marry Jean."

"Oh?" Perhaps there was some truth to Paul's belief that Rosina had a bit of a crush on Jean.

"Rosina will be a force to reckon with when she's grown." Anaïs sighed. "But for now, I'm afraid she's inherited my stubbornness."

Nico had lost count of how many times Jean had called *him* stubborn. "I'm sure there's a useful side to that trait," he replied diplomatically.

Anaïs nodded. "No doubt."

They walked quickly over to the stables. In the distance, the battle sounded muted, like the rumble of distant thunder. If Rosina had heard, wouldn't she already be back at the house?

The response to Nico's silent question came in the form of a shouted "No!" from the stables.

Anaïs and Nico ran, arriving at the entrance to the stables just in time to see a seven-year-old Rosina stomp her foot and tell a very uncomfortable-looking Charles Duvalier, "I *won't* hide. I've been practicing with my sword. I can help—"

"Mistress Rosina"—Charles's overly sweet tone made Nico cringe—"this isn't a situation for a young lady like you to be involved in."

"I am *not* a baby!" Rosina shouted as Nico and Anaïs stepped inside.

"Of course you're not, ma chère," Anaïs said evenly. "You've gotten very good with your sword."

"So I can fight too?" Rosina's warm eyes bright with excitement.

"I think it's too early for you to—" Anaïs began.

"But you said I was strong." Rosina put her hands on her hips and glared at her mother—a gesture Nico had seen several hundred times and which nearly made him laugh out loud.

Nico had never seen Charles look so helpless. Anaïs looked as though she was about to lose her temper.

"My lady." Nico kneeled so his face was at the same level as Rosina. "I've heard you're very strong."

Rosina considered Nico, the hint of a wary frown on her pursed lips. "Jean—Lord Lambert," she corrected as Anaïs raised an eyebrow, "tells me I'll be as powerful as Papa when I'm grown."

"I've no doubt you will." He smiled at her and nodded. "Your brother Paul tells me you're a fine rider too."

Rosina beamed. Over her shoulder, Charles's eyes grew wide. *Little does he know I have a few dozen lifetimes of memories of my sister!*

"There are evil men here," Nico continued. "They want to hurt your mother."

"I will kill them!" Rosina shouted.

"I need your help. To protect her." Nico paused a moment for effect. "There's a secret place I want to take her where she can be safe," he explained in an undertone. "But to get there, we need to use stealth. We don't want the bad men to find us. Can you help me protect her? Please?"

Rosina nodded fervently and drew her sword, a beautiful weapon with a jeweled hilt. An impressive feat for a vampire so young. She gazed at her mother, and Nico blinked back tears as he reminded himself that *this* time, Rosina would grow up with Anaïs to watch over her.

They left Charles near the gardens, where he would wait and make sure that none of the hunters followed. They rounded the corner of the house near where the entrance to what had once been a wine cellar. Nico was just about to open the stone door when a shot of fire landed a few feet away from them.

"Stay behind me." Nico shot back at their attacker.

"I am not an invalid in need of protection." Anaïs drew her own weapon. "I can—"

Rosina screamed as a fireball several feet wide fell toward them. Nico grabbed Anaïs and Rosina and wrapped them both in a cocoon of ice. He waited for the impact and prayed the defense would hold, but instead he heard someone shout. The attack didn't come.

"Are you all right, Maman?" Blaise touched the ice, which promptly melted, creating a rainbow of moisture in a ring around them.

"I'm fine. Thanks to you all." Anaïs rested her hand on Rosina's shoulder.

Nico opened the door to the passage. "Through here." He motioned Anaïs and Rosina.

"I'll go with them." Blaise flashed Nico a reassuring smile. "Paul told me of your plans. He said to tell you he'll meet you upstairs."

"I…. Thank you." Nico hesitated, but Anaïs said, "Blaise is quite good with casting wards to keep others out. And with my daughter"—she smiled proudly at Rosina—"I'm sure we'll be quite safe. Later, perhaps, we can speak. I have many questions I'm anxious to ask you."

"I'd like that." Nico hoped there *would* be a later.

He waited until Blaise, Rosina, and Anaïs descended a few steps, then closed the door behind them. A moment later the door glowed silver and blue, then completely vanished into the side of the house, leaving only the regular pattern of the stonework wall in its place.

Nico ran to the house, slipped inside, and worked his way through a crowd of visitors who'd taken cover behind the platform where Blaise and Jean were to exchange their vows. It took him far longer than expected to reach the stairs the servants used. He climbed them three at a time and burst through the door at the end of the western wing of the house.

Immediately a shot of fire soared from the other end of the hallway, near Paul's room. Nico had no time to counter. Instead, he turned his weapon sideways and did his best to deflect the fire and shield his face. The fabric of his shirtsleeve ignited, and he quickly tamped it down with a layer of ice. His skin stung and began to blacken. Not a life-threatening wound, but he would need treatment or it would not fully heal.

His attacker launched another volley, but this time Nico was prepared. He pointed his sword and a shower of ice flew toward the hunter, extinguishing the blaze and attaching itself to his body. Before his opponent could extricate himself, Nico charged. Not the safest move, but if he was protecting someone inside Paul's room, there wasn't time.

The hunter recovered just as Nico grabbed him by the throat. Hunters were strong, but vampires were far stronger. The man ceased his struggling at Nico's blow, dropping to the floor with a resounding thud as Nico released him, heart pounding with fear at what he might find when he reached Paul's room.

Please…. You have to survive.

CHAPTER THIRTY-SIX
NEVER ENOUGH

ADRIEN BRUSHED aside his fear for Nico. Jean was right. Nico was far more powerful than Adrien gave him credit for. By now he'd have rescued Paul and—

A fiery blaze of energy sped by Adrien's head, the heat of the attack stinging his cheek. *Focus!* This wasn't the time to give in to distractions. This was about creating a future where Nico and those he cared about could live peacefully.

He launched a volley back toward the storehouses. Through the cloud of debris, he caught the outlines of several hunters. From the shots fired off in rapid succession, he guessed there were at least a dozen. Add to that another six or seven running toward the wall, and Adrien and the vampires were outnumbered.

Adrien ran toward the nearest outbuilding, hoping to better assess their attackers. He dodged a blast and deflected another back where it had come. He'd nearly made it when a shower of silver and blue ice shot past him, blown by an unseen wind. The ice met a fiery hunter attack head-on, stopping it completely, then shifted course, descending on one of the hunters like a thousand tiny blades. The hunter screamed in pain.

A familiar attack.

"Go on." Adrien turned to see a much younger Jean Lambert motioning to him. "I'll keep them at bay while you take a look."

"Thanks." Adrien jumped onto the roof of the building. Through the smoke and thick fog from the vampires' attacks, he counted three dozen hunters—men and women—some of them working in teams and others flanking the perimeter as if waiting to take their turn. *Not good.*

Adrien looked toward the house to see if Roland and Jacques had made it outside. If they had, he couldn't see them. Even with their numbers, the hunters would have little chance at defeating two ancient vampires and three immortals. But to turn the tide, they needed a strategy.

Adrien returned to Jean's side. Some of the guests had now joined the fray, but they were no match for the hunters' weapons.

"Get back!" Adrien jumped in front of one of the vampires. The beam of fire glanced off the hilt of Adrien's blade, burning his hand before causing another tree to erupt into flames.

Adrien hissed in pain and dropped his weapon.

"I can handle this," Jean said. "You should be treated."

"I'll be fine." The wound would heal quickly.

Jean charged forward to counter several attacks headed their way, covering for Adrien while he retrieved his sword and pulled his belt from his trousers, wrapping it around his wrist and the hilt and pulling it tight with his teeth. It would do until the muscles healed.

Adrien took a few deep breaths and willed the pain away. The wound hissed, but already the skin had begun to knit together. He met Jean's gaze and saw the question there.

"Do I know you?" Jean asked as he, then Adrien, shot off a new round of volleys at the hunters.

You will soon enough. "I'm a friend" was all Adrien said.

Whatever Jean intended to say was lost in a barrage of fire from the hunters. One of the guests who'd joined the fight took a direct hit to the chest and fell. "Help her!" Jean shouted to the guards.

One of the men pulled the vampire out of the line of fire. He bent over and tried to stem the bleeding, but the wound on the woman's chest refused to heal. He looked up at Jean, his expression grim.

Adrien ran over to where the woman lay. He cut the skin at his wrist and his blood dripped onto the wound, which hissed and smoked. Jean stood above them and gave them cover as the woman's skin gradually began to heal.

Hunter weapons had grown more powerful over time, but they had yet to experiment with vampire blood to enhance them. If they failed to defeat Pelletier here, the future would bring far more frightening consequences.

Adrien turned to the guard. "She'll need more healing, but she'll survive."

The guard nodded and gathered the woman in his arms. He ran toward the house through a cloud of smoke as Adrien and Jean launched simultaneous attacks on the hunters. They shouted and retreated behind what was left of one of the storage buildings.

Adrien jumped and deflected another attack, this one aimed at Jean.

Nearby, another vampire fell, this one by the blade of a hunter's sword. Adrien gritted his teeth. There were more vampires than hunters now, but they'd lost at least seven so far, most of them dead or dying.

More of the guests stood in the doorway of the kitchen. "Stay inside," Stéphane ordered, causing them to retreat.

"My lord, you should be inside as well," Jean told Stéphane.

"This is my home. My responsibility." As imposing a figure as he was, Stéphane dodged an attack with surprising grace. "I will not—"

A ball of fire at least two feet in diameter streaked across the courtyard and exploded near the house, causing Adrien's ears to ring. Jean waved his hand, extinguishing the bales of hay that had caught fire where the attack landed. "Where is Lady Rousseau?" he asked.

"Safe," Roland said as he and Jacques joined the fight. "She and Rosina are with Blaise. Six guards are protecting the front of the house."

Jean's glacial expression flickered, and relief replaced the tension in his jaw. "If I may, my lord?"

Stéphane nodded.

"Best we form two groups. You, my lord, Jacques, and Roland will defend the guests from this vantage point." Jean turned to Adrien. "You—"

"Claude Clement," Adrien supplied, shouting over another barrage of attacks.

"—monsieur Gilbert and I will work our way around the back of the storehouses and try to cut the enemy off from their point of retreat. We'll work our way forward and surround them."

THE FUTURE had already changed. The attackers hadn't managed to surprise Stéphane or Anaïs, and without Anaïs to protect, Stéphane could hold his own.

It was time for Pelletier to make an appearance, and Adrien knew where he was headed. Better not to think about it. Instead, he focused his attention on a small group of hunters at the periphery who'd been slowly moving toward the corner of the house.

CHAPTER THIRTY-SEVEN
DEATH AND THE CONSPIRATOR

NICO REACHED the end of the long hallway to find the door to Paul's suite ajar, hanging off its hinges, the wood black from fire. He entered, sword at the ready. A shadowy figure jumped out from behind a high wood wardrobe, meeting his blade and causing the sound of metal to echo in the small room.

Nico pushed hard, forcing his attacker to take several steps backward. He'd expected to see another nameless hunter or even Pelletier himself, but when light from an attack outside streaked the sky, Nico gasped in shock.

"L—Lord Rousseau?" Nico had hoped to avoid his uncle Reynaud. In his own timestream, Reynaud had been killed long before the massacre at the Council of Hunters, but Nico knew him from Adrien's memories as an ally to Pelletier.

"Who the hell are you?" Reynaud growled and swung his weapon.

"Someone who won't let those hunter bastards destroy my family." Nico gritted his teeth and met Reynaud's blade once more.

Reynaud knitted his brow, and both of them stepped back. This wouldn't be easy. The Reynaud in Adrien's memories was older and weaker. This Reynaud was in his prime.

Nico glanced over to the bedroom, but the door was closed. Was Pelletier already there, stealing Paul's lifeblood? Nico needed to finish this quickly. He wouldn't lose Paul.

Reynaud had fought in the long-running war between the vampire clans, and his fighting style reflected a battle-hardened approach to combat. Short, powerful strokes, excellent aim. The Rousseau general he would soon become was already evident in this younger man.

Were you the one who fanned the flames of the war between our clans, Uncle? How many Lamberts and Rousseaus had died because of him? Nico had seen loved ones perish in a war fought for what? A lie Pelletier and Reynaud created? Anger surged red-hot in Nico's chest. He wanted to kill Reynaud, punish him for all the grief he'd inflicted.

I'll stop you here, before you can poison this future.

Reynaud charged and swung his weapon wide, taking Nico by surprise and striking his forearm. Nico pressed the wound with his free hand to staunch the bleeding. He'd been too busy thinking about revenge. A mistake that could be fatal.

"I can feel your hatred burn." Reynaud wore a self-righteous expression the way one might wear a ceremonial cloak. How long had he plotted with Pelletier to destroy Stéphane? Had he meant Pelletier to murder all of Stéphane's bloodline?

"Battle is not about revenge, nor is it about strength. It's about exploiting your opponent's weakness and magnifying your strengths."

In a space as small as the antechamber, long-range elemental attacks were impossible. This fight was about swordplay and strength. Nico and Reynaud flew about the room, charging, retreating, and clashing once more. Each time they parried, Nico followed the line of Reynaud's arm and observed the movement of his feet. Nico moved defensively, giving Reynaud room to negotiate the small space, allowing him to land several attacks and grow more comfortable with his dominance.

Reynaud was a competent fighter. Strong, but without creativity. His left attacks were weaker, leaving him more vulnerable on his right. He held his weapon a bit too tightly, permitting him less ease of movement.

Nico feinted left, purposely drawing Reynaud's stronger attack. Another blow—this to Nico's shoulder—smarted and drew blood. A calculated risk, but one that paid off. It looked far worse than it was, especially since Nico made sure to wince as Reynaud withdrew.

From time to time as they fought, Nico was sure he heard movement in Paul's bedroom. Once, he thought he heard a clash of steel.

Time for our little dance to end, Uncle.

Nico drew a quick breath, then aimed beneath Reynaud's arm and his unprotected side. Reynaud blinked in surprise as Nico's weapon sliced through his velvet jacket and met its mark. He shouted in anger and instinctively favored his wounded flank.

Nico had anticipated the opening. He kicked off the floor and flew upward, pushed off the ceiling, and fell toward Reynaud, the point of his sword aimed at the other man's heart. Too late, Reynaud realized he'd left himself vulnerable. Nico's blade pierced Reynaud's chest, causing him to cry out in pain.

Nico released his sword, then rematerialized it an instant later as he landed behind his uncle. "You will not succeed this time," he said as he swung at Reynaud's neck. "This ends now."

"No!" Reynaud's shout ended as Nico's sword severed his head. Blood splattered onto what was left of the furniture and pooled on the floor.

Nico charged into Paul's room, sword drawn. The smell of blood assaulted him as he rounded the corner. *Am I too late?*

"Thanks to you," Paul told Nico as he pulled his sword from Claus Bremen's chest, "I was ready."

Bremen grabbed at his chest and stared at Paul. "How…?" he asked, the word barely intelligible as blood bubbled from his lips.

Nico fought back a wave of revulsion for the man whose experiments with vampire blood had created the tools used to massacre most of the people Nico had loved. This man was the reason the Nicolas of Adrien's timestream had suffered endlessly. He was, without a doubt, the reason Pelletier was here, looking for the child Anaïs carried. The purest of ancient blood and the most powerful.

Paul nodded to Nico, who gritted his teach and swung his sword. Bremen's head tumbled from his body.

CHAPTER THIRTY-EIGHT
LOOSE ENDS

As ADRIEN sped atop the wall to follow some of the retreating hunters, he caught a glimpse of Nico and Paul at the doorway to the kitchens. A dozen hunters lay dead, while some of the guards tended to the injured vampires.

Nico frowned. *"Pelletier escaped. I was too late."*

Adrien jumped off the wall and ran to Nico. *You saved your brother, Nico. We'll find Pelletier. You've already changed the future.*

Paul nodded to Adrien. "I should see if my father needs help. Besides, he needs to hear about Reynaud before someone else tells him."

"What about Reynaud?" Adrien asked after Paul joined Stéphane across the courtyard.

A muscle in Nico's cheek twitched. "He's dead."

"Dead?"

"I met him outside Paul's room, guarding it while Pelletier.... I... took care of him."

Adrien sighed. Whatever Nico thought of his uncle, Adrien doubted he'd wanted to be the one to kill the man. "Are you all right?"

Nico nodded.

"There's something I don't understand, though," Adrien said. "I've seen Jean's memories. He never saw Reynaud in Paul's apartments. How's that possible?"

Nico shook his head. "I'm not sure. Things were different in so many ways this time. My guess? My uncle decided that given the commotion, it was safer to stay as close to Pelletier as possible. Knowing his penchant for self-preservation, he figured if Pelletier failed to steal the gift from Paul, he'd kill Pelletier to prevent him from pointing the finger of blame his way."

"I'm sorry. I never liked the man much, but I never guessed...."

"Nor did Jean. Or any of us." Nico glanced over to where Paul was speaking in hushed tones with Stéphane, whose expression was grim. "Much as I wish I hadn't been the one to discover that he helped Pelletier engineer the destruction of the Rousseau Clan, I'm ashamed to admit I enjoyed killing him. It was… satisfying." Nico drew a long breath and seemed to collect himself.

"There's nothing to be ashamed of," Adrien said without hesitation. "You did what was right, knowing what damage he might do if he survived."

Nico nodded. Adrien knew he didn't want to dwell on the subject of his uncle's treachery.

"And Pelletier?"

"Paul was expecting him." Nico smiled. "At the last moment, Bremen showed up and Pelletier fled. I'm sorry, I—"

"You have nothing to apologize for. He isn't going to leave without his prize. He's probably looking for Anaïs as we speak. Paul was an afterthought. He is after the you yet to be born."

"Saving Paul wasn't enough." Nico clenched his hand around the hilt of his weapon with such force that his knuckles turned white. The fact that he and Nico were still here in the past meant that the different futures they'd come from still existed. It meant that Pelletier would gain the power he sought some other way.

Nico's eyes darkened with anger. "Let's finish this."

Adrien nodded.

ADRIEN AND Nico walked past what was left of the storage buildings, through the gate, and down a pebbled walkway. Overhead, stars began to appear, dim at first, but becoming brighter with every passing minute. The hunters waited beyond the formal gardens. Adrien sensed them, although he could not be certain Pelletier was there.

Nico stopped Adrien before "Are you sure about this?"

"Absolutely." They'd planned for this possibility.

"But—"

Adrien took Nico's hands and met his gaze. "I have to be the one to confront them. Their weapons can't easily kill me."

Nico pressed his lips together.

"Nico?"

Nico nodded. "We do this together."

"Together. Just the way we planned it."

CHAPTER THIRTY-NINE
ENDGAME

EIGHT HUNTERS surrounded Adrien the moment he reached the trees that marked the edge of the property. None of the men presented much of a challenge as an opponent, but Adrien held back and fought using only those powers they might expect of another hunter. The restless thrum of power felt familiar, but there was nothing to chafe under his command. *He* himself was the demon now, the restlessness his own.

He ignored the footsteps of two other men who made their way toward him as he continued to fight. He sensed Nico's apprehension and determination. There was only one way this day would end, but they both needed patience to ensure the outcome.

Not long now.

Prescient words, for the moment Adrien thought them, a searing pain shot through his body. He coughed and choked as blood filled his mouth, glancing down to see the point of the sword protruding from his chest. A hunter's weapon, meant for vampires. The wound wouldn't kill him, since his body was only part vampire, but it pierced his heart and immobilized him.

Adrien blinked as the world blurred. He dropped his weapon and struggled to stay alert, allowing his vampiric power to sustain him as his human strength waned. When his vision cleared, a man stood in front of him, lips curving slightly upward.

Giovanetti. And to his right, Pelletier, who eyed Adrien with obvious contempt. Pelletier inclined his head and Giovanetti withdrew his sword slowly as the other men watched.

Adrien's body exploded into a haze of pain. His fingers tingled, instinctively reaching for Ianus. He fought the urge to call the sword and take Giovanetti's head. *Focus!* Giovanetti was an afterthought, Pelletier the goal.

Already Adrien's heart had begun to heal, its irregular beat steadying. Adrien put his hands to his chest to hide his body's response, then dropped to his knees and gasped. Giovanetti chuckled as Adrien coughed up blood.

"*Adrien!*"

He's here. Just a little longer.

Giovanetti retrieved Ianus and held it up for Pelletier to see.

"A hunter?" Pelletier pulled Adrien's chin upward. "I don't recognize you." He tossed the weapon aside.

Adrien spat in Pelletier's face. Giovanetti responded by kicking Adrien hard, causing him to fall onto the moss-covered ground. Adrien writhed and moaned, then lay, panting and grasping his belly.

"May I kill him for you?" Giovanetti offered.

"I'll take care of him." Pelletier pointed to the forest. "Take some of the men. Make sure this one came alone."

"Of course." Giovanetti called three of the men by name, and they followed him into the trees.

Just a little longer. They're headed your way.

From his vantage point on the ground, Adrien counted six men, including Pelletier. Two stood close to Pelletier, while the other three appeared to be keeping a lookout for movement headed toward them from the castle. Once the wounded had been treated and the building was secured, Jean and the others would come looking for the rest of the attackers. Pelletier would leave his followers to fight while he headed back to the castle in search of another victim.

Pelletier must have motioned to some of the men, because the next minute two of them were slipping their arms under Adrien's and pulling him to his feet. Adrien let his body go slack and allowed his eyes to flutter closed.

Almost there.

"Where have they hidden Lady Rousseau?" Pelletier demanded.

Adrien opened his eyes to narrow slits and continued to gasp for air. "As if... I'd... tell you."

This garnered a hard slap across the face. The men released their hold on Adrien, and he collapsed onto the ground.

Just another minute.

"*They're here.*"

Time's up, Nico. Adrien rolled onto his side and materialized his sword. He swung wide, hitting the two men who'd held him in the chest. They shouted and fell where they stood.

"What the hell? Restrain him!" Pelletier shouted.

Adrien focused on a spot behind the three lookouts, disappearing and reappearing as he swung his weapon again, piercing the shoulder of the closest and stabbing the other two in the abdomen before they could even figure out where the attack had come from.

At the same time, the sounds of shouts from the forest echoed across the field, followed by the grinding of metal against metal. Then, nothing.

Pelletier turned to see what was happening, but Adrien moved like lightning to where he stood. He didn't hesitate but charged with his sword pointed at Pelletier's chest. Pelletier raised his own sword, too late to stop Adrien but not too late to wound him.

Pelletier's sword pierced Adrien's side as Adrien ran his weapon through Pelletier's heart.

"Adrien!" Nico was at his side an instant later, his strong arm around Adrien's waist.

"Giovanetti and the others?"

"Dead." Judging by the look in Nico's eyes, he'd enjoyed killing Giovanetti.

Pelletier dropped his sword and stared at them. "Who…?" His voice was barely a whisper.

Adrien pressed his hand to his wound. Already the blood had stopped. Sucker hurt like hell. "You wouldn't know us."

"Not yet," Nico added with the ghost of a smile. Then he looked at Adrien and nodded.

Adrien twisted the sword, then pulled it free. "Not ever."

Pelletier fell in a heap, his heavy breaths beginning to slow.

Adrien lifted his sword, then released it one last time. He grabbed Nico and held him tight. His body tingled and felt suddenly light. "Strange."

"Like floating. Warm." Nico's eyes filled with tears, but he was smiling.

Adrien kissed Nico as the world around them faded. *I love you. I will love you forever.*

"*And I you.*"

CHAPTER FORTY
THE DREAM

Saint-Gervais, France—March 1895

"GET OUT of bed!"

Adrien blinked hard, rubbed his eyes, and sat up. He felt as though he'd been sleeping for days. Everything felt fuzzy, and his head hurt. He put a hand to his chest and tried to remember. *Something terrible.*

"Get out of bed!" someone shouted again.

The dream faded and Adrien looked up to see François frowning at him, lips pressed together in frustration. "You promised you'd come with me to Lyon, Addie. At this rate, we're going to be late."

"Lyon? Why are we going to Lyon?"

What had the man in his dream said? Something about the past. Adrien struggled to remember. He'd been dreaming of something. Of someone.

"You're not escaping this time," François said. "All of the week's work is done. And if you think you can use a book"—he pointed to a pile on the floor by the bed—"as an excuse, I'll use them for practice. I bet they burn quite well."

Adrien stood and stretched, then walked past François to the small mirror by the window. He brought his hand to his face and traced the sparse stubble on his cheek. He could almost imagine the echo of a beard there.

"Addie!" François cuffed him on the back of the head just hard enough to get his attention.

"I hate when you do that," Adrien snapped.

François shook his head and laughed. "All the more reason not to stop. These days it seems the only way to keep you from dreaming." He picked up one of the books and raised an eyebrow. "King Arthur?"

Adrien pulled the book from François's hands and clutched it to his chest. "Touch it and I'll run you through."

"Be my guest." François pointed at the sword propped against the bed.

174

Adrien picked it up and weighed it in his hands. The cool metal of the hilt warmed to his touch, and for just an instant, Adrien saw it glow bright blue. He blinked, and the sword was once again as it had been. "Did you see that?" he asked François.

"See what?"

"The sword, it glowed somehow and—"

"Glowed? All by itself?" François rapped his knuckles on Adrien's skull. "Papa shouldn't have let you have that second glass of wine last night."

Adrien rubbed the bridge of his nose. The pain at the back of his eye sockets eased somewhat. The feeling was somewhat familiar. Something about time. *No... something about....* Adrien tried to remember the name that had lingered at the back of his mind. He'd dreamed of someone, but as the dream faded, so did the name.

"Addie." François glared at him. "The carriage is ready. I packed some food for the trip. But if we don't leave now, we'll arrive too late for the fête."

"Fête?"

"The Council's ball." François shook his head in disbelief. "We've planned this for weeks. Please don't tell me you're going to back out again this year. You promised once you had your commission, you'd go with me."

"Back out? I... no." He'd told François he would go.

"You're far too set in your ways. For once, you need to take a chance. See the world beyond this tiny town."

"I am." Adrien wouldn't tell François that he'd dreamed of the dance several nights in a row. He *wanted* to go. He felt almost compelled to do so.

"You're daydreaming again." François laughed and pushed Adrien playfully. "Breakfast? Maybe then your head will clear."

"I'll dress and eat," Adrien said. "Then we can leave." François stared at him with such a comical expression that Adrien laughed out loud. "Have I surprised you?" He tossed the book at François, who caught it and looked at him in obvious shock. "You might try reading it," Adrien added. "Far more enjoyable than practicing swordplay. You might even learn a few new things."

François chuckled, then shrugged and left the room. He didn't return the book.

"You slept a long time."

"Isabelle." Without thinking, he rushed to embrace her. He held her until she pushed him away, a quizzical look on her face.

"Are you sure you aren't still asleep?" she said, giggling. "You act as though you haven't seen me in ages."

What was he doing? He'd seen her just the night before. "I guess I'm still a little sleepy." He took the cup of café au lait she handed him and sighed as the liquid warmed his chest. He buttered a piece of bread and dipped it in the coffee, then proceeded to finish half the baguette.

"I told your father the wine was a bad idea." Charlotte Gilbert set a basket full of vegetables on the counter and clucked like a hen.

"It wasn't the wine," Adrien shot back.

Isabelle and Charlotte laughed, and Adrien laughed too. Charlotte leaned over Adrien and hugged him. "I packed a bag for you," she said.

"I could have done that myself, Maman. You didn't need to—"

"I enjoy taking care of my children," his mother said. "Besides, your brother is still afraid you'll back out."

"He needs to stop worrying, and so do you." Adrien shoved one last bite of bread into his mouth, washed it down with the rest of the coffee, then got to his feet. "Thank you, though," he told his mother as he kissed her on the cheek.

"You'd better go," Isabelle said. "François is so excited that you finally agreed to go with him, he may burst into flames, sword and all." She laughed, then picked something up from the table and handed it to him. "For the ball," she said.

He unfolded the bundle and held the deep brown jacket up to his chest. "It's beautiful," he said. "You made this?"

She blushed and giggled. "Maman and I did."

"Thank you." He swallowed hard and met her gaze, so bright and full of joy.

"There's a shirt and trousers as well," she said, looking away as the pink on her cheeks deepened.

He leaned in and kissed her on the cheek. "Thank you," he repeated, at a loss for words.

"Get going now," his mother said with mock sternness. "I expect you to tell me all about it when you return." She turned back to the table and rearranged several plates stacked there.

"I will," he said. "I promise."

Ten minutes later he and François tied their bags to their saddles and led the horses out of the barn.

"Ready for your big adventure?" Jacques attempted to wipe a bit of dirt from his nose and ended up smearing it all over his nose and cheek. Adrien guessed he'd been up early tending to the animals, since he and François wouldn't be around to help today.

"It's a ball," Adrien said. "Not an adventure." Still, he couldn't shake the heady anticipation.

Jacques cocked his head to one side and seemed to consider something before saying, "That all depends on who you meet there."

"Meet?" Adrien snorted. "I know all the hunters who'll be there."

"You probably do." The edges of Jacques's mouth quirked upward in something approaching a grin. "But this is the annual hunter ball, so you're likely to meet a few vampires as well."

Adrien noticed that François's cheeks pinked in response. *Interesting.* Was François hoping to meet someone there?

CHAPTER FORTY-ONE
THE FATED ENCOUNTER

THEY SETTLED into their hotel room with just enough time to bathe and dress before walking the few blocks to the Council of Hunters building where the fête was already in full swing. Someone shouted their names to the crowd, and they descended the long staircase leading to the ballroom.

An orchestra played as a number of vampires and hunters danced a lively mazurka on the parquet. Dancers dressed in lively colors and fantastical masks ran around, pulling people onto the dance floor and flirting. Adrien found himself whistling along to a familiar tune and wishing he had the courage to join the group.

"Excuse me," François said as helped himself to two glasses of champagne from a passing server. "Will you be all right if I leave you to your own devices?"

Adrien frowned. "I'll be fine." Just because he hated parties didn't mean he was incapable of fending for himself! François just chuckled and waved before making his way across the ballroom.

Adrien had expected François would join the group of hunters, male and female, near the food tables. Adrien recognized some as François's friends who'd stayed with their family when passing through their small town. François sometimes spent time with Victor Sauvage, who'd studied with Roland Günter a few years before. But tonight François gave Victor a friendly tap on the back, waved to the rest of the group, and continued to walk until he came to a man standing by a pillar at the far end of the room.

No. A vampire. Charles Duvalier had been staying in Saint-Gervais for several weeks. Although he appeared to be only in his early twenties, Adrien knew him to be hundreds of years old. When François flashed him a brilliant smile, the deep worry that troubled Charles's youthful face eased. Adrien watched as they conversed, their manner comfortable and familiar.

That explains a lot. More often than not recently, François had been absent from the vineyard. He'd told their parents he was helping a hunter who worked in a nearby town, but now Adrien was sure François had been spending time with Charles.

They're in love. This thought filled Adrien with relief he couldn't explain. That, and the certain knowledge that these two men were meant to be together. But how strange was that? He'd never thought much about François's heart. But it warmed his own to realize what he was seeing.

You've been reading too much Alfred de Musset.

Adrien shrugged off the thought.

"Champagne?" a server asked him.

"Thank you." He took a glass and sipped it as he looked out over the room. Already, couples filled the dance floor, moving in prescribed steps to a lovely waltz. He watched the dancers for some time, then deposited his empty glass with another server and walked toward the entrance to the patio to get some fresh air. Just observing the merriment made Adrien uncomfortable. He'd do the bare minimum, greet some of the guests, then slip out and explore the city.

"May I have this dance?" said a warm voice behind him.

The newcomer, a handsome man dressed in a burgundy velvet suit that flattered his warm brown eyes and pale skin, bowed low. *An ancient vampire.* Familiar, and yet they'd never met—as beautiful as he was, Adrien would have remembered.

"I'm not much of a dancer," Adrien admitted as he held out his hand in greeting. "Adrien Gilbert."

"Nicolas Rousseau," Nicolas said as he grasped Adrien's hand.

He'd heard the name, of course. The Rousseaus were an ancient clan with close ties to the Council of Hunters, but he couldn't recall ever having been introduced. "Have we met before?" Adrien felt the pull of something inexplicable with Nicolas's touch. Something that made his body thrum with need, hunger. Something that made Adrien think of... *bloodlust? But that's impossible. Bloodlust in hunters is rare, and—*

"I know your parents, Charlotte and Jacques," Nicolas said when Adrien remained silent.

"You do?" Not surprising. Jacques had recently been elected to a seat on the Council.

179

Nicolas smiled. "My family and I attended their wedding. Before you were born, of course."

"Of course."

Roland often spoke of the ancient clans. He'd even suggested Adrien consider spending time with the Lamberts as an apprentice, continuing in the long tradition of hunters and vampires teaching each other and learning about their different traditions. Roland once told Adrien that Adrien's father, Jacques, had lived with the Lamberts when he was young, although when Adrien had pressed him for details, Roland was surprisingly tight-lipped.

An image flashed through Adrien's mind of Nicolas jumping high into the air, twisting and turning like smoke from a fire before landing gracefully on a limb.

"You still haven't answered my question, monsieur," Nicolas pointed out.

"Question?" Why did his thoughts keep wandering? But as Nicolas smiled at him, all Adrien could think about was how close Nicolas was and the rhythmic beat of his own heart.

"Will you dance with me?" Nicolas's eyes flashed with humor as he pulled Adrien toward the dance floor. He'd been holding Nicolas's hand the entire time. "I'm quite good, they say."

"They do?"

Nicolas shrugged and bowed to Adrien.

"I'll be sure to let you know if *they* are right, monsieur Rousseau," Adrien said as they began to dance.

"I seem to be doing quite well so far. You appear to be enjoying yourself," Nicolas countered, a ghost of a smile on his full lips. "Please call me Nicolas."

"Nicolas," Adrien teased, "I'm just eighteen. Some here might think you're taking advantage of my youth."

Nicolas chuckled. "If I might be so bold, you're far more mature than your eighteen years."

"My father tells me I'm an old soul."

"Indeed." Nicolas's eyes sparkled, and for a moment Adrien saw pain reflected there. But his bright smile returned an instant later. "And do you agree?"

Adrien nodded as Nicolas spun him around. "I suppose. I've never felt comfortable with men my age. With you, though, I feel quite at ease."

"I'm glad to hear it." The music ended and Nicolas bowed deeply. "I've been looking forward to meeting you for a very long time."

"You have?"

"Yes." Nicolas met Adrien's gaze, his expression open and kind. Sincere.

"It's not as though I'm difficult to find. Certainly with your status, you'd have been able to find me whenever you wished." Adrien sensed there was a point to this verbal waltz.

"There's a time and place for everything, monsieur Gilbert."

"Adrien."

"Adrien," Nicolas repeated. "Much as I would like to dance with you again, I was hoping you might join me for a walk in the gardens. You see, my dance card is quite full, and I'd rather escape before someone else claims me."

Judging by the withering looks they garnered from some of the onlookers, Nicolas wasn't joking. "I'd love to walk," Adrien said.

Nicolas guided him out the large glass doors at the back of the ballroom and down the steps to the gardens. Above, the stars shimmered. Gas torches lit the main pathway through the beds and around the fountains. Here and there, other revelers from the dance also made their slow way around the paths.

"Have you been here before, Adrien?" Nicolas asked as they walked around a large fountain carved in smooth marble.

"Several months ago. My master, Roland Günter, presented me to the local Council." Adrien smiled at the memory. "My brother stood at my side as I took the oath to become a hunter."

"So you enjoy the work?" Nicolas seemed genuinely interested.

Adrien tried to focus on the conversation, but his eyes kept straying to Nicolas's full lips and the slight throbbing of a vein under the soft skin of Nicolas's neck. Adrien's cock strained uncomfortably in his britches. He wasn't sure which he wanted more, those lips or Nicolas's blood—

"Adrien?"

"Huh?"

Nicolas chuckled. "I asked if you enjoyed your work."

Adrien's cheeks heated and his mind once again seemed capable of intelligent thought. How strange, to be discussing killing vampires with a vampire.

"It's not odd at all."

"What? Did you read my mind?" Adrien face was on fire. If Nicolas could read his mind, did he know what Adrien had been thinking just before?

"I can hear some of your thoughts." Nicolas appeared unruffled. He drew closer and traced the hollow of Adrien's cheek. "Especially," he added, his lips so close to Adrien's ear that gooseflesh rose on Adrien's body, "those sentiments I share."

"Y-you… you… ah… *heard* what I was thinking?" *And he feels the same?* Adrien swallowed hard and shifted to accommodate his traitorous body.

"Not as much *heard* as *felt*." Nicolas leaned in and brushed Adrien's lips with his own. "There's nothing to be ashamed of. I take it as the highest compliment that you find me desirable as well."

"I…." Adrien swallowed again, his throat suddenly dry. He'd never wanted anyone the way he wanted Nicolas. And had Nicolas just repeated that he wanted him too? "I'm not experienced," he said far more quickly than he'd intended. He'd never been with a man before, although he knew a little about pleasuring women from the encounters he'd had with some of the women in Saint-Gervais.

Several women, hand in hand, ran laughing through the gardens. But instead of retreating or suggesting they return to the ballroom, Nicolas said, "I know a place that's less crowded. Will you join me?"

"I… I don't know if…." Adrien wasn't sure he could restrain himself if he was alone with this man.

"I'm sorry," Nicolas said quickly, his eyes wide with recognition. "It's dark, and I realize you don't know me. To ask you to trust me—"

"It isn't that," Adrien replied. Nicolas seemed so experienced, so seeing him suddenly flustered surprised Adrien. He took Nicolas's hand and squeezed it. "I trust you. Besides, I'm stronger than I look. Even if you were to…." *To… what? To kiss me? To make love to me?* God, would his face stop heating up like some pathetic child's?

"Thank you." Nicolas seemed to understand Adrien's discomfort, because he added, "I have no doubt you're strong."

Adrien had no idea what to say to that. He shifted from one foot to the other, then coughed and said, "Lead the way."

They snaked around a small pond and over a wooden bridge. Here Nicolas led them off the gravel onto a dirt path and through the privet.

"The maze. They don't illuminate it at night, so only vampires can see their way around."

"And if we become lost?"

"I enjoy a challenge." Nicolas gripped Adrien's hand tighter, and the sounds of music from the ballroom faded.

The moon had begun to rise, and the inky blackness lifted. Light silhouetted Nicolas's face, drawing Adrien's attention to his high cheekbones, long lashes, and pale skin. An image of Nicolas baring his neck flickered through Adrien's thoughts, and once again the bloodlust rose in him. *Where did that come from?* Like the other, this felt like… *a memory?*

Adrien pushed the thought away. He'd just met Nicolas. Still, he'd met plenty of other vampires, and he'd never before felt the urge to taste blood. Nicolas was different. "It's beautiful here."

"It is." Nicolas eyed him with apparent curiosity and motioned him to a bench tucked into the high hedge. "I've spent far more time alone here than dancing."

"I can't blame you." Adrien leaned toward Nicolas without thinking, and Nicolas did the same. Their lips met and Adrien's hunger surged.

Nicolas gasped but did not shy away from the kiss, instead pressing his tongue against Adrien's lips until Adrien acceded to the intrusion. Nicolas's bloodlust rose, although Adrien couldn't explain why he knew this. He only knew that he wanted Nicolas, *needed* to taste him, and that if he didn't taste him, he would—

No! Adrien pulled away and got to his feet. His mind and body warred with his intense hunger for Nicolas. "What are you doing?" He'd studied vampires enough to know they were capable of creating lust in unsuspecting humans.

Nicolas blinked his surprise. He seemed hurt, even offended at the insinuation. "I assure you, I've done nothing to create the bloodlust in you. I doubt I'm capable of doing so in a hunter."

"I'm sorry." Whatever he felt for Nicolas, he hadn't meant the insult. "It's just that I've never…." Adrien struggled to find the words and finally gave up. He wanted this. He wanted this man more than anything he'd ever wanted before.

François is right. I'm too cautious. This time he'd take a chance.

Nicolas watched him, jaw tensed. Waiting.

Adrien inhaled, then met Nicolas's gaze. He leaned in and kissed Nicolas again, this time allowing himself to fall into the sensations. The outside world blurred and the sweet scent of Nicolas's blood danced around Adrien in colorful wisps, like sunlight refracting as it meets water.

Nicolas's voice echoed in Adrien's mind like a memory: "*We're better together.*"

Someone laughed, bringing Adrien back to himself. The kiss broke and he pulled away, dizzy and out of breath.

The guests who'd interrupted them whispered to each other and walked quickly away, disappearing a moment later behind a privet hedge.

Nicolas bowed. "Dance with me?"

Adrien nodded, and they ran, hand in hand, back toward the hall.

CHAPTER FORTY-TWO
ECHOES

"ARE YOU sure I can't offer you something to drink, Lord Rousseau?" Charlotte Gilbert gestured for Nicolas to sit at the rough-hewn kitchen table. "Water? Wine, perhaps?"

"You're too kind. But really, I'm fine." Nicolas struggled not to stare. She looked so much like Adrien, with her long blonde hair and bright blue eyes. She was as beautiful as he was handsome.

A moment later Adrien stood in the doorway to the kitchen, his face smeared with sweat and dirt from working the vines. When he saw Nicolas, his face lit with a brilliant smile. "Nicolas? I didn't expect to see you again so soon. I'm glad you're here."

"I had some business nearby and thought I'd make good on my promise to call on you again." Not a lie, but not entirely the truth. Nicolas had used a visit to his sister, Rosina, who was studying philosophy at the University of Toulouse, as the excuse for the visit to Saint-Gervais. She'd seen through his ruse, of course, but other than gentle teasing, she hadn't dissuaded him from seeing his "handsome young hunter."

Adrien blushed and quickly wiped his cheeks with his sleeve. "If I'd known you were coming," he finally managed, "I'd have made myself more presentable."

Someone giggled—Adrien's little sister, Isabelle, who watched them from the stairway.

"Isa," Adrien's mother chastised, "aren't you supposed to be helping your father with the horses?"

Isabelle blushed furiously, then scampered past Adrien and out of the house.

"My apologies, Lord Rousseau. My daughter's never been particularly discreet about matters of the heart." Charlotte glanced at Adrien, whose dirty cheeks were nearly as pink as his sister's. "Will you be joining us for dinner again tonight?"

"I would love to, madame. If it's not too much trouble." Nicolas smiled at the thought of another comfortable dinner. Much as he loved his own family, the Rousseaus' idea of a meal was born of centuries of tradition and hardly an informal affair.

"Perfect." Charlotte smiled and turned to Adrien. "Then enjoy the beautiful day while you can. I'll see you both later."

"She's wonderful," Nicolas said a few minutes later as Adrien washed his face and hands by the well. He hopped onto the stone wall, feet dangling above the thick green grass, and admired Adrien's powerful shoulders and swordsman's arms.

"My mother? Is she that much different than yours?" Adrien looked up at him, eyes bright with interest.

"In some ways, she's much the same. In others…." Nicolas closed his eyes and delighted in the warmth of the sun on his face.

"You've never been comfortable with your status."

Nicolas opened his eyes and stared. They'd never spoken of his dislike of formalities. "I… no."

Adrien stood momentarily still, then seemed to collect himself. He dried his face with a cloth and smoothed his hair back. Was his skin flushed from the cold water, or was it something else?

As often happened when he was with Adrien, a memory flickered in Nicolas's mind: Adrien, hair wet as they bathed in small lake after they'd made love. The memories were his, and yet they weren't.

Nicolas forced his thoughts back to the present only to find Adrien frowning and staring off into the distance. "Are you all right?"

Adrien looked at Nicolas. "I… I think so."

Nicolas offered his hand. "Why don't you show me around?"

"I'd love to." Adrien laced his fingers through Nicolas's and they ran, laughing, following the path that snaked through the vineyard until they reached the top of the hill.

Nicolas looked out over the town and beyond to the lush hills covered with terraced farms and dotted with herds of sheep and cows. The sun hung low in the sky, and shadows from passing clouds danced across the landscape.

"I like you like this." Adrien wrapped his arms around Nicolas, who sighed in reply.

"Like this?"

"Happy. At ease."

"Have you ever seen me anything *but* happy when I'm with you?" Nicolas grinned.

"No, but…."

"But?"

"I don't know. There's something… I can't really explain…. Sometimes I can see your face in my mind and I…." Adrien chuckled. "It's nothing."

Nicolas turned and met Adrien's gaze, the ache in his chest intensifying as he traced his fingers over Adrien's jaw. "You missed a spot," he gently teased as he brushed away a bit of dirt from Adrien's cheek.

Adrien captured his hand and kissed it. This close, Adrien's stuttered breaths heightened Nicolas's desire and his bloodlust blossomed red-hot. He leaned in and licked Adrien's neck, reveling in the saltiness, wanting so much more and struggling for control.

"Please," Adrien whispered. "Take my blood."

"I can't—"

"I want you to have it."

Nicolas hesitated. He'd never wanted anything more, but he knew the power an ancient could wield over a human.

"This is my choice," Adrien said as if he'd read Nicolas's thoughts. "I want this. *I want you.*"

Nicolas wasn't sure if Adrien had spoken these last words aloud, but this time he didn't hesitate. He bit Adrien's neck and plunged headlong into Adrien's soul, allowing himself to fall into the color and passion that was Adrien. Love, longing, and the eagerness of youth collided and blurred, like a river rushing toward the ocean, fearless and free.

He saw glimpses of himself in Adrien's soul. As he was now, as he was in another lifetime. Buried memories, perhaps, or something more. But there was no time to stop and understand as he fell deeper into Adrien, whose heart opened to him and held him captive.

If you only knew how much I've wanted this. If you only knew the secrets of my soul! There would be time for the past later. For now, Nicolas wanted nothing more than to lose himself in Adrien's brilliant, shining soul.

Epilogue

May 2018
Saint-Gervais, France

ADRIEN INHALED the sweet fragrance of the vines as the sun broke rose over the horizon. So fragile now, the clusters of flowers would soon die, replaced by fruit barely the size of a pea, which would then grow into grapes for the fall's harvest.

He gently picked several blossoms and cupped them in his hands, allowing the heady aroma to fill his nostrils. He smiled and walked down the hillside to the large sycamore tree that shaded his mother and sister's headstones. He placed the flowers atop the graves and sat, resting his hand on the soil, and smiled.

"Spring is the hardest," he whispered as a strong hand clasped his shoulder. "It reminds me of them and the years they spent here."

"I'm sorry." Nicolas sat beside him. "I wish I could to ease your pain."

"They lived long and happy lives and left this world on their own terms. My grief is selfish. I want them back."

Nicolas leaned in and kissed Adrien. "Wanting their love is hardly selfish."

"Remembering them here keeps their memory alive." Adrien stood and offered Nicolas his hand. "Isa's oldest great-grandchild, Marc, emailed. He'd like to spend the summer here, learning about the vines."

"The little monster who chased you up and down these hills and nearly fell into the well when you weren't looking?" Nicolas chuckled.

Adrien nodded. "The little monster is nearly twenty-six. Got his MBA at the Wharton School and is working in New York."

"And, like his great-uncle, he's restless."

"His great-uncle is happy here." Thirty years before, he'd hesitated to take over the vineyard when his father had accepted a permanent position at the Council of Hunters. Now, as Jacques prepared to assume the position of regent, Adrien couldn't image a life other than this.

"And all he wants is to learn about the vines?"

"He might also want a bit of help learning how to fight," Adrien said. "Seems a certain sword appeared for him when he was younger. He ignored its call for a while, but…."

"Your mother's sword."

"How did you know?"

Nicolas shrugged. "Just a good guess. But from what your father told me about your mother when she was young, seems she was a bit of a handful as well."

"Roland says he'll be checking in on me. Just to be sure I'm as good a teacher as he was."

"I don't doubt he will. And François? Last I heard from Charles, they were thinking of stopping by for a visit," Nicolas said as they headed down the path toward the house.

"He texted. He said they'll be coming for Jean's birthday."

Nicolas pulled Adrien close and kissed him again.

"What was that for?" Adrien grinned.

Nicolas shrugged. "No reason."

"You're hiding your thoughts from me." Adrien nipped at Nicolas's neck until Nicolas hissed in reply. "Better fess up."

"Just… ah… thinking how about how I don't think I'll ever get bored of this. Even after a dozen lifetimes." Nicolas put his hands to Adrien's cheeks and met his gaze.

"Mmm."

"Are you happy?"

Adrien sighed. "Do you have to ask?"

Nicolas nodded. "I know you've regained most of your memories."

"You want to know if I regret the future we created?" Adrien laughed and shook his head.

"You've always lived for a challenge. You crave it."

"Challenges aren't all I crave." Adrien kissed Nico. "This life's a good one."

"A quiet one as well."

Adrien shrugged. "As long as there are vampires and hunters, there will be work to do. Perhaps there's room on the Council for a slightly jaded immortal hunter."

"You're thinking of taking your father's place." Nicolas stepped back and stared at Adrien.

"Roland approached me about it," Adrien admitted. "Someone needs to fill my father's seat now that he'll be installed as regent."

"Blaise has been pressing me to take the Rousseaus' seat. He and Jean are talking about moving back to Lyon."

"You'll take it, won't you? I'd be miserable without my husband at my side." Adrien grinned. Much as he loved Saint-Gervais, he'd been dreaming of traveling again. Paris would be a start. And if the news out of the United States of a new vampire clan rising to power was true, there'd be plenty of work to forge alliances.

Nicolas gazed past Adrien for a moment, and Adrien wondered if he was thinking of another past.

"The past doesn't weigh me down," Nicolas said, no doubt having read Adrien's thoughts. "It's the future that holds the promise. *Our* future."

"So you'll take the seat on the Council?"

Nicolas nodded. "Of course. But what of the vineyard?"

"Maybe it's time my brother and Charles take a break from their travels." Adrien grabbed Nicolas's hand and pulled him toward the house. "I think I'll call him later."

"Later?"

"Breakfast first," Adrien announced. "I picked up a few croissants in town. And even if you think it's a vile human concoction, I'm going to have my coffee."

Nicolas screwed up his face in mock horror.

"I bought you a pain au chocolat."

"You did?"

Adrien laughed. "And they say vampires don't need food to survive. Clearly they weren't talking about you and chocolate."

"There's one other thing I need to survive," Nicolas said against Adrien's ear.

Adrien shivered. *Eternity will never be enough.*

"Eternity is just the beginning, beloved."

SHIRA ANTHONY was a professional opera singer in her last incarnation, performing roles in such operas as *Tosca*, *Pagliacci*, and *La Traviata*, among others. You can hear Shira sing an aria from a live performance of Puccini's *Tosca* by clicking here: "Vissi d'arte" (http://www.shiraanthony.com/wp-content/uploads/2012/06/tosca-visse-darte-exceprt1.mp3)

Shira's given up TV for evenings spent with her laptop, and she never goes anywhere without a pile of unread M/M romance on her Kindle. When she's not writing, she is usually in a courtroom trying to make the world safer for children. Her favorite place to write is at the Carolina coast aboard *Land's Zen*, a 35' catamaran sailboat, with her favorite sexy captain at the wheel.

Whether contemporary romance, high fantasy shifters, or time-traveling vampires, Shira writes what she loves and never writes a story without a HEA. Her Mermen of Ea trilogy book *Into the Wind* was named one of the best books of 2014 by both Scattered Thoughts and Rogue Words and Hearts on Fire Reviews, and was a finalist in the 2014 Goodreads M/M Romance Member's Choice Awards. Her Blue Notes series of classical-music-themed gay romances was named one of Scattered Thoughts and Rogue Words' best series of 2012, and the most recent book in the series, *Dissonance*, was named one of the best books of 2014 by Hearts on Fire Reviews. Her book *A Solitary Man*, coauthored with Aisling Mancy, won a 2016 Rainbow Award Honorable Mention for Best Gay Mystery/Thriller.

Shira can be found on:
Facebook: www.facebook.com/shira.anthony
Goodreads: www.goodreads.com/author/show/4641776.Shira_Anthony
Twitter: @WriterShira
Website: www.shiraanthony.com
Email: shiraanthony@hotmail.com

BLOOD
AND RAIN
SHIRA ANTHONY

BLOOD
SERIES

Blood: Book One

Vampire hunter Adrien Gilbert never dreamed he'd fall for his prey or that his love, Nicolas Lambert, would give him the gift of immortality. But when a hunter bent on destroying the truce between vampires and hunters throws the gauntlet at Adrien's feet, Adrien must travel through time to save Nicolas, and with him, the entire vampire race.

Born in the 1800s into a clan of vampire hunters, Adrien once wanted only to tend his family's vineyard or read a good book. Then his older brother is murdered. Bound by his hunter's oath, Adrien sets out on a path that will change his life when he agrees to execute his brother's killer, the vampire Charles Duvalier.

After months chasing Charles, Adrien reluctantly makes a bargain with ancient vampire Nicolas Lambert. Adrien will escort Nicolas to Paris for his marriage to a rival clanswoman, and Nicolas will help Adrien find Charles. Nicolas's quiet strength and gentle heart soon convince Adrien that Nicolas is nothing like the vampires he has sworn to destroy. But as the wedding draws nearer, a sinister figure threatens the already fragile peace. To secure both past and future for those he loves, Adrien must find a way to stop the looming war. But first he'll have to let Nicolas go.

www.dreamspinnerpress.com

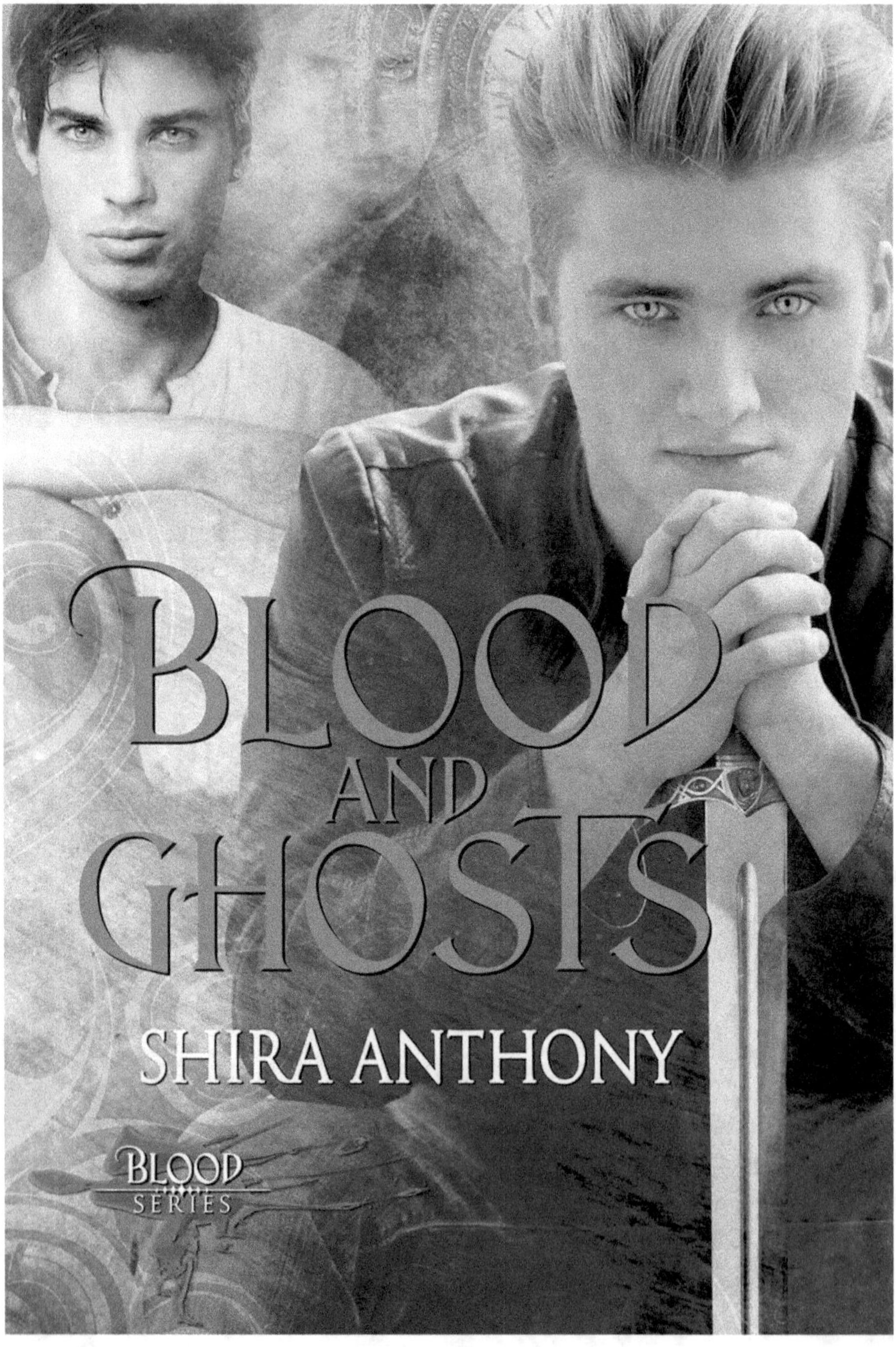
BLOOD AND GHOSTS
SHIRA ANTHONY
BLOOD SERIES

Sequel to *Blood and Rain*
Blood: Book Two

Vampire hunter Adrien Gilbert never dreamed he'd fall for his prey or that his love, Nicolas Lambert, would give him the gift of immortality. But when a hunter bent on destroying the truce between vampires and hunters throws the gauntlet at Adrien's feet, Adrien must travel through time to save Nicolas, and with him, the entire vampire race.

With Nicolas's marriage to a rival clanswoman only weeks away, Adrien struggles to come to terms with his defeat at the hands of Verel Pelletier, a vampire hunter and an immortal like himself. Adrien and his former teacher, Roland Günter, begin to explore his newly acquired abilities, but without his soul's sword, Adrien flounders.

Then, on Nicolas's wedding day, his brother reveals a two-hundred-year-old secret, sending the wedding party into a blazing battle between hunters and vampires. Once again Adrien finds himself facing Pelletier's superior strength. Just as Adrien believes all hope of a future with Nicolas is lost, he finally learns his true gift—he can turn back time. But time travel comes with a high cost. To save Nicolas, Adrien must become strong enough to use his power without descending into madness.

www.dreamspinnerpress.com

A Heart's Gate Story

The truth might ruin his dreams—or make them come true.

When Zane moves into an old gothic brownstone, he discovers the house comes equipped with a caretaker—Kit, who lives in the basement. Zane is immediately drawn to the charming and attractive Kit. But Kit is much more than he seems. He is a two-hundred-year-old half-human, half–red-fox spirit who guards a Gate between the mortal and spirit worlds—a fact Zane should recognize, but doesn't.

Orphaned at a young age, Zane never learned he comes from a long line of mystical Keepers. Kit needs Zane's help to protect the Gate, but how can he tell Zane of his legacy when that will crush Zane's dreams of traveling the world? If he takes up the mantle, Zane will be bound to the Gate, unable to leave it. But when Zane realizes Kit's true nature, and his own, he'll have to make a choice—fight to protect Kit and the Gate, or deny his destiny and any chance of a future with Kit.

www.dreamspinnerpress.com

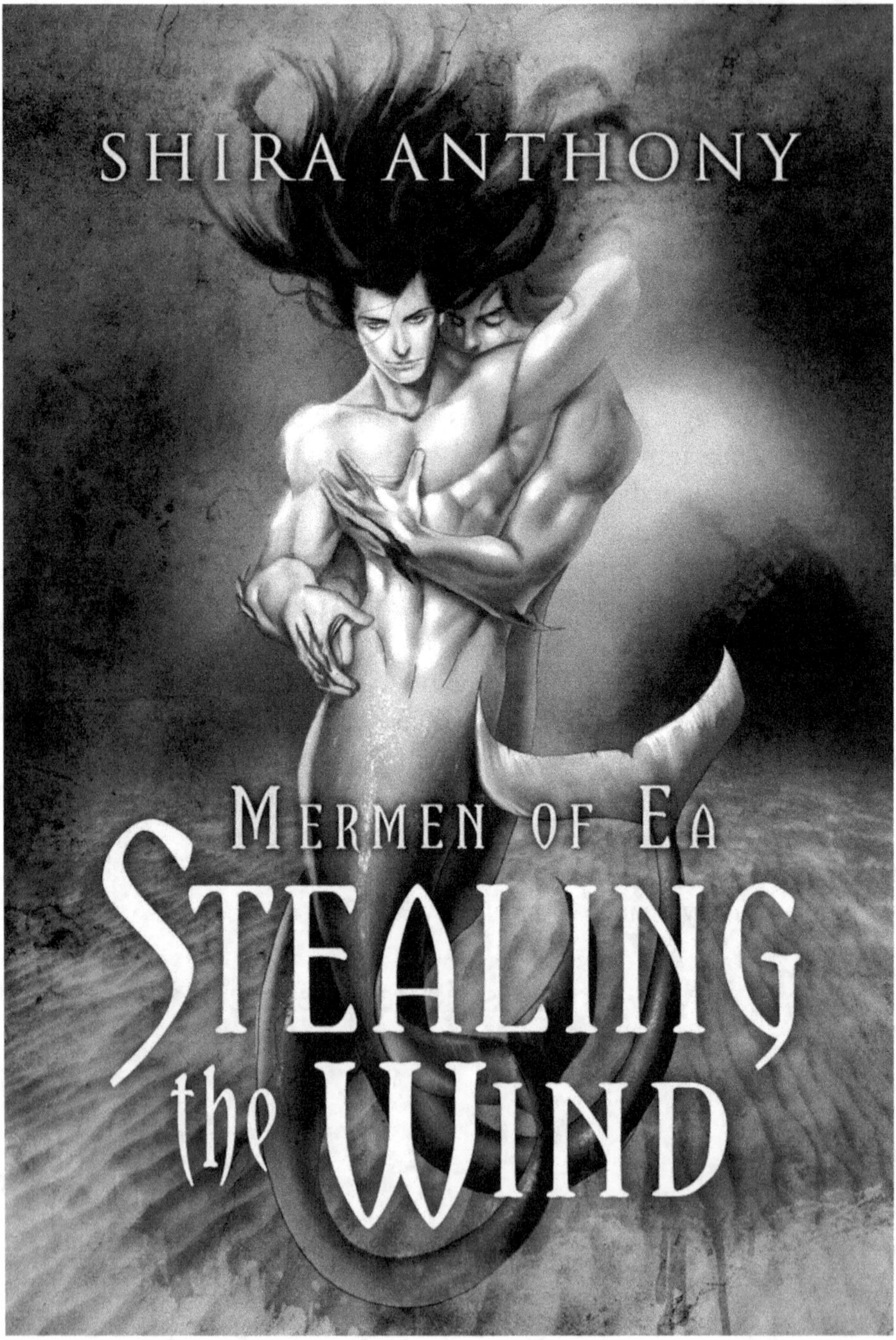
SHIRA ANTHONY
MERMEN OF EA
STEALING the WIND

Mermen of Ea Trilogy: Book One

Taren Laxley has never known anything but life as a slave. When a lusty pirate kidnaps him and holds him prisoner on his ship, Taren embraces the chance to realize his dream of a seagoing life. Not only does the pirate captain offer him freedom in exchange for three years of labor and sexual servitude, but the pleasures Taren finds when he joins the captain and first mate in bed far surpass his greatest fantasies.

Then, during a storm, Taren dives overboard to save another sailor and is lost at sea. He's rescued by Ian Dunaidh, the enigmatic and seemingly ageless captain of a rival ship, the Phantom, and Taren feels an overwhelming attraction to Ian that Ian appears to share. Soon Taren learns a secret that will change his life forever: Ian and his people are Ea, shape-shifting merfolk… and Taren is one of them too. Bound to each other by a fierce passion neither can explain or deny, Taren and Ian are soon embroiled in a war and forced to fight for a future—not only for themselves but for all their kind.

www.dreamspinnerpress.com